The Red Oak

Part Three of The Searight Saga

R.P.G. Colley

R.P.G. Colley

Fiction:

Love and War Series:
Song of Sorrow
The Lost Daughter
The Woman on the Train
The White Venus
The Black Maria
My Brother the Enemy
Anastasia
Elena
The Mist Before Our Eyes
The Darkness We Leave Behind

The Searight Saga:
This Time Tomorrow
The Unforgiving Sea
The Red Oak

The DI Benedict Paige Crime Series
by JOSHUA BLACK

And Then She Came Back
The Poison in His Veins
Requiem for a Whistleblower
The Forget-Me-Not Killer
The Canal Boat Killer
A Senseless Killing

The Red Oak

Part Three in
The Searight Saga

Rupertcolley.com

June 2004

Chapter 1: *The Day Everything Changed*

The strong acidic smell hit Tom Searight in the back of the throat as he groped through the darkness of the museum exhibit. The sound of artillery fire shook the stillness of the room. He passed a dugout and listened as the officer inside bellowed down a telephone, his clipped English accent cursing at the sudden loss of signal. A dim lamp flickered on the shelf, next to the tins of condensed milk and a half-full bottle of wine. Tom moved on through the trench, one careful step at a time. The noise of the attack died down. He came to a soldier standing stock-still on the 18-inch-high fire step peering through a periscope into No Man's Land. Tom stepped up next to him, conscious that even in the dark if his head peeped over the parapet, he risked being caught by a German sniper. The soldier, wearing a greasy waterproof cape, held his rifle in his right hand, the steely point of the bayonet glistening in the semi-light.

Tom heard a commotion to his left. He turned to see a small group of schoolchildren brush hurriedly by, no more than about twelve years old, all commenting on the horrible smell and complaining of boredom. Would he have been so dismissive at their age? Probably not. But then, maybe at the age of thirty-eight, Tom was already turning into a younger version of his intolerant, octogenarian father. If nothing else, he would have thought a trip to the Imperial War Museum was a good excuse to get out of school for the day.

At least his own daughter appeared motivated. Granted, her motivation stemmed from wanting to impress her history teacher, who seemed to be the current flavour of the month. In two weeks' time, Charlotte was doing a recital of war poetry in a class presentation marking the ninetieth anniversary of the start of the First World War in front of the whole school. She'd suggested a half-term trip to the museum as a means of gathering background information. This teacher, Mr Moyes, was obviously quite something, thought Tom. Not wanting to discourage his normally work-shy daughter, he had volunteered to accompany her during his week off work.

Tom left the trench exhibit as the officer yelled down his radio for the umpteenth time that day and the sentry kept up his watch, his gaze forever fixed on the invisible foe on the other side. He found Charlotte nearby studying a group of medals in a glass display. 'Found anything interesting?' he asked her.

She shrugged her shoulders and curled her lip. 'Not really. Can we go now?'

'Already? We've only just got here.'

'Whatever.'

Tom couldn't help but feel disappointed. He'd been looking forward to a morning out with his daughter; they talked so rarely now. The First World War project provided a connection; the trip to the museum a shared venture, an opportunity to talk. But his efforts to engage her in conversation on subjects pertinent to her life came across as either patronising or invasive. He was trying too hard and she let him know it by her monosyllabic answers. He wondered whether Julie would have had more success but she had the convenient excuse of a pre-arranged lunch date. 'Have you seen everything you want to see?'

'Yeah. There was nothing on the poets anyway.'

Tom's attention was caught by a mug made out of a golden syrup tin. 'Look, sweetheart, ninety years on and they still use the same logo.'

'Dad,' said Charlotte, lowering her voice and glancing around. 'Do you have to call me that?'

'Sorry, petal, am I embarrassing you?' It was only meant to be a little joke but her scornful look reminded him that irony wasn't Charlotte's strongest point. But it was true; at fourteen, she was already too grown-up and self-conscious for pet names. Fourteen going on seventeen, Charlotte was a pretty girl; she had inherited her mother's fine bone structure with her cheekbones and delicate nose, and the long blonde hair. Despite the semi-permanent scowl, Charlotte's natural attractiveness was cause for a mild dose of anxiety for Tom; she was already receiving far too much attention from ill-suited boys.

'Right,' he said. 'Can we at least go to the museum shop?'

The shop was packed, far more than the exhibition they'd just left, with people more interested in buying branded rubbers or key rings than viewing the exhibits themselves – anything to show they'd done their bit, shown a passing interest and had the souvenir to prove it. Tom gave Charlotte a fiver, with which she bought a small book on First World War poetry. He could tell she would have far rather pocketed the money and used it on something else. For himself, he bought a lightweight account of the Western Front. At least it showed willing and, if nothing else, would impress his father.

Half an hour later, they were on the stifling tube, heading back to Holloway, both half-heartedly reading their respective purchases.

'Dad,' said Charlotte, in a depressingly familiar tone that Tom knew all too well. Charlotte was never one to initiate a conversation unless she wanted something. 'Y'know you said you'd take me out for dinner after the museum?'

'Lunch you mean, what about it?'

'I was wondering, would it be OK if I could go and see Abigail instead? I could show her the book; y'know, read the poems and that.'

Hmm, likely story, thought Tom. But he'd taken the father-daughter thing far enough for one day and his disappointment was deepened by the realisation he was relieved by its premature end. She'd said Abigail: the two girls had been friends since nursery and, like an automatic reflex, whenever Charlotte mentioned her friend's name, he thought of her mother, Rachel. 'Well…'

'Thanks, Dad.'

'But only if you're back by four – and you actually *do* some work. OK?'

'Yes, I promise. I am your "sweetheart" after all.'

Fourteen years old and she thinks she can twist me around her finger, thought Tom with a wry smile.

Two stops later, Charlotte bounced up from her seat unaware of two adolescent boys in logo-emblazoned sweatshirts watching her. 'I'll get off here,' she said, giving her father a peck on the cheek. 'Thanks, Dad, see ya later.'

'Four o'clock, OK?'

'Yep, four o'clock.'

Tom watched her as she disappeared into the throng of people. He spotted her book of war poetry wedged against the armrest of her vacated seat. He snatched it, rose to his feet and fought against the tide of incoming passengers, calling out her name just as the doors snapped shut, leaving him pawing at the glass door. As the tube picked up speed he saw a glimpse of her striding purposefully along the platform, her eyes fixed on the phosphorus-green screen of her mobile. He turned and leant back against the curved door. The two adolescent boys caught his eye and sniggered.

He got off at the next stop and emerged into the oppressive London heat. He zigzagged his way along the Holloway Road avoiding the abundance of semi-clad youngsters – men stripped to the waist, pale legs and fresh tattoos; girls with exposed midriffs, large earrings and pierced bellybuttons. He popped into his local newsagent, the place decked with England flags ahead of the European football championship due to start in a few days. He bought a copy of *The Times*, Tony Blair's serious face dominating the front page. As Tom ambled back home along their quiet, tree-lined road, he felt saddened by the way the morning had gone. She was a good kid, but if only he could breach the widening divide of misunderstanding. And he hated the way that his daughter's cool detachment made him feel gauche and unsure of his actions. He pined for the little girl who was forever gone and no number of how-to-parent-a-teenager books could alleviate that longing.

He set his mind to the rest of the day; the sun was out and he had the house to himself. He could sit in the garden with a cup of tea and read the paper or his new book. Tom returned home feeling quietly smug.

*

At first, he didn't notice anything. He closed the front door behind him, threw the newspaper on the small telephone table in the hallway and was greeted with yelps of excitement from Angus, the family's white Highland terrier. 'Hello, boy, you all alone?' He put his head around the sitting room door. Empty. 'Is anyone at home?' he yelled. He walked through to the kitchen, noticing the smell of bleach, put the kettle on and let Angus out into the garden. Julie had left three envelopes on the kitchen table propped up against the vase of flowers – the flowers he'd given her on their recent anniversary. He glanced at them quickly. One was a gas bill, another a clothes catalogue for Julie, but it was the third one that intrigued him. It had a French stamp on it and, handwritten, was addressed to him. Who in the dickens would be writing to him from France, he wondered. He was about to open the letter when he saw it: a briefcase at the foot of the telephone table. He padded over to inspect. It was a big scruffy brown thing that had obviously seen better days. It was a man's briefcase. Whose was it? He'd definitely not seen it before. Did it belong to a friend of Julie's? The more he stared at this brown briefcase, the greater his sense of unease. And suddenly he knew that it shouldn't have been there; that something was wrong. The soft brown leather was heavily scuffed with deeply embedded lines like cracks in the parched earth of a dried-out riverbed. He wanted to flick open the scratched silvery latches, to rummage inside for clues as to why it was sitting there, leaning against the telephone table in his hallway. It owed him an explanation for its presence but somehow an inbred respect for privacy held him back. He turned to peer up the stairs. 'Is anyone home?' he shouted out again. But this time he was convinced he wasn't shouting to an empty house. The silence was overwhelming, unnatural. Tom knew there was someone else in his home.

*

Julie Searight lay on the bed in the spare bedroom, her fingers gripping the hot crumpled sheet beneath her. She was naked. She hadn't moved; pinned to the bed by panic, immobilised by the thumping of her heart. She could hardly breathe in the humid closeness of the room, melting into the cloying stickiness of the sheets, her back drenched in sweat. She would have opened the window if she hadn't felt so frozen with panic. Her mind blank, she stared at the ceiling, her mouth gaping, her breath coming in short staccato bursts. Her world was about to collapse around her at any moment. How could she have been so stupid? She lowered her eyes and looked at Mark. She hated him for having put her in this position. Mark too hadn't moved an inch since they heard the door key turn in the latch. He was kneeling on the bed between Julie's opened legs, his hair stuck to his forehead, a bead of sweat glistening on his upper lip. The smell of illicit sex hung in the air like an accusing spirit mingling with the early afternoon heat. She looked at the pile of hastily discarded clothes on the wicker chair in the far corner of the room: a dark blue tie, a black sock, his favourite boxer shorts (which he wore on every occasion), and her bra coiled half in and half out of the snake-charming laundry basket. She could hear Angus yelping outside – Tom must have closed the back door on him.

At least, she thought, Charlotte hadn't come back. But what was Tom doing at home anyway? They weren't due back for ages yet. What could she say? Introduce them? Mark meet Tom; Tom, this is Mark; Mark and I have been having a rampant affair these last eighteen months; you don't mind, do you, love? She almost laughed; what an absurd situation she found herself in – caught red-handed by her husband in bed with her lover. This had been the first time she had invited Mark to her house. It'd been Mark's idea. Or had it been hers? She couldn't remember. Usually, when Tom said he'd be back at three, you could depend on him being back at three, not two hours earlier.

'Is anyone home?' Second time around, Tom's voice had an edge to it – he knew something was wrong. The first time, there was still a chance. A chance he might have gone out into the garden and cut the lawn, or fallen asleep in the sun-lounger. A chance he might have gone out again, taken Angus out for a walk, anything. Mark could have slipped away. She could have pretended to have been stood up by her lunch date, returned home early and had a snooze. In the spare bedroom? She could have fluked it. Tom would never have known. She would have taken the sheets and put them in the wash – just doing the domestic chores. But not now. The second shout was more real, more urgent. What had given the game away? Maybe he heard something, but she and Mark had barely moved a muscle from the moment he came in.

Julie and Mark looked at each other, both lost in their own fearful thoughts, Mark's hand resting on Julie's bent knee. Averting her gaze, she concentrated on the reflection of Mark's slender back in the long mirror opposite the bed, the hollows in the small of his back, the arch of his spine, the top of his smooth buttocks. They heard Tom moving around downstairs. Even his footsteps sounded different as he carefully and deliberately checked each room: the sitting room, the living room, back to the kitchen. Julie's heartbeat, already unbearably fast, quickened at the sound of Tom's muffled footsteps on the carpeted stairs. She tried to control her breathing as Mark's hand tightened its grip on her knee. With Tom at the top of the stairs, they both felt the need to appear slightly more dignified. Mark covered his lap with his tee shirt. Julie pulled the warm sheet over herself, covering her nakedness.

Tom was on the landing. Julie wanted to scream: 'Just get it over and done with'. She heard him cross the landing and check their main bedroom and then heard him say 'hello?' as he looked in Charlotte's room. Two bedrooms gone, one to go. I'm sorry, she thought, I'm so sorry. As Tom approached the spare bedroom, Mark put his hand to his mouth and Julie gripped the sheet tighter still. They both turned to face the door. The bed was behind the door as it opened, so Tom would have to open the door fully or put his head around it before seeing them. It was the last room of the house. His presence lingered on the other side. What a sight to behold, she thought, as her self-pity transferred itself to Tom. Poor man, he'd done nothing wrong; nothing to deserve this indignity, this shame.

Holding her breath, Julie watched as the doorknob moved slowly around. The door opened an inch, maybe two. And then paused. What was holding him back, was it the mirror? But no, it was too far to one side. Then, miraculously, the door slowly closed again. The doorknob moved back to its original position, finishing with a tiny clunk. Tom had let go.

Her heart still thumping furiously, Julie breathed out. She heard Tom walk back across the landing and quickly back down the stairs. Mark raised an eyebrow and looked as if he was about to speak. She put a finger to her lips and listened as Tom went through to the kitchen and let Angus back in from the garden. To her eternal relief, she heard the jangling of the dog lead, the sound of an excitable dog and Tom saying,

'Come on, let's go for a walk.' He was going out after all. The front door closed and Julie sighed loudly and resisted the urge to scream out. She rubbed her eyes and groaned.

'Christ,' breathed Mark, running his fingers through his hair. 'That was close, too damn close. He must've known; why didn't he come in, could he smell us? I mean, what stopped him?'

'Shut up a minute.' She needed silence, not the sound of Mark theorising on the obvious. What was he so worried about anyway, what did *he* have to lose?

Mark didn't take the hint. 'I'm sorry, Julie, that was too much. Too much. I told you it was too risky; we're not doing it here again.'

Julie sat bolt upright, clutching the sheet over herself, seized by a sudden sense of anger for compromising her marriage for the sake of idle sex. She wanted Mark to go and to go now. 'Mark, get out, just piss off. We're not doing it again here or *anywhere*. I'm through with it. Just *leave*.' She grabbed his shirt from his lap and threw it at him. She fell back against the pillow, exhausted and close to tears.

Mark recoiled at the harshness of her words. He'd expected her to be upset, but not to so vehemently take it out on him. He climbed off the bed and grappled furiously with his clothes, fighting back his own anger at the injustice of her comments. 'You bitch,' he muttered, as he hastily pulled on his boxer shorts. 'You bloody bitch. I know you're upset, but don't take it out on me. I mean, at the very least, I thought I meant *something* to you. But no, obviously not. I was just a bloody shag to you, wasn't I? Well, thanks, Julie; thanks a bloody bunch.'

Julie rolled her eyes. She knew Mark deserved better, but she didn't care, not now. 'Go, Mark, just go.'

'I'm going all right. I just hope for your sake I don't bump into Tom on the way out,' he said menacingly. He stuffed his tie into his trouser pocket, grabbed his jacket, and paused at the bedroom door. 'I'll see you at school sometime then.' Julie lay still, unable to move, unable to make any response.

Mark hurtled down the stairs and saw his briefcase in the hallway beneath the telephone table. Damn it, he thought, what a stupid place to leave it. Tom must have seen it. He paused briefly at the hallway mirror and brushed his hair back into place, rearranged his collar, and gave himself a pitiful look. Taking a deep breath, he opened the front door, looked up and down the street, and walked hurriedly up towards the end of the road where he'd parked his car. The visitor's parking permit had run out barely fifteen minutes ago, and already stuck to the windscreen of his Ford Fiesta was the familiar yellow penalty notice. Mark cursed – what a crap way to end a crap day.

*

Meanwhile, Julie, realising she might have little time before either Tom or Charlotte returned, snapped out of her state of self-pity. She began by hunting for a clean, nondescript bra and knickers, placing the more alluring set neatly in her drawer. With a pang of guilt, she realised how her sexy underwear saw the light of day more for Mark's benefit than Tom's. She desperately wanted a shower to remove the smell of sex and sweat but she knew time could be against her; a quick wash would have to suffice.

Once fully dressed, she began maniacally making the bed, stuffing the crumpled sheets into the laundry basket, replacing them with ironed duplicates and puffing up the pillows. Half an hour later, both she and the spare bedroom looked as they should in the middle of a weekday afternoon. Only the faint aroma of sweat remained. She opened the window and then cruised around the house picking up dirty mugs and plates and stuffing them willy-nilly into the dishwater. Tom would have a seizure. He liked the dishwasher to be loaded properly to his exacting standards. The main plates went here, the bowls there, the mugs at ninety bloody degrees from the sodding side plates. One of the mugs slipped, fell to the floor and broke. Julie swore; her nerves were on edge. To her horror, it was Tom's favourite mug, his Arsenal football mug, celebrating the 'Double' of 2002, a Christmas present from Charlotte. Fortunately, only the handle had snapped off, the mug itself was still intact. She put the handle in the mug and hid the evidence behind the tins in the food cupboard.

Still feeling jittery, Julie made herself a coffee and went outside into the garden to try and enjoy the sun. Sitting in the sun-lounger beneath the shade of the laurel hedge, she closed her eyes, breathed deeply through her nose and tried to compose herself. She promised, to whatever greater being might have been eavesdropping, that she had learnt her lesson. From now on, she was going to be the perfect mother and the model wife. Things were going to change.

Chapter 2: *The Library*

Tom had seen them all right.

From the moment he saw the briefcase he knew something was amiss. Aware of the stilted silence, he had begun climbing the stairs, conscious of the slightest sound, the tiniest creak. As he trod carefully across the carpeted landing, his heart pounding, he told himself he was being irrational. What did he expect to find – a burglar? But burglars don't leave briefcases in the hallway. Having checked his and Julie's bedroom, and then Charlotte's, he relaxed slightly. But perhaps he should check the bedroom at the back of the house as well. He placed his hand on the doorknob – white and shiny with a small floral pattern on it but with a crack straight down the middle he hadn't noticed before – and slowly turned. He thought he heard a small sharp intake of breath from within. He paused. Angus was yapping outside in the garden. He opened the door a fraction, barely an inch or two, and then stopped. Tom peered through the gap between the edge of the door and the doorframe. There, through the slither of view, he could clearly see her lying on the bed. Between her legs, the crouching knees of a man, a tee shirt on his lap, and the dark hairs on his painfully pale legs. What should he do? Burst in and confront them in their humiliation? Instead, fearing his own humiliation, Tom did nothing. He gently closed the door, wondered momentarily where he could find replacement doorknobs with the same pattern, walked slowly back along the landing and down the stairs.

He stood in the hallway and tried to control his breathing. His throat felt dry, his head spun. The familiar surroundings seemed oddly out of place. The hallway mirror seemed too big for the limited amount of space within its reflection, the rug seemed too dark, its triangular pattern too fussy, the small crack in the ceiling looked menacingly large. He needed to get out and get some air. He whistled for Angus and remembered the dog was still outside in the garden. Letting him back in, Angus ran straight past him, headed for his basket in the corner of the kitchen, and dived into the comfort of the chewed blanket, looking somewhat put out that Tom had forgotten him for so long. Tom picked up the dog lead and all was forgiven in an instant.

'Come on, let's go for a walk,' he said, trying to make his voice sound as natural as possible. Grappling with Angus's lead, he fumbled as he tried to attach the metal loop to the dog collar. Every action seemed unnatural and clumsy as if he was critically watching himself from the outside. He saw the briefcase again. He glanced upstairs and guiltily lifted the unlocked flap to see what was within. Inside, he saw a book, various files and *The Guardian* newspaper. Angus barked with impatience, making Tom jump. Without thinking, he swiped the book as Angus pulled on the lead and stretched for the front door.

The heat outside was as oppressive as the surreal tension inside. Someone said hello, a neighbour. Tom grunted an acknowledgement. Angus tried to scramble ahead as his master brusquely yanked him back. Tom strode forward, his mind incapable of taking in the vision of his wife in bed with another man. *Actually* in bed. Should he take comfort that it was only the spare bed, and not theirs? Perhaps he'd imagined it; it seemed too unreal. He felt like going back to check he hadn't been mistaken. But the knotted feeling in the pit of his stomach told him it was real all right.

Angus saw a pigeon and lurched violently towards it, twisting mid-lunge as the lead snapped him back. A few minutes later, they were in the park. Tom let Angus off the lead and the little dog charged off chasing an invisible prey. Being a sunny day during the half-term week, the park was predictably busy with children shrieking, boys playing football and grown-ups playing Frisbee. An ice cream van played its shrill tune; an elderly lady with a Yorkshire terrier tried to shoo Angus away. He wandered along the tarmac path and alongside the green wicker fence behind which was a café and an ankle-high paddling pool. He paused and watched the small children splashing in the sun-reflected water. He remembered Charlotte as a toddler doing exactly the same, while he and Julie sat sipping coffee wearing sunglasses to shield their eyes from the painfully white plastic tables. From the path, Tom cut across the grounds and breathed in the smell of the freshly cut grass. He headed for the large ancient oak tree that dominated the middle of the park, now in its full glory; its huge branches casting long shadows across the large expanse of neat grass. Only the scattering of litter spoilt the effect. It was, apparently, a red oak, not that Tom knew one oak tree from another, but he'd always loved the gritty lines of the bark, the twisted and gnarled branches.

Over the years, it'd become *their* tree, the Searight tree.

Charlotte still used it as a reference point when taking Angus out for a walk. When she was a toddler, Tom used to hide around the sturdy trunk and play peek-a-boo with her while Julie lay on the grass watching them, smiling with maternal contentment. In the days before Charlotte, Julie and he often used to take an early evening stroll during the summer weekends. Hand in hand, they'd wander up to the tree and lie within its shadows and idle away the time. Tom had always been tempted to carve his and Julie's initials into the bark. He smiled at the memory, stopped a few yards short of the tree, and sat down cross-legged within its looming shadow.

He looked at the book he'd taken from the briefcase. A strange little coincidence: it was a book on the First World War. Well, at least they had more than just his wife in common. Flinging the book to one side, he lay back, closed his eyes, and listened to the gentle breeze wafting through the leaves high above him. Meanwhile, Angus busied himself in his olfactory pursuits, occasionally checking back with his master, making sure it wasn't time to go yet.

Tom tried to think, but his mind was still a blank, his senses devoid of any comprehensible feeling. A strange numbness covered him like a lethargic blanket denying him any semblance of emotion or reaction. She was having an affair; he had failed her. *Why was she doing this?* He sighed; he'd failed her. The enormity of it suddenly hit him as his heart squeezed inside, leaving him gasping for breath, his eyes pricking on the brink of crying. Burying his face in his hands, he tried to hold back the tears.

'Tom? Are you all right?'

Angus barked. Tom opened his eyes to see a pair of feet in sandals with a ring around the left middle toe. Recognising the high-pitched voice, he looked up. 'What?' It was Rachel,

Abigail's mother, looking resplendent in a pink top and pale trousers. 'I'm s-sorry,' he stuttered, sitting up.

'My God, Tom, what on earth's wrong?'

'It's nothing, it's… Just some bad news, that's all.'

'Are you crying?' Uninvited, she kneeled down facing him.

'No, no. It's fine, really.'

He'd known Rachel for years but it had been a few months since he'd last seen her. He vaguely recognised a smartly dressed man hovering nearby, in neatly pressed chinos, polished brown leather shoes and an expensive shirt masquerading as casual wear. Seemingly overdressed for the park, his attire appeared at odds with his earrings and his beard dyed blue. Rachel looked embarrassed and twirled a long slender finger around a strand of her shoulder-length hair coloured different shades of red. 'I'm sorry, I shouldn't have disturbed you.'

'Doesn't matter,' said Tom, wiping his eyes with the back of his hand. She looked thinner than ever and as attractive as always with her bright lipstick and huge smile. Coughing to clear his throat, he asked whether Charlotte was behaving herself.

'You're asking *me*?' She looked genuinely puzzled.

'Yes, isn't she with Abigail?'

'No, why? Should she be?'

'Yes, she said she was seeing Abigail this afternoon. She left about an hour ago.'

Rachel shook her head. 'I'm sorry, Tom,' she said softly, 'but Abigail's out for the day. She's visiting her granny in Lewisham. And I certainly haven't seen Charlotte; Adrian and I only left the house a few minutes ago. Oh, by the way, this is Adrian.'

The man with the blue beard was stroking Angus. Yes, thought Tom, he'd seen him once at Tom's place of work; he'd come to see his boss. The man stood up and briefly acknowledged Tom before announcing, 'I'm off to get us an ice cream. Do you fancy one, mate?'

'No, you're all right, thanks,' said Tom.

Bluebeard sauntered off, hands in pockets, jangling his loose change.

'So tell me, how's Julie?' asked Rachel. Tom grimaced at the question as the slithered vision of his wife with some strange man flashed across his mind. He tried to cover it up with a smile, but she'd spotted it. 'Something's wrong, isn't there?' she asked softly, her head tilted earnestly to one side.

'Nothing. Really,' he replied, too quickly, avoiding eye contact.

She glanced around as if making sure Bluebeard was out of earshot. 'Come on, Tom Searight, I've known you long enough and well enough to know when something's not right. Tell me, what's up?'

He could feel his eyes pricking again. He couldn't cry; not in front of Rachel; not in front of her. He didn't want to tell her but he knew that she, of all people, would understand and he knew one way or another, she would winkle it out of him. He always used to tell her everything. And right now, he needed someone to take his side, to sympathise.

'Tom?' He could tell she was dying to know, desperately trying not to appear too eager.

He could feel his heart pounding within. 'I think she's seeing someone.' The words came quickly as if trying to deny their existence. And why, he wondered, had he said, "I think", as if implying there was still room for doubt? What clearer evidence did a man need?

He caught her immediate reaction, the gleeful glint in those hazel eyes, the suppressed smile. 'Oh dear, I am sorry.' She didn't mean it; he could tell. 'I knew something was wrong. Oh, you poor thing. How long have you known?'

There was no room for doubt in Rachel's mind, no acknowledgement of his "I think". Tom looked at his watch in mock seriousness. 'About half an hour,' he said, sardonically.

'Oh my word; how did you find out?'

'I… I just did.' He couldn't tell her, not that; it was too humiliating. 'I'm still in shock, I suppose. I don't know what to do.' He rubbed his eyes again, taking a deep breath. 'I just don't know what to do,' he repeated to himself with a sigh.

Rachel put on that familiar half-smile of sympathy. 'I understand,' she said, nodding earnestly. 'Look, later on, why don't you come back to mine and–'

'No, no, it's all right, I just… you know.'

She nodded again. 'Look, I can see you need some space, but I'm still at the same place. I'm sure you haven't forgotten my number.' No, thought Tom, he hadn't forgotten, it was still there, embedded in his memory. She ran her hand over his sleeve. 'If you ever want to talk about it, give me a ring.'

'Yeah, thanks, Rach.'

She lowered her head and peered up at him. 'I mean it. Anytime, OK?'

'I ought to go,' he said, although he had no idea where to or why he ought to. Calling for Angus, he struggled to his feet, his whole body feeling suddenly rather heavy and awkward.

'Lovely to see you again,' said Rachel, with that huge painted smile of hers.

'Yeah. You too.' He turned to leave, conscious she was watching him as he strolled away, Angus bounding nearby.

'Tom!' shouted Rachel after him. 'Your book.' She scooped the book off the ground and looked at the title. 'Reading about the First World War, are you? Isn't that the history project they're doing at school at the moment?'

'It's his.'

'His?'

Tom nodded. 'I found it in the house.'

'He was inside your...' She stopped herself. 'Oh dear.' Opening the cover, she noticed the date label inside. 'It's a library book, from Valentine Road library. Do you know who he is?' Tom shook his head. 'Why don't you use this to find out? Just take it back to the library, it's only up the road.'

He looked at her. 'Really?'

Bluebeard reappeared clutching two ice cream cones. 'Here you are,' he said gruffly, handing one to Rachel. 'One pound, twenty.'

'I think, Adrian, you're meant to say "my treat".' She looked at Tom, smiling sympathetically at him. 'Nice to see you again,' she said softly.

Tom returned the smile and wondered whether she was also thinking about that time all those years ago.

Bluebeard licked his ice cream, looking from one to the other. He seemed slightly ill at ease, thought Tom.

As Tom walked away from the oak tree with Angus at his side, he looked again at the book cover. The picture showed a soldier, rifle at the ready, leaning against a sloping muddy trench wall, gingerly peering into No Man's Land. Tom hadn't given a moment's thought to the First World War for years, probably since he left school, and yet the subject seemed to be dominating the day, following him around like an unwanted companion. He glanced at the contents page: there was a chapter on the art and literature of the Great War, including, of course, the war poets. He flipped to the page and saw the familiar names: Brooke, Owen, Graves, Sassoon, and others he didn't recognise. His eyes settled on a poem by Sassoon, one he knew bits of by heart. For some strange reason, he'd never forgotten the final stanza. Perhaps Charlotte could use it in her recital. He closed the book and muttered the words to himself: "'Have you forgotten yet? Look up and swear by the green of the spring that you'll *never* forget".'

He looked at his watch; it was only a matter of four hours since he was standing in the mock trench in the museum. Four small hours. And in that time, his life had inexplicably changed. Four hours ago, he'd been a normal dad taking his daughter out to a museum, with a wife who loved him, or so he thought, and a happy, normal home to return to. In a matter of an afternoon, everything had been turned on its head. To what was he returning now? A manipulative, conniving daughter and a deceitful, adulterous wife. As he approached the library, Angus pulled on his lead and wagged his tail enthusiastically. At least someone seemed happy.

Presumably, thought Tom, if the man frequented Valentine Road library, it meant he was local. Looking at the date label again, Tom noticed the book was almost a fortnight overdue. He felt in his pocket and found a fifty pence piece. That should cover the overdue fine, he thought. He hadn't been to a library for years and did not possess a library card. He tied Angus up to a wooden bench outside, promising the dog he'd only be a few moments and went inside. It was a small, dark library with heavy wooden shelves and peeling notices; a typical municipal affair opened only a few hours per week. As he entered, he noticed a small display of books and pictures on football, a rack of videos and DVDs, and a sign with a large *X* over a picture of a mobile phone. The place was almost empty. A few users congregated around the shelves marked '*Returned Books*'. He approached the deserted counter. Behind it stood a young, tall, black girl, her white blouse neatly pressed, her hair tied tightly back. She smiled politely at him. 'Can I help?'

'Yes, I'm just returning this book.'

She opened the front cover, scanned the barcode with a light pen and peered into the computer screen in front of her. 'It's a few days overdue, I'm afraid, and there's another nine books due on the same day, I might as well renew all of them for you.' She pressed a few buttons and the computer bleeped. 'There,' she said, 'all due now on the twenty-third of June, that's three weeks' time. That'll be nine pounds, please.'

'How much?' Tom had no idea library fines could be so expensive. 'Are you sure?'

'Yes sir, it's fifteen pence per book per day, that's ninety pence per book. Ten books altogether, so that's nine pounds exactly,' she said with a flourish.

'Heck, can I pay next time?'

'We'd rather you pay now, sir, otherwise it affects your borrowing rights.'

Typical, thought Tom; he screws my wife, I pay his library dues. Anyway, he needed to get the man's name and address. He handed over a ten-pound note, and, trying his best to sound casual, remarked: 'I think you may have my old details on there, can you tell me what address you've got for me?'

'I'm sorry, sir, I can't because of the Data Protection Act, but I can *confirm* an address. What details do you think we have?'

This was going to be more difficult than anticipated. He tried to quickly think up a fictional address – the street next to his. 'Er, twenty-four Crescent Road?'

'No, that's not it. Previous address?' she asked, handing him back his change and a receipt.

'Forty-four East Avenue?'

'No, that's not it either. Perhaps you should bring in some proof of address next time you're in, like a gas bill or a recent bank statement.'

'Can't you just tell me?'

'No, I'm sorry, sir, it's the—'

'Data Protection Act, I know.' It hadn't worked. £9 for nothing – no name, no address. 'OK, thanks anyway,' he said, turning away from the counter.

'A pleasure, Mr Moyes.'

Tom stopped. Mr *what*? He knew that name. He turned back to face her. 'What did you say?'

Tom's odd reaction took the smile off her lips. 'Erm, I said it was a pleasure.'

Mr Moyes? Wasn't that the name of Charlotte's history teacher? 'Do you have my first name? I think it's Mark.' He wondered whether that sounded as ridiculous as he feared.

She glanced nervously at the screen. 'Er, yes, sir, Mark.'

'Oh bloody hell,' Tom muttered under his breath.

'Are you… you all right, Mr Moyes?'

But Tom had stormed out, clutching the one-pound coin and the crumpled receipt, his head spinning. The young library assistant stared at the computer screen, trying to work out what she had said to suddenly upset Mr Moyes. He seemed quite nice at first – before he turned all weird on her.

Chapter 3: *The Letter*

The bright morning sun streamed through the thin curtains and into the bedroom. Tom opened his eyes, smiled at the prospect of another day off, and turned his head on the pillow to look at his still-sleeping wife. His stomach lurched at the sudden remembrance of the preceding day; those few seconds of somnolent morning optimism quickly draining away.

Why Mark Moyes?

Julie stirred next to him. 'Hello, darling,' she yawned. He felt Julie's clammy hand rest on his stomach. Slowly, her hand inched down, her fingers crawling, spider-like, over his skin.

'Julie, I've got to get up.'

'Hmm,' said Julie dreamily.

'No, no, really…'

'Get up for what? It's half-term; you're not going to work, I just thought that we could, er, you know…'

'Maybe later, eh?'

'Go on, you know you want to,' she purred as her hand slid gently under the elastic of his pyjama bottoms.

Out of principle, Tom did not want to give in to her erotic intent. She had that look he knew so well; when her eyes glazed over, her pupils dilated and the way she bit her bottom lip. Is this how she looked when she was with him? Despite himself, he felt a twinge of anticipation as her warm fingers crept delicately down, while her other hand undid the buttons of her pyjama top.

'Christ, Julie, I said no.'

Julie reeled back. 'Heck, all right. Jesus, Tom, what's got into you?'

'I'm sorry; I… I didn't mean to shout. Sorry.'

She looked at him from the corner of her eyes. 'It's all right, I guess.'

While Julie had a shower, Tom came downstairs to find Charlotte sitting at the kitchen table, eating a bowl of cereal while reading the cereal packet. The radio was on, blaring out Peter Andre's old hit, 'Mysterious Girl'. He switched the kettle on. 'So then,' he said loudly, trying to compete with the music, 'did you enjoy the museum yesterday?'

'Yeah, all right,' Charlotte replied without looking up from the packet.

'All right,' repeated Tom, chewing the phrase. 'Look, can you turn that down?' With a slight tut, she reached for the volume dial. 'And, er, have you decided what poem you're going to use for your recital?'

'No.'

'Didn't Abigail help you choose one?'

Charlotte blushed and stuffed a large spoonful of cereal in her mouth. 'No, couldn't decide,' she spluttered. 'Probably one by Wilfred Owen,' she said by way of adding some authenticity to her lie.

'How were Rachel and Bluebeard?'

'What?'

'Rachel's new boyfriend – he's got a blue beard. He works for a rival firm. Anyway, I'm sure Mr Moyes will be impressed, whatever poem you choose. Your mum and I are looking

25

forward to seeing him on Tuesday, the dreaded parents' evening, eh Charlotte?' He made his tea and sat down next to her.

'Yeah, whatever,' she said, immediately standing up and taking her bowl to the sink.

'Hang on a minute—'

'Sorry, Dad, I'm meeting someone.' She darted past him and out of the kitchen. 'See ya later,' she called as she pounded up the stairs.

Tom sighed; his mere presence was enough to drive her away now. He noticed the letter at the end of the table and tried to remember if he knew anyone in France. He opened the envelope fully expecting to be disappointed by its contents. Inside was a word-processed letter with an address in a place called St Omer, and an email address. He turned off the radio, having no desire to listen to Britney Spears. As he was about to read, he heard Charlotte running back down the stairs, calling for Angus. The dog jumped up from his basket and with tail wagging, waddled towards her. 'Later,' she yelled as she breezed out of the front door.

> *Dear Mr Searight,*
>
> *My name is Maria Dubois. You do not know me and you must excuse me writing to you like this. But I am trying to find an English family with your name. I shall explain why.*
>
> *A year ago, my grandmother died. She was an old lady, over 90 years old. She had been an archivist here in St Omer. Many years ago, the archive needed more space. They threw away some old books and documents. One of them was a diary which my grandmother saved. It was a diary written by an English soldier of the Grande Guerre. His name was Guy Searight. He wrote it during the war, then donated his medals and the diary to the*

archive. Before she died, she asked me to find Guy's family and return these things to them.

She always wished to do so herself, but she could not bear to part with them.

Guy was an ordinary soldier who belonged to the Essex Regiment. So I looked up the telephone pages in Essex and London on the Internet. It is lucky for me his name is not Smith! If there was a Guy in your family, please let me know, so that I can return you his diary.

It is of no value, but I think it is most interesting to you. Please write to me or use my e-mail address.

Many good wishes and thank you,
Maria Dubois.

Not the sort of letter one receives every day, he thought. Tom had never shown any interest in his family history, but he vaguely recalled his parents talking of a Guy Searight. He would have to ask his father who, presumably, would have received this letter too, so he could deal with it, the sort of thing he would enjoy. Or were his parents still ex-directory? Tom couldn't remember.

*

It was another hot day and Charlotte wished she'd remembered her sunglasses. She popped into the local newsagents and bought a can of Coke and a pack of Spearmint chewing gum. She looked at the time on her phone – it was ten, if she didn't hurry up, he might think she wasn't coming and give up on her. She quickened her pace. Hopefully, he'd have something on him today. Yesterday had been such a disappointment. She'd been looking forward to it all day, kept thinking about it at the museum, but he'd come empty-handed. It wasn't his fault, she supposed, he wasn't always successful in getting some and sometimes he simply didn't have the money. She once offered to pay something towards it, but he wouldn't take it. Charlotte often wondered how he could afford it – surely a paper round didn't pay *that* much. Maybe he stole to pay for the stuff, but it wasn't something she could ask, and anyway, perhaps it was best she didn't know. Yesterday had been an effort. Once she realised there was nothing forthcoming, she had to endure his limited company for half an hour before she felt comfortable enough to make her excuses and leave. Had she left immediately, he would have realised how fickle she was, how she was simply using him; 'cupboard love' her mother would call it. And that, of course, would jeopardise future supply. In fact, all round, yesterday had been a waste of time. Her dad had suggested a trip to the Imperial War Museum and she only accepted because she thought it would impress Mr Moyes. She liked her history teacher. He seemed so intelligent and sensitive, unlike all the retarded boys around her at school. One day, she would marry him or, at least, someone very much like him.

Once inside the park, Charlotte let Angus off the lead. He immediately ran off, squatted down near the paddling pool and did a huge poo. Had her father been with her, he would remind her whose dog Angus was, produce a plastic bag and make Charlotte scoop it up. But without her father, Charlotte had the rebellious satisfaction of leaving it where it was – just waiting for some poor sod to step in it. As she turned the corner, she could see the oak tree looming in the distance. It always embarrassed her how her parents insisted on calling it *their* tree, as if they had a God-given right to it just because they used it so often as a picnic place. She scanned the park, looking for him. Surely, he hadn't gone already, she wasn't that late. Angus trotted a few yards ahead of her. As she approached the giant tree, someone stepped out from behind it.

'Boo!'

Charlotte jumped, Angus barked. 'For Christ's sake, Gavin, what are you playing at?' she snapped.

The chubby youth with spiky dyed black hair and an earring sniggered. 'Watchya.' As always, he was wearing his black tee shirt with bold red lettering on it, which read: 'Swivel on it', and a pair of fresh, white trainers and an Adidas bag slung over his shoulder. 'Why did you bring that stupid mutt?' he asked with a sneer.

'He's *not* a "stupid mutt".'

'I 'ate dogs. Stepped in some dog shit yesterday. If I'd seen the bugger, I'd have kicked the bloody thing.'

Charlotte smiled at the thought of Gavin stepping in Angus's poo. 'Guess you didn't step in it with those lovely white trainers, didya?' She knew his trainers were too new and clean for his liking.

'Piss off,' he said.

There was a lull. She was desperate to know whether he'd brought anything, but she had to maintain her cool. But having a conversation with Gavin was difficult. Unless he was mouthing off about one of his numerous pet hates, he had virtually nothing of interest to say, at least nothing of any interest to Charlotte.

'Shall we go then?' he asked.

'What? You've got some?' asked Charlotte, trying not to appear over-enthusiastic.

'What do ya think, baby? Do you want some?' He was relishing his moment of power.

'Yeah, fuck it; why not.' She always swore when she was with Gavin; it was like a prerequisite. It didn't come naturally, but she hoped it made her look cooler. 'Look, I'll give you some money towards it soon, I can always nick a bit from my mum's purse; she'd never know.' The thought appalled her.

'Nah, don't worry 'bout it,' said Gavin, 'I'll think of some other way you can pay me… one day.'

Charlotte didn't know why, but his choice of words made her feel uneasy. Maybe noticing her discomfort, he immediately qualified it. 'You can do my history homework if you like. What do you know 'bout the Great Fire of London, 1665?'

'1666,' she corrected him.

'Whatever.'

'Not much, but I could find something out on the Internet if you want.'

'You're on. C'mon, let's go.' Gavin led the way towards the path at the far edge of the park, away from the café and the paddling pool. Charlotte called for Angus and followed. They walked silently along the path for a small distance until they came to a stretch of bushes. They fought their way through the waist-high thicket and found the large boulder they always sat on; the bushes around them providing a degree of shade from the glaring sun and shielded them from passers-by. Even if they were spotted through the scrub, no one ever challenged them. They sat down. Angus scuttled off sniffing for new olfactory delights, but stayed within close range of Charlotte.

Gavin produced the familiar green and gold tobacco tin from his bag. Inside were a couple of cigarettes, a packet of long cigarette papers, a lighter, and a little block of the shiny dark substance. Charlotte watched as Gavin split one of the cigarettes down the middle with his fingernail and spread its contents evenly down the length of a cigarette paper. He then produced the dark cube of resin and carefully softened it by holding it above the lighter flame.

Charlotte noticed the picture of the sprawling naked woman on the lighter. In any other circumstances, she might have objected to this small but blatant example of pornography, but this wasn't the time. With the resin sufficiently softened, Gavin crushed the corner of the block between his fingers and, like a stock cube, sprinkled it evenly over the loose tobacco. He then expertly rolled the extra-long cigarette, licked it secure, and twisted the paper at one end. Finally, he tore a small piece of cardboard from the packet of cigarette papers, which already had a number of similar-sized pieces missing from it, rolled it up tightly, and pushed it down the other end of the joint.

'There!' he said triumphantly. 'You first.'

'No, no, after you.' Having waited all this time, Charlotte wanted to delay the pleasure for a few more seconds.

'Right you are.' Gavin lit the joint and took a couple of long puffs. 'No effect yet,' he said, passing it to Charlotte. She took it and inhaled deeply, waited for a few moments, and inhaled again. She smelt the acrid smoke and derived great pleasure from it, symbolising as it did her act of rebellion. After the third draw, she began to feel the tingling sensation slowly cascading through her insides. She took another drag and her head began to swim. She handed it back to Gavin and hunted around her bag for the can of Coke. She swallowed a couple of large swigs to try and counter the burning sensation on her tongue. Like an unspoken rule, conversation was prohibited during the ritual of smoking. For the next ten or so minutes, the two of them sat in total silence, passing the joint to and fro. She contemplated Gavin's bag. The joke at school was that Adidas stood for 'after dinner I dream about sex' or 'after dinner I do a shit'. She grinned to herself.

'You finish it,' said Gavin passing the frazzled end to Charlotte. She drew on the last possible bit, burning her fingertips in the process, and then threw the butt into the undergrowth where they watched it slowly burn itself out. They remained silent, Charlotte enjoying the relaxing warm feeling that seemed to reach to the very end of her fingers and toes. But then she suddenly felt nauseous; the last heavy draw had tipped her over the edge. She tried desperately to suppress the urge to be sick, not wanting Gavin to realise. But the urge became too strong and she retched.

'Oh shit,' said Gavin. 'You're not gonna be sick, are ya?'

Charlotte couldn't talk. She tried to stand up but felt dizzy in the heat and sat down again. Her head throbbed. She groaned and retched again. She put her head between her knees and tried to catch her breath. Finally, after a couple of minutes, the nausea began to recede. She looked at Gavin from the corner of her eye, too shamefaced to look at him directly. 'Sorry,' she muttered.

'Don't worry 'bout it. Happens to all of us.'

Charlotte was taken aback. She'd never heard him admit to the slightest hint of weakness before, and she certainly hadn't expected any sympathy from him. Angus nudged her elbow; he wanted to go. She stroked him and Gavin almost smiled. 'I'd better go,' she said.

'Right.'

She took a last gulp of warm Coke and flung the empty can into the undergrowth – it would have looked too uncool to put it in her bag. She stood up. She felt unsteady still, but she needed to leave. 'I'll be seeing ya then.'

'Yeah, I'll text you when I get some more, all right?'

'Cheers, Gav.' She made her way through the bushes back to the path and, with Angus running in circles around her, headed back towards the oak tree.

Once out of the park, she put Angus back onto the lead. As she ambled home along the backstreets of Holloway, she chewed on her chewing gum; she needed to freshen her breath before getting back. Her cheeks still burned with the heat of the day and the embarrassment of having almost been sick in front of Gavin. The nausea had subsided but she was left with a throbbing headache; she needed to lie down in a cool room. As she turned into her road, Angus saw something on the opposite pavement, his ears pricked up and suddenly he darted off, the lead slipping from Charlotte's light grasp before she had time to react.

'Angus!' she screamed as the terrier charged across the empty road. Whatever had pricked Angus's attention had vanished, leaving the dog barking at nothing, his tail wagging furiously. 'Angus, you naughty dog,' said Charlotte as she caught up with him, slapping him with the end of the lead. She took Angus home, the dog sufficiently cowered, holding his lead with a firmer grip. By the time she reached home, his tail was wagging again, the incident already forgotten.

*

Tom sneaked out of the house while Julie was still getting dressed. He had no desire to stay in while Julie was around. It was another glorious day; the sun seemed to bounce off the pavement, bleaching the paving stones. He phoned Rachel on his mobile and asked if he could come round for a coffee. At first, Rachel hesitated, said she had an appointment at the bank. Tom said it didn't matter; he'd catch her some other time. But no, Rachel insisted on cancelling the appointment and yes, she was sure, totally sure. Strange, he thought – having arranged to see her he was immediately regretting it.

Fifteen minutes later, Tom was sitting on a squashy settee inside Rachel's living room, re-familiarizing himself with his surroundings while she made him a cup of tea. The settee was far too big and soft for Tom's liking and covered with oddly coloured cushions. Beams of sunlight highlighted the layers of dust; the room was cluttered with papers, newspaper supplements, schoolbooks, and various coats and items of clothing. The stereo was almost obscured by a jungle of CDs and records; all jumbled around with discs lying out of their cases and on the floor. The walls were painted a bright mauve colour decorated with prints of impressionist paintings. Next to the fireplace stood a foot-high brass figurine of an angel. 'Where's Blue... Adrian?' He shouted through to the kitchen.

'I don't know,' Rachel shouted back. Even when she shouted, her voice sounded gentle and slightly high-pitched.

'Doesn't he live with you?'

'God no, he's far too messy.'

Tom suppressed an ironic laugh. 'I've seen him before. He knows Claudette.'

'Who?' she yelled from the kitchen.

'My boss.'

A coal-black cat wandered in and greeted Tom with a gentle meow. Rachel appeared with two mugs of tea. She looked lovely, he thought, even slopping around at home; she was always so alluring, almost mysterious. He wondered how she managed financially. She probably didn't – hence the trip to the bank. She seemed to flit from one lowly paid job to another. Abigail's father had bolted the minute she was born. He'd been a roadie for a rock band and obviously, the allure of casual sex and life on the road appealed more than the responsibilities of fatherhood. Rachel was wearing a thin, rainbow-coloured top and black leggings which accentuated her slenderness, and a pair of long decorative earrings. He remembered how struck he was the first time he met her. 'Herbal tea, OK? I'd offer you a biscuit if I had any,' she said, handing Tom his tea.

Had she forgotten, he wondered, he hated herbal tea? 'So how long have you been going out with Adrian?'

'Why do you assume we're going out?'

'Well, aren't you?'

'Sort of,' she said, sitting down on the squashy settee next to Tom. 'How well do you know him?'

'He's been round to our office a couple of times. He works for a competitor. What I want to know is what he and Claudette are talking about. Our two firms are meant to be deadly rivals.'

'Your boss is called Claudette?'

'Yeah. Why?'

'Don't know. It just sounds like a bossy name, that's all. So tell me, did the library book provide any clues?' She pulled on an earring.

Tom closed his eyes for a few moments and nodded. 'Mr Moyes,' he said quietly.

'What? Abigail and Charlotte's history teacher? But he's a drip with floppy hair. You are joking me.'

'How I wish I was, the bastard.' Her instinctive reaction depressed Tom further. If Julie was desperate enough to fall for a drip with floppy hair, where did that leave him?

'Oh, Tom, I'm sorry. Do you know how long it's been going on?'

'The library couldn't tell me that,' he said tonelessly.

Rachel laughed her little delicate laugh that he'd always loved. 'What are you going to do?'

'I don't know.' He sipped his tea; it tasted like flowery soap. 'I can't believe she's doing this to me, I really can't. I keep asking myself – where have I gone wrong?'

'Tom,' she said, sidling up to him, 'you've done nothing wrong. She doesn't deserve you, you know I've always thought that.' She rubbed his leg reassuringly. She'd always been a tactile person. This was why he had come. This is what he wanted to hear; to have his leg stroked and his shattered ego caressed.

The cat brushed against his shin as if in sympathy and purred. He leant down and stroked it. 'I thought we were doing OK; I had no idea this was happening. How stupid of me.'

'She's greedy, Tom, always has been. If she wants something, she thinks she can just click her fingers and it'll come.' She clicked her fingers to emphasise the point. 'I'm sorry to say this, but I never thought you were right for each other.'

He ran his fingers through his hair and groaned. He had expected nothing less from her. But she was wrong; he and Julie *were* right for each other, they'd been married fifteen years, and they had a happy existence, a happy life. He loved her and she… well, he thought she loved him, but how could he be sure any more? 'I'm not sure what to do.'

'Confront her; what else can you do?'

'I'm scared. I know that sounds silly but I'm scared of what I might find out. I don't want to lose her; I don't know what I'd do without her.'

She placed her mug on the floor and looked at him directly, her face inches away from his, her bright crimson lipstick glistening. 'You'd come back to me, Tom, that's what you would do,' she whispered. 'Back to me where, in your heart of hearts, you know you belong. I'd never do this to you, you know that, never.' She leant slightly forward and kissed him delicately on his closed lips. He could taste the lipstick and camomile tea on her lips. The cat purred. Then, almost with a jolt, he came to his senses.

'Rachel, no. Please.'

'I know it was a long time ago; sixteen years is a long time. But I've never forgotten and I know you haven't either. And then there was that night in Lewisham.'

'Lewisham?'

'You know full well,' she said quietly.

*

Yes, thought Tom, wandering home in the sun, he remembered it well – a drunken, intoxicated kiss at a party in Lewisham three years previously. He'd regretted it immediately. He and Rachel had finished sixteen years back; he'd met Julie, got married and that was it. Lewisham was a mistake. He was out with friends, got drunk, gone to a party, bumped into Rachel and had been swept along in a drunken haze of nostalgia. That's all it had been – a nostalgic kiss with an old flame – nothing more.

Chapter 4: *The Café*

'Perfect mother and the model wife,' Julie muttered for the umpteenth time as she made herself a cup of coffee. 'As well as holding down a full-time career,' she added resentfully. 'Bloody superwoman.' How in the hell she managed to find time to have an affair, she had no idea. Her whole life was an admirable example of time management; she could write a book on the subject – if she had the time. She could call it "How to keep your husband *and* your lover satisfied, whilst cooking, cleaning and doing all the housework, teaching 30 adolescent kids and looking after one truculent teenager of your own". How do *you* do it, all the other mums would ask. Simple, would be her caustic reply, you drink too much, eat too much, resent the things you love, and have the occasional breakdown. But having a lover with a tongue like a lizard *has* its compensations.

She sat at the kitchen table and looked at the pile of exercise books awaiting her attention; the radio in the background playing 'Everybody's Changing' by Keane. She glanced at the vase of flowers at the end of the table that Tom had bought her for their wedding anniversary the previous week. They were beginning to look faded – said it all. Her mobile phone rang, the tinny sound of 'The Ride of the Valkyries' bringing her back to the present. She glanced at the number – it was Mark. He was forever phoning her on her mobile, sometimes at the most awkward of times, and however many times she told him not to, he'd always forget – or pretended to. She wondered whether he did it on purpose, hoping to force the issue by exposing their secret. This time, she'd been expecting his call and was relieved he hadn't phoned in the middle of supper; she wouldn't put it past him. But she wasn't sure if she could face him yet. She let it ring until the answering facility kicked in and listened back to his message after he'd hung up. Unsurprisingly, Mark sounded hesitant. It was a "we-need-to-talk" type message. He suggested they meet for lunch at "the usual place" at one o'clock.

No, not any more, she thought. She'd had too close a shave and it'd brought a few truths home to roost. The affair was finished, and that was it. She never wanted to go through that again. OK, she felt sorry for Mark; it was going to be hard for him. If he had his way, she'd up and leave Tom and Charlotte today, and move in and set up a new life with him; he really had a shine for her. She couldn't call it love, she felt embarrassed even thinking of the word, and anyway, she did not want Mark to be in love with her. Things were complicated enough as they were. But for her, Mark was a distraction, an occasional screw – an enjoyable screw, but no more than that.

The phone rang again, this time the main telephone in the hallway. She picked it up. 'Yes,' she said impatiently, knowing it was Mark.

'Julie? It's Rachel.'

'Rachel? Oh, Rachel, I'm sorry, I thought… it doesn't matter.'

'I know it's a bit out of the blue but I wondered if you fancied a coffee.'

And so it was arranged. But Rachel was right, it was out of the blue; they hadn't seen each other in ages. Julie didn't want to go out so she persuaded Rachel to come over. She quite fancied the company; any excuse not to do the marking. Julie quite liked Rachel, even if she was a bit dippy and too flirty with Tom. Not that Rachel was Tom's type, she was far too fey and girlie for him, too much of a modern-day hippie. Oddly enough, thought Julie, she'd be more suited to Mark, what with his earnest social conscience and his left-wing credentials.

Back in the kitchen, she opened the first exercise book and flipped to the last pages. What terrible handwriting, she thought. She wondered whether to meet Mark. Perhaps after eighteen months, he deserved an explanation. They had met two years ago at a teachers' conference in Brighton. He may've looked a bit vacant, but he was clever. He was delivering a lecture on meeting the needs of multiculturalism in the Special Needs classroom, but Julie couldn't concentrate. He wasn't particularly attractive in any normal sense of the word, but he possessed a conviction, a passion even, for what he did and what he spoke about. Later that evening, she bumped into him in the conference bar. She complimented him on his talk but because she hadn't been listening, she couldn't keep up with the resultant conversation. Her attempts to steer the subject to less politically charged topics appeared obvious and ham-fisted. Feeling disadvantaged by his conviction, and unable to bluff her way out, Julie made her excuses and left. But six months later, she saw him again. He'd come to her school for a meeting between regional secondary schools. It transpired that not only did he teach locally, but that he actually taught at her daughter's school and Charlotte was soon due to be in his class. This time, being on home territory, Julie felt more at ease. They hit it off and followed the meeting with lunch at a local pub, the Rose and Crown. Within a fortnight, they had slept together for the first time.

Turning the radio off, Julie picked up a small pile of exercise books and, with her coffee, went through to the sitting room. She sat down on the plump sofa with a sigh and wondered why she was risking so much. Why was she having an affair with Mark when she couldn't wish for a better husband than Tom? He still made her laugh, they enjoyed each other's company, and their love life was still good, albeit routine. And, most importantly, she still loved him. Yes, she still loved him. So, what was the reason? Was it purely the sex? Her face flushed at the thought. Even admitting it to herself, it seemed so immoral, so dirty. As a teenager, she'd been in no hurry to lose her virginity and when finally she did, it was to the man she would later marry. Yes, there'd been a couple of other boyfriends before they married, but she'd never slept with them and they'd been so brief, she could barely remember their names let alone their faces. Then she met Mark and she realised that after thirteen years of marriage, she wanted to experience sex with another man. She needed to satisfy her curiosity and once she had, she became addicted to Mark's lovemaking and his surprisingly daring attitude to sex. Julie smiled at the thought. On impulse, she snatched her mobile, rang Mark and said, 'Yes, I'll meet you at one, see you there.' She hung up before Mark had a chance to say anything – just as the doorbell rang.

*

Julie Searight was not the only woman reminiscing about a man. Rachel had thought of nothing but. Adrian rang and said he'd be around later, but she said no, she was going out to the bank. Yes, she had got the time mixed up. There was no way she wanted to see Adrian, not now with Tom back on the scene. It had been sixteen years since their relationship ended, but she remembered every detail. Their dates, their nights out, the long conversations, the sex. She was heartbroken when she broke it off, but what choice did she have? He'd started seeing another woman behind her back and she wasn't prepared to play second fiddle, without a future, without his full devotion. She met a new man and had a child just at the same time as Tom and Julie, his new woman, had Charlotte. Living nearby, the two women got to know each other from various playgroups while their daughters were still toddlers. If truth be known, Rachel had engineered it, purposely bumping into Julie. They became friends of sorts, if only because of the girls. She couldn't stand the woman. She was a self-centred, devious cow and so obviously mismatched with the kind-hearted Tom. Over the years, she'd kept in touch from a safe distance while Abigail and Charlotte became best friends and were often at each other's houses.

In the meantime, Rachel had had her fair share of boyfriends, but none that mattered. She resigned herself to the life of a single parent. The thought of rekindling her relationship with Tom had entered her mind many times but never as a serious possibility. At least, not until now. The fact Julie was having an affair came as no surprise. What luck, she thought, surely even Tom couldn't be that forgiving; he'd leave her and destiny would take care of the rest. But first, she had to give destiny a helping hand.

Julie answered the door, greeting Rachel with a hug and a peck on both cheeks. 'Rachel, long time no see, come in, do come in.' Rachel followed Julie through into the kitchen. She sat down at the large wooden table that dominated the oversized room and noticed the poor excuse for a bunch of flowers. She accepted Julie's offer of a coffee. While Julie rinsed out a couple of mugs, Rachel reacquainted herself with the kitchen. It was all far too chic for her taste, spotlessly clean, always had been. Everything had its place; everything neatly ordered and organised. It was nauseating.

'So, Rachel, it's so nice to see you after all this time. It's been ages. How are tricks?'

'Not bad, not bad.'

The two women talked quickly, catching up on their news – Rachel's work, Julie's work, house prices, Rachel's ex-boyfriend with the blue beard; Tom, the lovely Tom.

'And how's Charlotte?' asked Rachel.

'Oh, she's fine, enjoying her half-term. Decaffeinated all right? She's out at the moment, don't know where. I think she said she was going to see the new Harry Potter film this afternoon.'

'Oh yes, it's just come out, hasn't it? *The Prisoner of Azerbaijan*. Decaffeinated's fine.'

Julie laughed. 'Azkaban. Azerbaijan's a country.'

'Oh, yes. Mmm.' She pulled on her earring. Typical Julie, she thought, always such a know-it-all.

'So, how's Abigail?' asked Julie. 'Is she doing this First World War project?'

'Yes, she's forming a girl group, three of them. They're calling themselves the Passchendaele Sisters.'

'Passchen what?'

'It was a battle, apparently. Abigail asked Charlotte to be part of it but I think Charlotte's keen on doing some poetry.'

'Yes, silly girl, she'll be terrified on stage by herself, but she thinks she can do it so who am I to argue?'

'Perhaps she's under pressure from the teacher, what's his name?' She wanted to hear her say his name.

'Mr Moyes. Sugar? Milk?'

No hesitation, thought Rachel, not a flicker. 'Neither, thanks. Do you know him, this Mr Moyes?'

'Yes. Occasionally we have these meetings between local schools; I've met him on a couple of those.'

I bet, thought Rachel. 'What's he like?'

'Oh, you know, nice enough. A bit serious.'

'Don't forget it's parents' evening this week. Wednesday, isn't it?'

'No, Rachel, it's Tuesday.'

'Ah yes. Of course.'

The women continued speaking at length about their daughters and their friends at school, about their preferred choices for GCSE subjects, the teachers and the standard of teaching. Rachel noticed Julie glance at the clock a couple of times. She needed to push the conversation on. 'I saw Tom yesterday in the park.'

'Oh, he didn't say.'

'He was walking the dog.'

'Was he? He often does. Fancy a top-up?'

'I'm fine thanks. We all go back a long way.'

'Of course.'

'You're so lucky to have someone as kind as Tom; he's a good man. And so handsome. He hasn't lost his looks, has he?'

Julie laughed. 'No, I guess not. Bit greyer round the edges.'

'Aren't we all? It was nice to see him again after all this time. He does make me laugh sometimes, always did. We all ought to go out again, like we used to.'

'Did we go out that much?'

'Why, yes. Don't you remember that party we all went to in Lewisham, about three years ago?'

'Yes, I do – someone's fortieth. But I didn't go, remember? Charlotte was ill, or something.'

'Oh, of course. Pity, you should've been there. We all got so drunk, it *was* funny.'

Julie laughed again. 'Yes, I think I remember Tom rolling in, his shirt stinking of smoke and cheap perfume.'

'Did he?' Rachel grimaced at the description of her perfume being cheap, but she was almost there. 'Did you suspect something?'

'No, of course not. Why? Ha, don't tell me there's something I should know.'

Rachel finished off her coffee and purposely averted Julie's gaze. 'Well…' she said, elongating the word as far as she could stretch it. This was it, she thought, a minor confession of a drunken kiss, with perhaps a few doleful glances thrown in. Then a throwaway comment about regret, followed by a full confession of her love and declarations of guilt and remorse, qualified with 'best-to-clear-the-air'-type platitudes. Then leave destiny to do the rest.

They heard the front door open. Rachel shot a look at the kitchen door and strained her neck to see down the hallway. If this was Tom, his timing was perfect.

'Hiya, I'm back.'

'In here, Charlotte, I'm with Abigail's mum.'

Rachel sighed.

Charlotte breezed into the kitchen. 'Hello,' she said to Rachel. 'Is Abigail here?'

'No, she's out practising with the Passchendaele Sisters,' said Rachel, with little enthusiasm.

'They don't want to make it a foursome now, do they?'

'I don't know; you'd have to ask her.' She looked at her watch. 'Look, I'd better go. Thanks for the coffee, Julie, it's been lovely to see you again.'

Julie smiled. 'Yes indeed,' she said. 'It has been lovely. We must do it again sometime.'

*

An hour later, Julie was making her way to meet Mark at the Café Noir on Holloway Road. She'd put some make-up on and, despite the heat, wore her new and rather expensive coat. She wondered why she'd been so extravagant with the make-up – she was going in order to finish the affair, not to entice him back into bed. But applying excessive make-up when she was about to meet Mark had become a subconscious habit and she had to stop herself from changing into more alluring underwear. She'd enjoyed Rachel's visit. Over the years she'd lost touch with all her friends – life just got in the way. She'd never been particularly friendly with Rachel, but still, it was nice of her to get in contact. And so out of the blue. She must make the effort and nurture her friendships more.

She paused outside the café, slipping off her coat. This was their usual meeting place; the staff there knew them both by sight. She remembered how once Tom suggested they popped in there for lunch, and the lengths she had to go to, to drag him elsewhere while trying to remain calm. She looked at the time on her mobile; she was five minutes late, but she usually was. How many times during the last eighteen months had they met here and how many times had she been on time? But this, she decided, was going to be their last occasion. It was over; this was 'closure'. She took a deep breath and entered.

She glanced around at the familiar congenial décor – the primary coloured walls, the framed black and white photographs of Hollywood stars and Parisian street scenes, the large potted plants, the jazz CD playing in the background, the staff buzzing around, dressed in black and white, the cramped atmosphere of cooking and cigarette smoke, and the hum of conversation and shouted orders. As usual at lunchtime, the place was heaving, every table taken, but Mark was there reading a newspaper at their favourite table – one small enough not to have to share with anyone else, next to the fish tank full of various brightly coloured fish darting in and out between the vegetation and fake stones. How familiar it all was. Her adulterous life had become even more routine than her married life. Same man, same rendezvous, same table, and probably, knowing her and Mark, the same choice from the menu, washed down with the same drinks. As she approached the table, Mark looked up at her, smiled, folded up the newspaper and stood up. It was one of the things she'd always liked about Mark – his old-fashioned courtesy. It made her feel just a tiny bit special. Tom used to be very gentlemanly as well, but over the years it had slowly dissolved. In fact, now that she thought of it, it rather quickly evaporated soon after they got married. It was probably a generic fault within men, part of their courtship ritual, something to impress the ladies, but not built to last.

'Hello, Julie, five minutes late again?' He suddenly looked awkward. 'Sorry, I didn't mean that as a… '

Poor Mark, he was nervous. 'Don't worry. Sit down.' She draped her coat over the chair and tried to smile, but Mark's expression was grave. They sat in silence for a couple of minutes. Julie saw the picture of David Beckham on the back page of Mark's folded *Guardian*. She took a cursory look at the menu, which she could recite word for word whilst Mark looked down and fiddled with his napkin.

'I'm sure it gets smokier in here every time,' she said. 'I don't see the point in having a no smoking bit; the place is too small for it to make any difference. Are there any interesting specials on the board today? Not that I feel hungry, I had a late breakfast. I wish they'd open the windows; it's very hot in here. Oh dammit, I can't decide, I think I'll just have what I usually have. Adventurous to the last, eh? What're you having? Don't tell me – sausages and chips in the onion gravy. But don't choke on the mustard this time.' She chuckled at the memory, but Mark hadn't been listening. 'Mark?'

'What do you think we should do?' he said without looking at her.

'Have sausages and chips in the onion—'

'Julie, please.' He glared at her.

'I'm sorry, I suppose I'm on edge too.'

'It was a silly mistake going back to yours.'

'Ready to order now?' a voice interrupted. Julie looked up at the young, skinny, Mediterranean-looking waitress dressed head to toe in black and white, a ring in her nose.

'Yes, er, I'll have the...' she paused. She really wasn't hungry. 'No, second thoughts, I'll just have a side salad please.'

'What type?' asked the waitress, shifting her weight onto one leg, sucking on the end of her pencil.

'Caesar.'

'Same for me please,' said Mark.

'Is that it? Anything to drink?'

'Two café lattes,' said Mark. Julie nodded. The wickedly slim waitress flounced off without a word.

'Heck, I suppose she thinks it's not worth us taking up a whole table just for side salads,' said Julie.

'Does Tom know?' asked Mark leaning towards her.

'No. At least I don't think so.'

Mark fiddled with his napkin again, trying to find the right words. 'We can still carry on seeing each other if you want.'

'No, Mark,' she said quietly, 'I don't think we should. Not now.'

'But why not?' he whispered urgently. 'If he didn't see us, if he doesn't know…?'

'I don't know for sure that he didn't see us. And anyway, that's not the point, we've had a warning.'

'A warning?'

'Yes. Look, Mark, I had the scare of my life when that door almost opened, I almost peed myself.'

'But that doesn't mean we have to stop just like that. We can still carry on, surely, we just stick to my place, he'd never know.'

'I know, I know.' She twisted a salt pot around in her fingers and sighed. 'It's made me think and the point is…' She didn't want to have to say it.

'The point is?'

But she was going to have to. 'Oh, come on, Mark, you know I've never hidden the fact that I still love Tom.' She saw him flinch at her words. 'Mark, I'm a married woman for Heaven's sake, a happily married woman with a fourteen-year-old daughter who, by the way, happens to dote on you, in case you hadn't realised. I've got a fairly decent job and a lovely home. I can't just, just…' She waved her hands about, trying to find the words that summed it up without sounding trite. 'I can't just throw it all away.' She'd failed and she could tell she hadn't convinced Mark. 'Anyway, it's all right for you,' she said, changing the focus of her argument. 'You're single. You're not risking anything; you don't stand to lose everything.'

'Apart from my job, perhaps? Anyway, I'm losing you.'

'Come on, don't do this, you know full well what I mean. It's time to move on, Mark, you deserve better.' Oh God, she thought, did she really have to say that? Mark momentarily turned his head away in disgust, she couldn't blame him; he was not a man who could be fobbed off with clichés.

'Spare me,' he spat. 'I'm not a bloody teenager, I mean, please…'

'I know, I'm sorry; I didn't mean to come out like that. It's *true* though. Look at yourself. You're five years younger than me, you're good-looking, you're an all-round decent bloke, you're single and you're solvent. You could have them falling at your feet. I mean, don't you ever ask yourself what you're doing knocking around with some forty-year-old married woman who once thought puffball skirts were the height of fashion?'

Mark laughed. 'Now that you mention it…'

'There you go then. I know it sounded hackneyed but seriously, that's what I meant – you do deserve something better from life.'

'I know, but, but…' His eyes fell back to the napkin.

Julie felt a surge of panic. Please don't say it, she thought, just don't say it.

'But I think I love you, Julie.'

Oh, Christ help me, he'd said it. Julie's reaction was immediate. 'No,' she said firmly. 'No, you don't, Mark. We've come to know each other, we like each other, we have a lot in common and I'm great in bed–'

'Caesar salad for you, sir, and Caesar salad for…' The nose-ringed waitress raised an eyebrow at Julie. 'For madam.' Julie felt her face go crimson as she snatched the napkin as a child does a comfort blanket. 'And two café lattes. Enjoy!'

'Oh, how embarrassing,' said Julie. 'She couldn't stop smirking. "Madam" indeed!'

'She was taking the mick,' said Mark. They both giggled into their respective salads. 'And we do have a laugh,' he added.

'Yes, we do,' smiled Julie. 'But mainly I'm great in bed.'

They ate in silence. Enough had already been said, there was nothing else to add and further conversation seemed inappropriate somehow. What else can one say after the end of an affair? She would miss it. It started off as a great adventure before turning routine and predictable, but she still enjoyed it. She enjoyed having this huge secret. It would still be a secret, but a secret with which to remember a past, a secret without a present. Did it make it safer? Hopefully. Why come all this way and fall at the last hurdle? Even coming to this café was a risk. But no one had ever spotted them in here before; no one was going to now.

Eventually, having finished their salads, Julie said, 'We ought to go.'

'Yes,' said Mark reluctantly. 'You're right, of course. It's not love, it's just, I don't know, infatuation?'

'Yes, and likewise,' agreed Julie, leaving her napkin neatly to the side of the plate.

'Oh well,' he said. 'See you next Tuesday, I guess.'

'Yes, the dreaded parents' evening. Thanks for reminding me.' Julie picked up her coat. She took Mark's hand from across the table and squeezed it gently. 'See you Tuesday then.' As she stood up and turned to leave, she paused and smiled at him. 'Thanks,' she said, and then she left, leaving Mark to settle the bill – as usual.

Outside Julie walked briskly along through Holloway, past all the familiar shops and grocery stalls spilling their wares out onto the pavement – racks of fruit and vegetables, shops selling fake leather bags and sports bags shining in the sun. She felt relieved; she'd managed to finish it yet still leave on good terms. Why had she thanked him like that at the end? Was she saying thank you for being so understanding; thanks for the meal; thanks for taking her beyond the limits of her sexual imagination? No, she was thanking herself. Thankful for having had the courage to say what had to be said. It was over, now she could go back to her old life as a perfect mother and the model wife, safe with her secret.

Chapter 5: *Parents' House*

The last weekend of the half-term passed by in a vacuum for Tom. Every time he stirred himself to confront Julie, his courage seemed to melt away. Although still driven crazy with all the questions bombarding his mind, part of him elected to remain in ignorance. He still couldn't face the inevitable bust-up, the recriminations, the fallout. He told himself not to be such a coward, but what really held him back was the fear of finding something out about himself he preferred not to know. He imagined being presented with a list of his inadequacies and that was something he would rather do without.

And so he spent the weekend keeping his distance – mending that garden fence, something he'd been meaning to do for weeks; cutting and raking the lawn; buying things he wouldn't use from the DIY store. On the Saturday evening, Julie rewarded his dutiful work with a fine roast duck, accompanied by an expensive bottle of red wine. Afterwards, they all watched a family blockbuster Tom had hired from the local video shop. He would have gone to the library but couldn't face the young library assistant.

Sunday morning, the newspapers were full of obituaries for Ronald Reagan who'd died the day before. On the Sunday night, Tom rang his father and asked if he could pop over. So, after a dinner of leftover duck and a bottle of cheap beer, Tom left Julie and Charlotte watching a television police drama and drove over to his parent's place in Enfield. Ten years previously, Robert and Alice Searight had moved out of the three-storey semi-detached family home in Charlton, which had become too big and moved into a newly-built suburban cul-de-sac. Tom and his older brother, Alec, had left home a few years before, gone to college, got jobs and settled down. Much to Robert and Alice's consternation, Alec married a Canadian and moved to Toronto. They liked Vanessa as much as they liked Julie, but it meant the Searight seniors rarely saw two of their three grandchildren. The plus side, of course, meant that they had had several holidays in Toronto, but their dearest wish was for Alec and his family to move back to England. The new house in Enfield was a low maintenance, characterless affair, with overactive central heating, wall-to-wall non-descript carpets and plastic-framed double glazing. The interior was far too chintzy for Tom's liking: too many little ornaments, silly knick-knacks and embarrassing family photographs.

His mother answered the door. She was a short, slightly rounded woman with curly hair that had maintained its colour. She always wore a subtle amount of make-up; Tom couldn't imagine her any other way. She greeted him with a kiss and routine 'how's the family' questions. She offered to make him a cup of tea and disappeared into the kitchen. Tom found his father watching the television, wearing his usual dark blue cardigan, and off-green corduroys and plain brown slippers. Never a man for sartorial extravagance, Robert had always maintained a rigid and limited scope in his choice of colours. He was glued to the same police drama Tom had just escaped from; the cops were gearing themselves up for an airport arrest. Tom plonked himself into the garishly patterned armchair and exchanged 'mustn't grumble' type pleasantries with his father who kept his eyes fixed on the television. He still had a full head of hair, albeit totally grey and usually dishevelled. The bad guys were coming through passport control; the plain-clothes policemen lay in wait. The adverts came on. Robert asked Tom about his work, which Tom managed to parry with bland answers. The familiar conversation took its usual course. Tom would complain about his boss, Claudette, and Robert would sympathise by making disparaging comments about bosses generally.

'Here we are then,' said his mother carrying a tray with two steaming cups of tea on saucers and a little plate of biscuits.

'Aren't you having one, Mum?' Tom asked as the police drama resumed.

'No, I'm just writing a letter to Alec in the kitchen. Sad to hear about Ronald Reagan, isn't it?'

'Yes, of course.' Tom sipped his tea – too sweet, his mother always put too much sugar in his tea.

'How's Charlotte?' asked his father. 'How's the war project coming on?'

'OK, but she needs to pick a poem to recite at the school concert. The whole theme is First World War – sound effects, songs, poems and so on. It's for the ninetieth anniversary.'

'I do know the dates, Tom.' His father still hadn't taken his eyes off the television. The police were closing in on the bad guys. He slurped his tea. 'Ugh, not enough sugar.'

'Ah, maybe we've taken the wrong ones. Here – swap.' They exchanged mugs and gingerly tasted the contents. Satisfied, they settled down to watch the unfolding events. A chase had broken out, shots fired, a bad guy hit, a screaming woman, then a sudden stop… 'To be continued after the news', voice-over and credits followed.

'I hate it when they do that,' grumbled Robert. 'Means you have to stay up to God knows what time to see the end and then you don't really care anyway.'

'Why do you bother then?' asked Tom, but Robert didn't answer. 'Dad, are you still ex-directory?'

'Yes. Doesn't stop all those bloody calls trying to sell us something.'

'So, you wouldn't have received a letter from France recently?'

'What's that got to do with the phone directory?' his father asked, trying to watch the television news.

'It's just that I got this letter. I thought you might be interested.' Tom fished the letter from his back pocket and handed it to his father. Robert read it slowly without expression.

'Hmm, that's us all right,' he said passing the letter back to Tom and returning his attention to the news.

Tom was disappointed; he thought his father would show more interest. 'So Guy Searight is related. I thought so.'

'So why did you ask?'

'I wasn't sure. You never talk about your past.' Whenever Tom tried to bring up the subject, Robert became almost bad-tempered and clammed up. The subject had long been a family taboo.

His father realised it. 'True,' he said sheepishly. 'Like she says, Searight is an unusual name. He was your great-uncle, but you wouldn't remember him – he died soon after you were born.'

'So he fought during the First World War?'

'Oh yes. Have you got back to this French woman yet?'

'No, I thought *you* might like to?'

'No, no, not me, thanks; I'll leave it up to you.'

Tom was surprised; he thought it'd be the sort of project his father would relish. 'Do you remember him?'

'Of course. Nice chap. He and my aunt lived not too far away from my parents in Devon. My father and he were cousins, not that they got on that well. He had a wooden leg. Biscuit?'

'A wooden leg?'

'Well, a false one, lost it during the war.' Robert laughed. 'I remember he took it off once to show me.' He helped himself to a biscuit and grinned at the memory.

'Anything else?'

'No. Actually yes, he had a brother – Jack. He was killed in the war. 1917.'

Alice reappeared, her letter finished. 'How's little Charlotte then?' she asked. 'Such a lovely girl.'

Tom remembered Tuesday evening was the night of the parents' evening. He asked if one of them would come over to 'babysit'. His father volunteered. It was settled. They discussed Charlotte's schooling and the general state of education. Robert compared it to bygone eras and used it as a springboard to start on his favourite pet subject of slipping standards in today's society. Tom felt relieved when, after the news, the police drama resumed. Robert turned the television volume up unbearably loud and Tom, taking his cue, departed.

So, thought Tom as he drove home, this Guy Searight *is* related. As soon as he got home, he went into what they called the study and turned his computer on. Charlotte had gone to bed and Julie was watching the continuation of the police thing. As Tom popped his head around the sitting room door, the cops were in hot pursuit. Julie seemed transfixed. He looked at her watching the television and felt a brief but overwhelming sense of resentment. How dare she carry on as if everything was normal? Had she no idea what she was doing to him? Determined to keep his mind focused on the letter from France, he returned to the study and re-read the letter while waiting for the modem to connect.

Connected, he wrote quickly:

> *Dear Maria,*
>
> *I recently received your letter concerning Guy Searight. I asked my father, Robert Searight, and apparently Guy was his uncle.*
>
> *My father told me that Guy lost a leg during the war and he ended up in Devon. Is this the same man? If so, I would be most interested in seeing his diary.*
>
> *I look forward to hearing from you,*
> *Best Wishes,*
> *Tom Searight.*

Satisfied, Tom logged off. Tomorrow, he was back at work and at the mercy of Claudette's whiplash tongue, what a prospect. He peeped into the sitting room. Julie was still glued to the box.

Chapter 6: *Parents' Evening*

It was Monday morning. The sun of the half-term had given way to drizzle. The Searight household was a subdued one – Charlotte was back to school, Julie also had to go back, and Tom was back to work. Tom worked for a company of office consultants based nearby in Islington. He'd been with Tooley & Hill plc for about five years. His job title was that of an Assistant Project Manager, commonly referred to as an APM. Tooley & Hill were, amongst many other projects, currently putting together a proposal as a tender to the local council for fitting out a new leisure complex. It was to consist of a swimming pool, an art gallery, museum, theatre and a public library. Tom had drawn the short straw – he'd been given the task of designing the layout for a "forward-looking, modern library" which was to occupy one whole floor. It all seemed a far cry from his little local municipal library on Valentine Road with its helpful, Data Protection-obsessed library assistant. The library patronised by Mark Moyes.

By the time Tom arrived at nine, the large, open-plan spacious office was already a hive of activity with the sound of tapping keyboards, ringing telephones, and urgent conversations. Clive, his immediate boss, passed him wearing his usual scowl. The two men grunted a 'morning' at each other. Tom sat down at his desk, which after just five days' off, was already piled high with various memos, reports, forms, letters, updates and unopened envelopes. He gazed at the two photographs on his desk – a school photo of Charlotte, and a jolly holiday shot of his wife and daughter hugging each other on a Spanish beach. It always made him smile because of the striking resemblance between mother and daughter. A harsh voice interrupted his thoughts.

'Where the hell have you been?' It was Claudette hovering over him. Claudette Tyler, Senior Project Manager and his boss's boss, always devastatingly made up and with an unending wardrobe of immaculate outfits, and a voice that could fell a moose at twenty paces with the choice and delivery of her words.

'I was on leave, of course,' said Tom, looking up.

'What? During such a critical time as this? Our biggest tender in years and you sod off for a week.' She was young, bright and absurdly confident with a head of long, multi-coloured corkscrew hair.

'When isn't it a "critical time"?' He was used to this; Claudette delighted in playing the role of the ruthless executive, and as long as Tom gave as good as he got, they seemed to rub along.

She repressed a smile. 'Well, whatever, you're gonna have to catch up. Clive's been tearing his hair out. While you've been swanning it, the rest of the team have made strides. You've fallen behind. We've got an APM progress meeting at ten where we can bring you up to speed with what's been happening, all right?'

'Don't worry, I'll catch up, but I've got to leave on time tomorrow.'

'What the bloody hell for?'

'Parents' evening.'

'Oh, for Christ's sake; you disappear for a week and then want to bugger off early as soon as you come back. Couldn't you have had this parents' thing during your time off?'

'Oddly enough, it's not up to me.' He enjoyed these silly games. She flicked her hair. Tom grinned; he always knew he'd scored a point when she did that.

'You don't say?' She smiled back; she couldn't help herself. 'Look, I don't really care, just get your final draft to me by Wednesday morning. The library department has finally gotten its act together and given us a list of their requirements.' She handed Tom a piece of paper.

He cast his eye down the list of prerequisites. 'Blimey, if they want a counter that big, it'll take up half the floor space. And surely they'll want more PCs than that.'

'That's what they want.'

He looked at her. 'Do you know a man called Adrian, has a blue beard, works for Dunstone, Cutler and Maine?'

Claudette glared at him, her eyes momentarily furious, but then immediately softened. She knew him all right. 'Someone at DCM? Never heard of him.'

'He knows you.'

'Like I said, never heard of him.' She turned abruptly to leave, her corkscrew hair bouncing behind her with each purposeful stride.

The young woman sitting at the desk to Tom's left smiled – Gabrielle, his very capable assistant. 'Welcome back,' she said with a wry smile.

'Thanks,' said Tom with a roll of the eyes.

*

Charlotte had had quite a good day at school, but she was dreading the prospect of Tuesday's parents' evening. She'd get a good report from Mr Parker ('Pick-a-Nose Parker') in geography, and Miss Baines in PE, although that probably didn't count for much, Mrs Moore for art and Miss Grossman in music (did those count?), and of course, the gorgeous Mr Moyes in history. And Mr Wodehouse (Mr Woodlouse) in English might be OK, but it was the science subjects she dreaded most. She perpetually mucked around with Mr Oparinde in physics, and Miss Bullock (Miss Bollocks) in biology hated her – she stood no chance there.

On the Monday, she had biology and Charlotte went out of her way to be well-behaved and attentive. She even volunteered to help Miss Bollocks wash out the Petri dishes. Abigail teased her; 'too little, too late,' she sniggered. On Tuesday, Charlotte had history with Mr Moyes. She told him about her trip to the Imperial War Museum with her dad, and Mr Moyes seemed suitably impressed with Charlotte's extracurricular activities. Charlotte brimmed with pride. Even Abigail singing "Born Too Late" failed to take the shine off her moment of glory. She even managed to behave during physics despite being bored stiff.

Charlotte saw Gavin briefly in the playground, but as a rule, they tended to ignore each other at school. He was in the year above. Any communication between them was conducted via text. She reluctantly declined Gavin's invitation to meet at the oak tree on Tuesday after school. It wasn't worth the risk with the parents' evening that night; she'd be too much the focus of attention.

And so the dreaded Tuesday evening was upon her. Her father was home early at 5.30 pm, and they ate the shepherd's pie her mum had prepared the evening before. Soon after 6.30

pm, her granddad arrived. She thought at the age of 14 she could be left alone in the house, but this wasn't the night to argue. And anyway, her granddad was a bit of a pushover; he always let her have the choice of what to watch on telly. Ten minutes after he arrived; her mum and dad were off, looking unnecessarily smart, thought Charlotte. She and her granddad always got on. She sometimes found herself telling him things she wouldn't tell her parents, and for an old man, he seemed to… well, understand. So when Robert asked whether she was worried about the parents' evening, she told him the truth – which teachers would be OK and the ones she was worried about. He soon cottoned on that the history teacher was a bit of a favourite.

'So what's so special about this Mr Boyes?' he asked.

'Mr *Moyes*,' she corrected him. 'I dunno, he's kinda nice, I guess.'

'Nice?'

Charlotte went all coy. 'Yeah, you know...'

'Yes, I know. I had a teacher at school, Miss Gilmore. I thought she was "kinda nice" too; the bee's knees.' He smiled at the distant memory. 'So, is this why you're so keen on doing your history project?'

'Yeah, but also cos we have to do this school performance about the First World War. Almost everyone in my year, anyone who does history, music or art.'

'Your dad says you're doing a recital.'

'Yeah, I've got to read out a poem. You can come if you like.'

'Thank you, Charlotte, I would like to very much. Are you worried about standing up in front of all your friends?'

'Bit, but it's only for a couple of minutes.'

'So, what poem are you doing?'

'Haven't decided yet. I got this book of war poetry from the museum, but they're either too long or got too many difficult words, and I don't really understand most of them. I suppose I ought to ask Dad for help.'

'Well, why don't you bring me the book and we could choose one together. I can try to explain what they mean.'

And so they did. Charlotte and her grandfather spent over half an hour going through the poems, dismissing most for a variety of reasons and making a shortlist of potentials. Eventually, they whittled it down to a list of six. 'More exciting than the Booker prize,' he commented. Charlotte understood this to be a little joke, but about what she had no idea. Robert suggested that she practised reciting all six to see which sounded the best. At first, she was reluctant, feeling too self-conscious to stand up and read in front of him, but, as he pointed out, she had to start somewhere and he was as good an audience as any. And so she did, gaining confidence as she went. In the end, they settled on three poems, but they agreed to keep it a secret. Satisfied with a good evening's work, Charlotte made her granddad a cup of tea and got herself a fizzy drink.

'Granddad?'

'Hmm?' Did she imagine it, or did he pull a face when he tasted his tea; maybe she hadn't put enough sugar in it.

'Dad was saying something about a woman in France writing to him 'bout your dad or something.'

'Not my father, my uncle, your great-great-uncle.'

'Was he in World War One?'

Robert sipped his tea and pondered the question. 'Yes, he was a very brave man. He had a brother called Jack, and a cousin called Lawrence who was my father. So I suppose Guy, I never knew Jack, was really a great-cousin, but they were all called Searight and it was easier calling him uncle. And then I had a brother called Clarence.'

Charlotte chortled. 'Clarence? Funny name.'

'He was older than me, born on the last day of the war; the first one, that is. He was the bright star of the family. Got himself killed during the Second World War – he was in the Navy. Another brave Searight. Then your grandmother and I had two boys – your father and your Uncle Alec, so it was a bit of a relief when you were born – too many boys!'

'Why was your brother a "bright star"?'

Her granddad appeared lost in thought at her question and she felt worried in case she'd said something wrong. 'Granddad?'

He sighed. 'I know you're an only child, Charlotte, but sometimes having brothers or sisters is not what it's cracked up to be. Believe me.' He took another sip of tea and tried not to grimace. 'Lovely tea,' he said. 'Shall we put the telly on now?'

*

Tom and Julie walked to the school arm in arm. The evening was still warm. He wondered what was going through his wife's mind, whether she was dreading the prospect of him and Moyes coming face to face. He'd never met him before, having missed the previous parents' evening.

'I didn't tell you,' said Julie. 'Rachel came round for coffee.'

'Good God. Rachel?' He managed to stop himself from swearing. 'Rachel came to our house?'

'Yes, odd, isn't it? Haven't seen her for ages and just out of the blue she rang and invited herself round for coffee. Nice though. She was trying to make out we shared this crazy past together. I knew her as a mum, not as a mate like that. Odd, very odd.'

*

'Charlotte has the potential to do well, but she needs to concentrate more and not let herself get so easily distracted.' Miss Bullock was summing up. 'And she needs to be more punctual with her homework. Too often she seems to think some glib excuse will suffice. Does she ever ask you for help with her biology homework?' She looked at Tom, but Tom's concentration had drifted. 'Mr Searight?'

'Tom,' prompted Julie.

'What?' said Tom, coming back to the present. 'Oh yes, all the time. Yes.' He had no idea what he was agreeing to. Something about Charlotte's homework.

'If you could encourage Charlotte to hand her work in on time, it *would* help. She's an intelligent girl, it would be such a shame to see it all go to waste.'

'Yes, of course,' said Tom. Feeling that Miss Bullock had come to an end, he looked at Julie, who nodded. 'Thank you, Miss Bullock, it's been most interesting.' Having heard the could-do-better patter for the fifth time that evening, Tom was beginning to feel bored.

'Where do you have to go now?' asked Miss Bullock.

'History,' replied Julie.

'Mr Moyes. Yes, you're on the right floor. Turn left out of this room and it's at the end of the corridor on the left. Room 3E.'

As Tom and Julie made their way down the corridor, the knot in Tom's stomach tightened. He was anxious but, he thought, probably not half as much as Julie. He looked at his wife and sure enough, she seemed apprehensive. She noticed

66

that one of the buttons on her blouse had come undone. She re-fastened it and forced a weak smile. He noticed the crow's feet around her eyes and wondered whether they were usually so prominent. He felt as if he was leading her towards a firing squad. This was all her own doing, but he suddenly felt sorry for her. A week earlier he would have been none the wiser, but now he felt crushed with the knowledge of what his wife was going through. He wanted to put an arm around her and say 'don't worry, I'll look after you'. But no, she was not deserving of his sympathy; he had to be strong. Let her suffer. The door to 3E was slightly ajar. Tom knocked.

'Come in,' said a firm voice from within. Tom opened the door for Julie and followed her in. The teacher, presumably Mr Moyes, stood up as they entered. 'Mr and Mrs Searight?' he asked, offering his hand to Julie. She smiled feebly. 'How do you do? I'm Mark Moyes, Charlotte's history teacher.' He turned to Tom, shaking his hand with a firm grip. 'Please… take a seat.'

Tom and Julie sat down on the two plastic school chairs on the other side of the Formica table from Moyes. Julie sat perched on the edge of her seat, her legs delicately crossed, her hands placed neatly on her lap, twisting her wedding ring around her finger. They waited a few moments whilst Mr Moyes shuffled his paperwork. Tom looked down beneath the table at Moyes's feet. He could see the brown, scruffy briefcase.

His papers sorted, Moyes looked up and smiled. 'Before I start, I was going to grab a quick coffee. Don't mind, do you? There's a machine at the other end of the corridor. Would you both care for one?'

They did. 'One sugar,' said Tom, rummaging in his pocket for some loose change.

'No, no,' said Moyes firmly, his hand held upright, 'my treat.'

'Thank you,' said Tom. It's only a cup of coffee, he thought, don't get too martyred about it.

Moyes opened his briefcase and took a few coins from his wallet. 'Erm, those cups are awfully thin and too hot to carry three at a time. Would one of you mind giving me a hand?'

'Yes, of course.'

Tom was amazed at how quickly Julie had jumped in, surely etiquette decreed that Tom should do it. 'No, no, darling, I'll do it.' But Julie was already on her feet and following Moyes on the way to the drinks machine.

Damn, thought Tom, what story are they hatching up? He looked around the classroom and wondered where Charlotte sat. At least this was one class where she'd get a shining report, not that they'd all been bad, but none of them had been particularly good. The walls were adorned with artwork depicting scenes from the First World War. He felt a little bit ashamed that he couldn't tell which one was Charlotte's.

A few moments later, Mark and Julie returned with the steaming coffees, Mark struggling with the heat of two polystyrene cups. 'Here we are,' he said to Tom. 'Yours is the only one with sugar,' he said. Marginalised by a bloody cup of coffee, thought Tom.

'Now then, Charlotte – my star pupil!' Tom tried to smile. And so Moyes launched into his report: what a clever girl Charlotte was; intelligent, attentive, good worker, a tendency to daydream on occasions, but generally a fine girl. Tom noticed how Moyes spoke only to *him*; his eye contact totally focused on him, never looking at Julie who sat quietly sipping her coffee. If Charlotte carried on with this much dedication, continued Moyes, she could expect a good grade at GCSE, but that was still a long way off. She mustn't lose the momentum, got to keep going. Moyes pointed to Charlotte's artwork on the wall. It was a copy of the painting he and Charlotte had seen in the museum – a line of soldiers, blindfolded, all victims of a gas attack, holding hands as they fumbled blindly onwards. 'Isn't it good?' said Moyes. Tom agreed.

'Charlotte is very excited by our Great War presentation but I do worry about her insistence on doing her bit solo in front of the whole school. She says she has no experience of performing or standing in front of an audience.'

'What subjects are you doing next year?' asked Julie.

'We'll be starting on the Romans in Britain, the coming of the Anglo-Saxons and…'

Tom lost concentration as Moyes talked about the Vikings and Normans. He noticed that having been asked the question by Julie, they were forced to look at each other and both were finding it difficult. Julie gave way first and fiddled with her coffee cup, scraping away the pink line left by her lipstick under the polystyrene rim. 'Er, another part of the curriculum is the erm…' He stopped to think. 'Ah yes, the Reformation and especially its effect in Britain.' Tom stared at him. What did Julie see in him with his tatty chequered shirt, his floppy hair as Rachel described it, the thickset eyebrows. Why was she risking it all on this man? OK, he seemed all right, if a bit wet, and under other circumstances, Tom might have liked him. His stare was unnerving Moyes, he kept glancing back at Tom. '…Leading to Henry the Eighth and the Dissolution of the Monasteries.' Would Julie leave him for this man, Tom wondered; was he looking at Charlotte's future stepfather as well as her favourite teacher? Moyes was struggling, his cheeks flushed, his hand ruffling his hair. Whatever confidence he'd begun with had drained away during a two-minute résumé of a history curriculum. Empires rise, empires fall, thought Tom.

'…And the development of Protestantism in Scotland, and er, finally…'

Tom had had enough. Enough of the history, enough of remaining silent, enough of being made a fool of. 'Can I ask you a personal question?' he asked.

His interruption stopped Moyes dead. The teacher knew the question was not going to be curriculum-related. Moyes looked at Tom, his expression etched with fear. 'Yes, er, by – by all means.'

But Tom remained silent. He could sense the anticipation in the empty room as Moyes and Julie waited, both staring at him, waiting for him to ask his question. They could hear the murmur of voices out in the corridor but in Moyes's classroom itself, everything seemed so quiet, so still. Tom felt like a conductor taking his podium centre stage, while an orchestra and audience waited for the sound of the baton to click against the metal of the music stand. He looked at Julie, how vulnerable she looked now, and how pathetic. His orchestra and audience were getting impatient; it was time to wield the baton. He leaned forward on the plastic chair and tapped his finger against the top of the Formica table.

Keeping his eyes fixed on Moyes, he spoke quietly, even politely. 'I hope you don't mind my asking,' he said softly, 'but how long have you been having an affair with my wife?' He held Moyes's startled gaze, the three of them caught in a bubble that seemed to transcend the physical confines of the classroom walls.

It was Julie who reacted first. Abruptly, she stood up. '*Fuck* you, Tom.' Without looking at either of them, she collected her handbag, turned and marched quickly out of the room.

Moyes called out her name. He got up too, his chair scraping against the floor behind him, his legs hitting the edge of the table violently as he rose. The table tilted forward and the half-empty cups of coffee tipped over, spilling their contents over the carefully typed sheets. The table would have fallen back into place, but Tom purposely caught it and held it still, causing the cups and piles of coffee-stained paper to slide off and scatter to the floor. Then Tom let go and the table landed back down with a loud clatter.

'Bugger it,' cursed Moyes, as he crouched down trying to gather his papers. In his haste, he scattered them further across the floor and into the slopping coffee. He glanced back up at the door, but Julie had gone. He gave up on the papers and sat down with a sigh.

At last, Tom stood up, satisfied with the immediate fall-out of his bombshell. He looked down at the mess of papers, stationery and polystyrene cups. Tom paused and savoured the moment with the air of the vanquisher over the vanquished.

'Thanks for the coffee,' he said. And with that, he walked out.

The war was far from won, he thought, but how sweet the victory of battle.

Chapter 7: *The Departure*

Tom trotted down the school stairway, bumping into other parents milling about, clutching bits of paper and working out where to go, and outside across the floodlit playground with its painted white lines and red circles. He found Julie leaning against the wall next to the main school gates staring up at the stars, clasping a tissue. He rather hoped she'd walk home without him but realised she wouldn't want to, not in the dark. It was a warm evening but she wore her new coat, dark blue and shiny with a large matching belt, her hair tucked into the collar. She turned and started walking without looking at him, hands deep in pockets. It was only a ten-minute walk from the school to home. Tom walked alongside her, waiting for her to say something – an admission of guilt, a declaration of regret, possibly even an apology – just something. But no, with her head down and her eyes focused on the pavement, it was obvious she meant to maintain this sullen silence. A low-lying car passed at speed, its windows wound down, music thumping, the driver jerking his head in time with the frantic rhythm. A cat scuttled past, alarmed by the intensity of volume.

Eventually, as the bassline faded down the street, Tom spoke. 'How long?' he asked quietly.

'Year or so,' she replied matter-of-factly.

'Why?'

'Usual reasons.'

He tried to keep his voice steady. 'And what are they, Julie, what exactly are the "usual reasons"?'

'I don't know. Adventure? Breaking the routine? Vanity? Take your pick.'

A couple ambled along the pavement towards them, giggling and clearly drunk, their hands intertwined, their heads touching, their faces obscured by her long hair. They didn't notice the forlorn husband and wife as they zigzagged past.

'Is it still going on?'

'No. Not any more.'

'Why not?'

'Because…' she paused as if trying to grapple for a semi-decent answer.

'Because?'

'Oh, I don't know. I'm tired. Can we discuss this another time?'

'No! I *want* to know, tell me.'

Julie stopped and glanced around as if worried that people might hear Tom's raised voice from within their homes. Somewhere nearby a dog barked, a deep bark, a mixture of threat and apprehension. 'Because it was a mistake,' she said quickly. 'Because I realised there was no real reason. Because I didn't want you to find out. Because I didn't want to hurt you.'

'Bit late for that now.'

'I know.' She started walking again, slowly, her shoes shuffling against the paving stones. A street lamp flickered on and off. Tom followed a few paces behind. 'How long have you known?' she asked.

'A week. You know when.'

'Yes.' She rubbed her eyes and for the first time turned to look at Tom. 'What should we do? What will you do?'

'What would you like me to do?'

Julie swallowed. 'To believe me when I say it's finished, and, I know it's a lot to ask but to forget it ever happened.'

'Simple as that, eh?'

She shrugged her shoulders as if she really didn't care. 'It's up to you.'

Tom leant towards her, his voice filled with spite. 'Did you forget we have a daughter; did you think of her while you were with *him*?'

Julie shook her head. 'I've had enough,' she said, turning away from him and storming ahead.

Tom watched her as she approached and opened their front gate. He trudged slowly behind. He didn't know what to think; all he knew was that his wife, whom he'd loved for so many years, had suddenly turned into someone he no longer knew. Someone he no longer liked.

*

The following morning, Tom was finishing his breakfast when Charlotte came down. He and Julie had already given Charlotte the feedback from the night before and told her in no uncertain terms that Miss Bullock and others expected better of her. She still looked apprehensive, as if expecting another blow-by-blow account of her misdemeanours at school, but Tom needed to get to work and left quickly. He felt tired. He'd slept in the spare bedroom with its bed that was too soft. He'd woken up at regular intervals, each time the events of the previous evening replaying in his mind. The showdown in the classroom, the polystyrene cups, the painting of the gas victims, the conversation with Julie on the way home, the drunken couple, Rachel's interference. The vision of coffee spilling on the scattered pieces of paper.

By the time Tom arrived at work, the open-plan office was still half-empty. He sat at his desk and gazed at the two photographs, their jolly faces smiling up at him. He switched on his computer, and while he waited for the machine to kick into life, his thoughts turned to the letter from France. He logged into his personal email, keen to see whether she'd responded to his message. There were six new messages: one that promised to wipe away his debts; another informing him he'd won $1,000; one offering the best mortgage deals in the States; one from 'Angie – see me naked'; and another that promised him a penis extension. But there amongst the pornography and dubious American financial scams, was one from Maria Dubois. Tom quickly deleted the junk mail and eagerly opened Maria's message, surprised by how excited he felt.

Dear Tom

Thank you for your e-mail. Yes, you must be the right Searight. I'm so pleased to have found you. My grandmother would be so happy. I have not read Guy's diaries for the writing is too little and difficult. But Grandmama did say he had a false leg, so it must be the same family. I think she also mentioned a boy called Robert. He must be an old man by now. I did receive a message from another Searight but they were for sure not of the same family.

If you give me your address I can post the diary and the medals to you, but my husband thinks they may get lost in the post. If only we could meet, but I shall use the special postal service and hope for the best.

I send you my best wishes,
Maria.

The office was beginning to fill up. Tom saw Clive go into his office and Gabrielle smiled as she sat down at her desk next to Tom's. Slowly the idea formed in his mind, and the more he thought of it, the more it appealed. He decided to write straight back to her and advise her not to entrust Guy's legacy through the uncertainty of the Anglo-French postal service. He could just go without telling Julie, he had no need to justify or explain, the moral prerogative was still on his side. What about this weekend? No, too short notice. Perhaps the following weekend. No harm in asking, she might be pleased by his serious interest. Tom wondered what she'd be like. Young, attractive? Not that it mattered. He would stay in a local guesthouse or whatever they have in St Omer, go and have a cup of tea, pick up the family heirlooms and leave, and have a nice, solitary weekend in the bargain. He clicked the reply button and started to type:

> *Dear Maria,*
> *Your husband is quite right. It might be unwise to trust such an important package to the post. It would be tragic if it was lost after your grandmother looked after it all so carefully for all these years. As it was, I was thinking of coming to France over the next couple of weekends to look at the battlefields. I know it is very short notice for you, but I need not take up too much of your time if you're busy.*
> *Regards*
> *Tom.*

He'd had no intention of visiting the battlefields but the idea of a day trip to France rather appealed. The exchange of emails cheered him up no end. It was like a beacon that shone out amongst the gloom that had suddenly engulfed him during the preceding week, and he was quite content to be guided by this French ray of light and to see where, if anywhere, it would lead him.

Tom entered the password to access his design files and stared at the 3-D image on the screen in front of him. There was so much to fit in and it all seemed wrong somehow. The specification for the library counter took up far too much room, squeezing the children's library into a corner and surely they were underestimating the amount of space needed for public computers. But most importantly, thought Tom, there seemed to be no provision for disabled access. The specifications he was working to wouldn't meet the requirements of the 1995 Disability Discrimination Act.

The phone interrupted his thoughts. 'Is that Tom Searight? It's Adrian from Dunstone, Cutler and Maine.'

'Hello, Adrian, unexpected call, how can I help?' He wondered whether Adrian's beard was still blue.

'You can help all right. By butting out.'

'What? I'm sorry, what are you talking about?'

'I think you know; I'm talking about Rachel. She's told me all about you coming round to her place, about your little liaisons and I'm warning you to keep your nose out, all right?'

'No, hang on a minute…' But Adrian had rung off. Tom stared open-mouthed at the telephone. He decided it was about time he and Rachel had a little chat.

It was also time to discuss the library plans with Clive; it was, after all, part of Clive's job to advise and encourage. But Tom knew that Clive would be of little use. He was all right on seeing the 'big picture' and could talk for hours on grand visions and long-term objectives, but when it came to the small stuff, the detail, he got bored. He was not a man for the minutiae. And, more annoyingly, whenever Tom set up a meeting to see Clive, the man always cancelled; something else always "cropped up". The only way was to bulldoze in and demand his attention there and then. Tom did just that. As usual, Clive talked in monosyllables while stuffing his face with crisps. Tom showed him his plans to date. Clive gave them a cursory flip through, muttering the odd approving sound, spluttering bits of crisp over the paperwork. Whenever he had to think, he ran his short chunky fingers through his stubbly hairline. Tom expected nothing but begrudging support; it was far easier to give everything a casual nod of consent than be bothered about thinking through possible changes or improvements.

Eventually, Clive looked up. 'Don't know what you're worried about, looks fine. Go for it.'

'Is that it?'

Clive shrugged his shoulders. 'What else is there?

'Well, I'm worried about disabled access. I'm not sure how to address the provision for it. I mean, a lift, for example, would have to be worked out in conjunction with the other departments.'

Clive rubbed his hair. 'No need to bother. Like you say, it has to be a centralised thing. Claudette's probably dealing with it.'

The phone rang and Clive seized the opportunity to answer it. It was obvious that Tom had used up his time and he wouldn't get anything else out of him, so with half-hearted thanks, he left and made his way back to his desk.

Soon after 10.30 am, Claudette breezed in; wearing another variation on her masculine suits, and headed for her office. As usual, her corkscrew hair bounced in time with her purposeful stride. Tom hated to admit it but she was damn attractive.

Tom gave it half an hour before deciding to go speak to Claudette about the disability access. The blinds had been pulled down. He was about to knock on the glass-fronted door when he heard her voice from inside. 'They've given us a date for the presentation – Friday, three o'clock… Yeah, of course, I can do it… I'm worth a lot more than that… If you like; it's for you to discuss but I'm not risking it for less...'

'Eavesdropping, Tom?' Tom jumped. It was Clive.

'I was going to ask Claudette about the disability stuff.'

'Relax man, she's doing it. Anyway, you know she doesn't want to be disturbed when the blinds are down.'

'Suppose. I'll try later.'

*

Tom didn't get to see Claudette and it was time to go home. He couldn't face it but equally, where else could he go? Forty-five minutes later, he opened the front door with a heavy heart. This wasn't going to be easy, he thought. Angus welcomed him home. He could smell dinner and hear the television blaring. He popped his head around the sitting room door where Julie and Charlotte were watching an early evening soap opera. Without turning away from the screen, Julie told him there was some cottage pie for him in the microwave. Tom went into the kitchen and looked at his dinner but wasn't the slightest bit hungry. He sat down at the kitchen table and glanced at the post. The anniversary flowers were still in their vase, next to Julie's mobile. He picked the phone up but on hearing Julie's footsteps in the hallway, quickly placed it back on the table. She came in, her arms folded tightly, avoiding his gaze. 'I'll make you a cup of tea,' she said.

Tom switched on the microwave as Julie rinsed out a couple of mugs and dried them.

'Look,' she said, 'I've mended your Arsenal mug.'

He wasn't aware it had been broken. 'Thanks,' he said picking up an envelope and opening it. Another bill.

'It didn't take long to stick it back together. Tell me again, what's a "double"?'

Tom didn't answer. He watched her and wondered where in the hell they went from here. 'I still don't understand why you did it,' he said eventually, looking back at the telephone bill.

She turned to face him, leaning against the sink, mugs in hand. 'It didn't mean anything.'

'Fine, but that still doesn't explain *why*.'

'I told you last night.'

'No, you didn't.'

She moved across the kitchen and clicked the kettle on. 'Tom, you were my first, the only man I'd been with. After almost twenty years together, it seemed so, so…'

'Inadequate?' he sneered. The microwave beeped.

'No, not "inadequate". But hell, Tom, it was just sex. I know that sounds morally awful, but why should it be just men who are motivated by lust? I had loveless sex, oh my, what a slag, how depraved I am. Lock me up! But it won't happen again, so you know where you stand. It's not as if I was in love, I was never torn between the two of you.' She put a teabag into each mug.

'So, was he any good then?'

'Oh, for Christ's sake, is that it, is that what you're concerned about? Worried you don't come up to scratch?'

Tom wished he'd never asked. 'If you must know, he's a bit wet,' she said. 'Frankly, I'm relieved it's finished.'

'Getting bored, were you? Looking for the next one?'

'Don't be ridiculous.'

'Can you blame me?'

The kettle boiled, the microwave beeped again. Julie was about to pour when 'The Ride of the Valkyries' rang out. He caught the worried look in her eyes. They both looked at it. 'Aren't you going to answer it?' he asked.

'No.'

'I will then.'

Julie leapt across the kitchen. 'No, I will,' she said, snatching the phone from Tom's hand. Without looking at the number, she answered. 'Hello?' Tom watched her, scrutinising her face. 'No, I'm a bit busy right now.' She looked flustered, he thought. 'I've got to go.' She switched the mobile off and put it into her jeans pocket.

'It was him, wasn't it?' He knew the answer.

Julie sighed. 'Yes.'

It took a few seconds for his anger to register, but then he thumped the table. 'So it's over, is it?' he yelled.

Julie looked startled. 'Yes, honestly, Tom, it is, *believe* me.' For the first time, she looked nervous, on the defensive.

He stood up. 'So why is he still phoning you?'

'Just because he rang, doesn't mean to say I'm lying.'

'I don't believe you.' He stepped menacingly towards her.

Julie gripped the work surface, a look of panic spread across her face. 'Tom, it's true.'

He moved within a couple of feet of her and glared into her eyes, his veins pulsating with rage, his fists clenched at his sides. He spun away angrily, stormed out of the kitchen and ran noisily up the stairs. Slamming the bedroom shut, he pulled a small dust-covered suitcase out from beneath the bed, flung open the wardrobe door, snatched various garments and stuffed them haphazardly into the case. His task completed, he went to the bathroom where he grabbed his toothbrush and shaving kit. Carrying the suitcase downstairs, he left it in the hallway, picked up the telephone and returned to the kitchen where Julie was sitting at the table, her head in her hands.

She spoke: 'What are you doing?'

'Going to my parents.' He tapped a number into the telephone.

'You can't just walk out on us.'

'Watch me,' he snapped back.

'What do I tell Charlotte?'

'Tell her what you like. Tell her you've been sleeping with her favourite teacher; I don't care.'

'Tom—'

Tom spoke into the phone: 'Hello… yes, can I have a mini-cab please… as soon as possible.' He glared at her. 'Enfield, yes… three minutes… that's fine, thanks.' He switched the phone off.

Julie rose from the chair, moved back to the kettle, and clicked it on again. 'Tom, you can't just walk out and expect you can get away with a quick cheerio to your daughter; it's not fair on her.'

He seized on her mistake: 'Oh, and was it fair on *your* daughter when you embarked on your little sexual adventure?'

Tom's jibe hurt. She grabbed a mug, spun around and hurled it at him. It missed by a good foot and hit the wall behind him, shattering on impact.

Tom looked at the broken fragments lying on the floor. It was his Arsenal mug. 'Doubt you'll be able to fix it this time,' he said.

Charlotte came into the kitchen. 'What was that noise?' She saw the shattered mug and looked worriedly at her parents. 'What's going on?'

'Charlotte,' said Tom, 'I'm going to spend a few days with your granny and granddad.' He tried to make the tone of his voice sound light-hearted.

Charlotte glanced confusedly from one parent to the other. 'But why; what's been happening?'

'Well…' Tom looked at Julie.

'Charlotte, I need to explain a few things…'

'Bloody right you do.'

'Your dad and I have had a bit of a falling out and your dad thinks we should spend a few days apart.' She turned her gaze onto Tom. 'Perhaps he's right. And please don't swear.'

'Don't look so worried, sweetheart,' added Tom. 'It'll be all right. Like your mum says, we just need to sort a couple of things out, that's all.'

'What sort of things?'

It was Julie's turn. 'Your dad and I… We still love each other, but sometimes… sometimes parents argue and–'

'Mum, stop treating me like a child, just tell me.'

'No,' said Julie firmly. 'I can't; it's between your father and me. All you need to know is that–'

'That you throw cups at each other?'

'Well yes, that may have been a bit rash.'

Charlotte looked at her father. 'You're not divorcing, are you?' Her voice was faltering.

'No, no, of course not,' said Tom, surprised at how quickly she'd advanced the situation. 'I'll probably be back within a few days.'

'So what's the point?'

Indeed, what was the point, thought Tom. What was the point in leaving one's wife in order to punish her while at the same time declaring you'll be back in a few days' time? She'd probably quite enjoy the peace. But having called the taxi, having told the whole damn family, he couldn't back out now, he'd committed himself. But somehow he needed to reassure his daughter while threatening his wife. 'I need to mull a few things over,' he said. 'Consider the future.'

'So you *are* separating,' said Charlotte.

'No, but I suppose you could call it a trial separation.'

'But what about me?'

Tom feared she was about to burst into tears. 'Whatever happens, Charlotte, I'll always be your dad.'

'You mean a weekend dad, like most of the dads at school.'

Tom realised he'd run himself into the ground. You can't be reassuring to one person, while at the same time appear threatening to another.

Charlotte couldn't bear to hear any more. She turned, ran out of the kitchen, up the stairs and to her bedroom, slamming the door shut behind her.

'Satisfied?' asked Julie.

'OK, no need to sound so smug, remember where this started.' Tom picked up the telephone again. 'If you'll excuse me…' He went into the sitting room and closed the door behind him. He decided to ring his parents and at least give them a few minute's notice of his impending arrival. His mother answered. 'Mum, it's me, Tom… Mum, I know this is a bit out of the blue but I need to spend a few nights away from home. Do you mind if I come to yours tonight? I'll explain later.'

Understandably, his mother was alarmed by this unexpected request. Tom parried her concerned questions as best he could. 'I can't really talk about it right now… no really, everything is fine, it's just that I need to stay out of the way for a while…' He heard the beep of the car horn outside. 'Look, Mum, I've gotta go, the taxi's here… yes, I'm leaving now… I'll see you in about half an hour.' Tom rang off. His poor mother, she'd be worried sick, she'd fear the worst. In some ways, the worst had already happened.

At the sound of the horn, Charlotte came back down and was waiting at the foot of the stairs with Angus and her mother. Tom looked at them all and suddenly felt the significance of the moment. The departure was for real and the thought struck him that perhaps he might never come back, not properly anyway. Julie stood behind Charlotte, her hands on her daughter's shoulders, Angus sitting obediently at their side. Tom felt jealous at this unexpected show of solidarity. He also felt aggrieved that anyone looking in from the outside would assume *he* was the guilty party in this pathetic scene. Maybe he'd been too hasty; this was, after all, his home too and here he was, about to leave; about to face the unknown.

Outside, the taxi beeped its horn again. 'Well, this is it,' he said at long last. 'I'll be off then.' He looked at Charlotte. She spent so much of her time trying to be older, more grown-up, but at this precise moment she looked every inch the child she really was. And here he was, about to destroy some of the security she rightly took for granted, unnecessarily exposing her to the truth that security wasn't always a given. And for what, so that he could make a point, so that he could punish his wife through punishing his child. Tom stepped forward and kissed Charlotte on the head. He looked briefly at Julie but her eyes remained expressionless. He was unsure whether he was relieved by the lack of histrionics or disappointed by her outer calm. He picked up his small suitcase and the briefcase he used for work. A nicer briefcase than Moyes's battered old thing, he thought.

'Right then,' he said, glancing around at the hallway as if taking it in for the last time. He opened the front door. Angus leapt forward and tried to squeeze out. Tom forced him back in. As he closed the door, he heard Charlotte say, 'Come back, you silly dog, *you're* not leaving me.'

Chapter 8: *The Prodigal Son*

Half an hour later the taxi pulled up in front of his parents' house in Enfield. As he paid and tipped the driver, he saw his mother appear momentarily at the living room window pulling back the Austrian blinds. She reappeared at the front door and waited for him.

'Hello, Mum,' he said, trying to sound casual.

'Tom, why are you here, what's going on?'

'Hang on, Mum, let me get in first.' He squeezed past her with his cases, and leaving them in the hallway, went into the living room where his father was watching the television.

'The prodigal son returns,' his father said huffily.

'Nice to see you too, Dad.' His mother followed him in. 'Any chance of a cup of tea?' he asked, remembering he never got to drink the last one offered to him.

'OK, but don't think you're getting off that lightly, Thomas Searight.' His mother disappeared into the kitchen. Tom sat down on the sofa at right angles to his father.

'So to what do we owe this unexpected pleasure?' he said, without averting his gaze from the TV.

'Small argument, that's all. It'll blow over.'

'People don't tend to move out just because they've had a "small argument", surely.'

Tom decided there was little headway to gain from this accusatory conversation; he would wait until his mother returned. 'Another earthquake?' he asked feebly, trying to divert the subject to the television news. His father didn't respond and the two of them sat silently watching the footage of a far-away devastation. It was thus ever the case, thought Tom. His father and he preferred not to talk about 'real life'. They talked about football, the war, useless politicians, the even more useless council, even the weather forecast was preferable to anything that might involve 'emotions'. Footballers' tears were the closest they ever got to talking about anything that hinted at feelings.

Alice returned with a tray of cups and saucers and a pot of tea. No mugs as usual, thought Tom. She placed the tray on the occasional table and then went straight for the television and turned it off. Robert opened his mouth to complain but decided better of it. She poured the tea whilst the two men watched passively. Tom began to regret coming, perhaps he should have gone to a friend's place, or better still just slept in the spare bedroom as he had done the night before. He was dreading his mother's inevitable interrogation. Whilst his father never attempted to understand anything emotionally charged, his mother tried too hard, to the point she would say "I see" to everything while not understanding anything. She passed him his cup of tea. He took a sip – it was Earl Grey.

'I'll go and make your bed up in the spare room in a minute,' she said.

Tom thanked her and, to his surprise, she said nothing else. The three of them sat in silence, delicately sipping their tea, each wondering how to broach the subject that hung awkwardly in the air between them. It seemed inappropriate to start with small talk. Eventually, Tom broke the silence. He felt he owed them an explanation.

'Julie and I…' He paused, aware of the air of expectancy surrounding him. He tried again. 'Julie and I have had a sort of falling out.'

His mother sighed. 'Oh, Tom.'

'A "sort of falling out". What exactly does *that* mean?' asked his father.

'It's not that serious.' He remembered his father's earlier jibe. 'I know it probably looks serious, otherwise, why would I be here, but really, it isn't. We just need a few days apart, that's all. A bit of breathing space if you like.'

'Bloody fool,' muttered his father.

'What's that meant to mean?'

'It's another woman, isn't it?'

'No, quite the contrary, in fact.' Damn, he thought, he'd said too much.

'So it's another man then,' said Robert, almost enjoying his son's slip-up.

'No, I didn't say that,' said Tom. She may have deserved it but Tom wasn't going to allow Julie's name to be dragged through it. 'It doesn't involve anyone else; it's just between Julie and me.'

'And Charlotte,' added his mother.

'Yes, and Charlotte,' Tom conceded. 'Look, we have discussed it.'

His father looked at him. 'And…?'

But Tom wasn't prepared to elaborate. 'It'll sort itself out, like I said, it's not that serious.' His parents looked at each other; they didn't appear at all convinced. 'Honestly,' Tom added. What was he saying, he thought. What hope did he have of reassuring his parents when he couldn't even convince himself with his string of platitudes? Here he was, split up from his adulterous wife, resorting to meaningless sound bites that convinced no one, let alone himself, for the lack of anything else to say. He should be at home, sorting his life out, instead of sipping Earl Grey from delicate china cups with the two people who brought him up, and with whom he now seemed to have so little in common. And, what's more, he never liked Earl Grey and he knew his father didn't either, but his mother always insisted on it, thinking it symbolised the height of sophistication.

'How long do you want to stay?' Alice asked, 'Not that we mind.'

'Don't know, a few days perhaps.'

'And then what will you do?'

'I was thinking I might have a weekend in France.'

'France? A bit vague. What for?' asked his father.

'Do you remember I told you about the French woman who wrote to me about—'

'Oh, you're not serious.'

Tom was startled by his father's reaction. 'Why not? She's even got his medals. I thought you'd be pleased.'

Robert sighed. 'The past is the past, man, let it lie. I mean, what's the point? I told you all you need to know. The man lost a leg during the Great War and ended up somewhere in Devon. And so what about the medals? They all got medals; it's not as if he won the Victoria Cross or anything. No, my advice, Tom, is tell this French woman to post them over to you if she wants, but all this gallivanting over to France, I can't see the point in it.'

Tom couldn't fathom why his father was so agitated. He felt disappointed at his crude dismissal of the idea; it was almost as if he was denying Tom permission to go and visit her. 'I'm sorry, but I didn't actually ask for your advice and I don't see the problem.'

'No? For one thing, you were never interested before, so why this sudden intrigue? It's not because you want to meet a young French bird, is it?'

Tom almost choked on his tea. 'Don't be silly; of course it isn't.'

Robert smiled. 'So you mean you'd still be going over if it was some old duffer like me, eh?'

Damn you, thought Tom. His mother intervened. 'Stop it, Robert. I think it's a lovely idea.'

Good old mother. 'Thank you, Mum.'

'But I do think,' she added, 'you ought not to stay away from home for too long.'

That was the idea, but his father's outburst and his accusation had unnerved him. Fortunately, Alice changed the subject with news about Tom's brother in Toronto. Thankful for the diversion, Tom vaguely listened and even accepted a top-up of tea. But his father spent the rest of the evening in a foul mood and stared intently at the blank television screen. Both Tom and his mother knew best not to try and engage him any further. Over the years from when he was a boy, the family had become accustomed to Robert's frequent bouts of moodiness. But as his father grew older, his mood swings were becoming increasingly more acute.

Chapter 9: *Playing God*

Tom didn't bother phoning her. He knew it was that time of day when she'd be in. He arrived straight from work, marched up to her front door and rang the bell. She answered, wearing the same rainbow-coloured top and dangly earrings. 'Hello, Rachel. I think we need to talk.' She tried to smile and stepped back to allow Tom through. He barged past and went straight through to her sitting room. He decided against sitting on the squashy settee and remained on his feet. Rachel had had a bit of a tidy-up. The newspapers and magazines were heaped in a pile in the corner of the room, most of the CDs had been put away, and there was even a slight hint of furniture polish. But it still seemed a far cry from the neatly organised arrangement of his own sitting room. 'Abigail in?' he asked abruptly.

'No, she's with the Passchendaele Sisters,' she said, in her softly spoken, high-pitched voice.

Tom was about to ask what she was talking about but realised he didn't really care. 'Bluebeard? Is he here?'

'No need to call him that. I haven't seen him for a few days. Can I get you a tea?'

He remembered her choice of herbal tea and shook his head. 'So what exactly are you playing at, Rachel?' The black cat sauntered in, purring to itself.

'Sorry, what do you mean?'

'Come on, you know damn well, cosy chats with Julie, gossiping with Adrian.'

She grinned. 'Well, you know, I thought it'd be nice to see her again.' Her voice seemed squeakier than normal.

Tom decided to sit down after all. The cat made a beeline for him and rubbed against his legs, arching its back. 'What, old friends together, that sort of thing?'

'Yes, why? What's wrong?'

'Julie's not stupid, you know. You were hardly friends in the first place, so why now, all of a sudden?'

Rachel stood still, her head tilted to one side. 'Because,' she said slowly, 'she doesn't deserve you.'

'What? What's that meant to mean? Is that why you went round for a cup of coffee?' She nodded. Tom stared at her, his mouth open. 'Oh God, what did you tell her? There's nothing to… Oh, you didn't, did you? About Lewisham?'

'Well… sort of. Charlotte came back.'

'Oh, for f… You mean, seriously, you told her about a drunken kiss? A one-off?' Rachel made no response, merely pulled on an earring. 'Please tell me you didn't.' She nodded her head. Tom rolled his eyes. 'For Christ's sake, Rachel, what are you playing at? You make out to Adrian as if it's still going on, and now you're bent on telling my wife. You're talking about my marriage here, what gives you the right to mess it up?'

In an instant, Rachel's coy tone of voice disappeared, replaced by venomous derision. 'I don't remember you having any reservations when you were kissing me the other day.'

The cat, startled by the sudden rise in volume, darted out of the room.

'What? I didn't kiss you; you pecked me on the lips.'

'Sometimes, Tom Searight, you can be such a coward. You're so damn spineless.'

'What?'

'You didn't finish it with Julie then and you're not finishing it now. Your marriage is messed up, has been for years, but you still need someone like me to expose it for the sham it really is.'

Tom screwed up his eyes in puzzlement. 'What?'

'She's having an affair for goodness sake and what have you done about it? Have you confronted her?'

'No, but–' He wasn't prepared to tell her.

'Exactly. Because you're worried about what you might learn. Well, perhaps you need to learn the truth. She's having an affair. What does that tell you, Tom? You can't just sweep it under the carpet and hope it'll go away. Something's wrong and you need to face up to it – but no, you're too spineless. That's why I went to see her.'

'No, no, I'm sorry; I'm still not with you. I got the spineless bit loud and clear, but I'm still none the wiser.'

'Because telling her – about you and me – would make her realise, both of you realise, how mismatched you two really are. I was trying to bring the inevitable out into the open.'

'Oh, so you took it upon yourself to play God.'

'She's fucking your daughter's teacher, for pity's sake. You can't forgive her for that; you can't call that a marriage. Don't you have any pride?'

'I give it to you, Rachel, there's a logic in there somewhere, a bloody *twisted* logic, but a logic nonetheless.'

'You'll thank me for it in the end.'

He stared at her incredulously. 'Not likely. Mind your own bloody business.'

'How can I, when I know she's not your destiny? She's just a fill-in.'

Tom laughed. 'Is she? We've been married fifteen years. That's one hell of a fill-in. So, come on, Rachel, tell me, where does my destiny lie?'

Rachel sat down at the far end of the settee. She looked at him and said quietly, 'I think we both know the answer to that.'

Tom scowled at her; did she mean that, did she really think there was still a spark, just because of one kiss? 'Oh God, you've been waiting for this, haven't you?' he said. 'Waiting for your chance and then, all of a sudden, it's there, handed to you on a plate. But you're wrong, Rachel, you're so wrong.'

'But you wouldn't go back to her after all this, surely?'

'No, but…'

'So what do you mean?' Her voice faltered.

'I mean, whatever happens between Julie and me, don't think I'm coming back here, cap in hand.'

Rachel drew her knees together and placed her hands neatly on her lap. 'But, but I thought…'

'Christ, it was sixteen years ago. And that kiss, in Lewisham, it was just a laugh, you know that…'

She sprang to her feet again. 'Oh, was it indeed? Well, I'm pleased you thought it was so amusing. I actually thought I meant something to you, I thought…'

Tom closed his eyes. He'd gone too far. She suddenly looked very small. 'OK, OK, I'm sorry.' He stood up. 'Look, I didn't mean to be so flippant. You did mean a lot to me, but hell, Rachel, it was a long time ago. When you finished with me, I was upset but I got over it; I sort of presumed you had too.'

She shook her head. 'I only finished it cos I hoped it would force the issue, make you realise what you were missing.'

'And now? Do you really think I could do it to Charlotte? I know Abigail's father walked out on her, but I couldn't do that. I'm not being spineless; I'm just trying to be a decent father to my daughter.' Tom surprised himself by the extent of his own sincerity.

She rolled her eyes and smiled ironically. 'That's what I mean when I say she doesn't deserve you; you're too good for her.'

'Perhaps.' Even in the midst of an argument, Rachel could make him feel positive about himself.

'Well, you've made your feelings perfectly clear and now I feel stupid.' She turned her head to avoid his gaze. 'Go on, you'd better go. Abigail will be back soon wanting her dinner.'

'All right. I'm sorry. You sure you'll be OK?'

She nodded.

'Will you get Adrian off my back?' he asked hesitantly, fearing he was pushing his luck too far.

She nodded again. 'Just go, Tom. Just go,' she said, softly.

Tom stepped outside and closed the front door gently behind him. He looked at his watch. It would take him ages to get back to Enfield. As he walked down the street, he sighed. He never realised that a passion could lie dormant for so long. He just hoped to God that she wouldn't try it again.

*

Charlotte sat at the mirror in her bedroom studying her reflection, singing along to 'Air Hostess' by Busted. She backcombed her hair, adding copious amounts of hairspray, but still, it wouldn't stay in the style she wanted it to, her hair was just too thin. She'd inherited her mother's hair and how she hated it. What she really wanted to do was to dye it black, but she knew she lacked the nerve to be so radical.

It felt strange not having her dad around. In fact, more than strange, she hated it; she really missed him. It must've been one hell of an argument for him to walk out like that. And so suddenly, no warning whatsoever. And did he walk out, or did Mum kick him out? Maybe their winning numbers had come up on the lottery and Dad had forgotten to buy the ticket. Whatever it was, it must have been serious. And what if Dad didn't come back? He'd become one of these weekend dads; might be quite cool, actually. Charlotte knew from her friends at school that the weekend dads (and it was rarely, if ever, the mums) always tried to make up for the guilt by buying them loads of presents and taking their kids to places they never went to when they lived at home. But given the choice, she'd have him back any day.

Charlotte tried on some lipstick. The colour was called 'dark auburn'. She puckered her lips and having applied lavish amounts of the stuff, kissed the mirror leaving a smudged kiss shape on the glass. She hadn't noticed much difference in her mum yet. She always seemed a bit short-tempered when she'd just got in from school, but that was nothing new. It must be awful having a job that always left you feeling pissed off. There was no way Charlotte would be a teacher. No, she wanted to be a vet or perhaps a dog trainer. The problem with being a vet, though, was that you had to pass exams and, frankly, Charlotte found it difficult concentrating at school. She was amazed she'd got off so lightly after the parents' evening; just the usual stuff when she'd been expecting a roasting. They'd only mentioned it in passing; they seemed too preoccupied somehow. Her dad had mentioned that Mr Moyes was pleased with her and would have shown them more of her work had he not spilt coffee all over it. It didn't surprise her; Mr Moyes was clumsy at the best of times. Anyway, Mr Moyes hadn't worried her because she enjoyed history – about the only subject she did, but what good was a history GCSE to a vet? But Mr Moyes was nice, really nice. It was the main reason for wanting to do well in the First World War project. He really liked the paintings she did. The second one was of a poppy field with one gravestone in the middle and an inscription that read: "To a brave soldier who died in World War One". She wished now she'd put the 'Great War' as her grandfather called it. How were *they* to know it'd be the First World War, it could've been the only world war. Some of the boys in her class were going to re-enact the trenches for the school performance. They were planning to use pillows and cushions as sandbags. They'd need hundreds, thought Charlotte. They were asking people to bring some in from home. Not bloody likely, she didn't want those smelly boys leaning all over *her* pillows. Now if it were Mr Moyes, well, that would be different!

Charlotte was beginning to regret her choice for the performance. It meant being the only child in the class doing a solo effort. She wished she'd taken up Abigail's offer and been part of the girl group singing songs from the war. She'd turned it down because she hated the songs; they all seemed so naff somehow. Charlotte had felt drawn by the story Mr Moyes told the class about Rupert Brooke and how he died following an insect bite. And so she decided to pay homage to the war poets, but there was no way she was going to recite by heart. She'd do a little talk first – just a few minutes on the poets and what happened to them, and then she'd read out a couple of poems, and that would be it. Goodnight. She already felt nervous about the prospect, she'd never been on stage before, but at least it would be over quickly. Hopefully, Gavin wouldn't be there, he'd become a dab hand at bunking off school and there was no way he'd want to sit through the performance.

Charlotte applied a layer of mascara onto her eyelashes, her eyelids flickering wildly with the effort of concentration. She'd been trying to avoid Gavin. Ever since the half-term week when she was almost sick on the stuff, it'd put her off it. It'd taken the shine off somehow. Gavin had promised to find "something stronger", but Charlotte didn't fancy it. She daren't admit it but she was scared of trying anything harder. She liked to be in control of herself, to know what she was doing. And there was always a chance she'd be caught. Her parents would go ballistic! She'd done what Gavin had asked her to do and got him some stuff on the Great Fire of London. In fact, she had almost written it. She was regretting that too. If he got a good mark for it, he'd be sure to ask again, and she had enough to do without doing his bloody homework for him. It's not as if she could sit his exams.

From downstairs, Charlotte heard her mother call – their favourite soap opera was starting. Charlotte wasn't bothered about it really; she only watched it to keep her mother company. She had wanted to pop out and indulge in her new habit – have a cigarette, followed by a strip of chewing gum. But tonight she felt obliged to keep her mum company. She was about to wipe the make-up off but then decided against it. If her mum made any fuss, she'd just change the subject and say how much she was missing her dad. That'd keep her quiet – play on the parental guilt. It always worked a treat, especially when it was true.

Chapter 10: *Dad's Story*

Tom and his parents were watching the same soap opera as Julie and Charlotte. His whole family seemed hooked on the same one. He couldn't see the point in them; his own life was too full of triviality without sharing fictional ones. But to his annoyance, he found himself enjoying the everyday intrigues of urban folk and asked his mother numerous questions to help fill in the gaps. His mother was only too glad to furnish him with full biographical backgrounds, while his father complained of not being able to hear the television and turned up the volume with the remote control. The possession of the remote had always been a source of parental friction and tonight, at least, Robert wasn't going to relinquish control. By the end of the programme, the sound was at full volume, but Alice didn't seem to notice, simply readjusting the volume of her own voice to compensate. It was only when the closing theme music drowned her out totally did Tom plead with his father to turn it down.

After his parents had stopped arguing whether one character deserved what another character had just done to them, Alice said she needed to go and write a letter. She offered to make Tom and Robert a cup of tea, which they accepted on Tom's proviso that it wasn't Earl Grey. Robert took the opportunity to confess, after all this time, that he too wasn't keen on the stuff either. As Alice went off to the kitchen, Robert flicked through the channels. There was a documentary about Hollywood stars having cosmetic surgery which Tom quite fancied watching, but he knew his father would be too squeamish to watch the obligatory surgical scenes. Finally, without asking his son's opinion, Robert declared there was 'nothing on', and reluctantly turned the TV off.

It now meant father and son had to find something to talk about. Robert, as usual, asked Tom about his work. Tom told him about the presentation coming up on Friday while Robert listened vaguely and made no response. Then, after an awkward silence, Tom asked his father whether he'd heard of Arsenal's latest French signing. Robert hadn't, and furthermore, he deplored this influx of foreign players into the English game. That was that then. Another silence. But then Alice came in with the tea. 'Not Earl Grey this time,' she said, obviously disappointed by her menfolk's distinct lack of taste. She left them to pour their own tea and hurried back to start her letter in the kitchen. Tom poured. Robert took a sip.

'Urgh!' he uttered. 'Is she trying to poison us?'

Tom gingerly tasted his tea. Heck, his father was right, it was one of those smoky-flavoured ones, Lapsang Souchong probably. Obviously his mother's idea of a little joke. But neither of them could be bothered to do anything about it and so they persevered in silence, grimacing with each mouthful.

It was Robert's turn to break the silence: 'Still planning to go to France this weekend?' he asked nonchalantly.

Ah, thought Tom, this is the rub, this is what he really wants to know. 'Yes, it'll get me out of your way for a couple of days. You can have your spare room back.'

'Back for what? I never go in there.'

Typical, thought Tom, his father was never one to take an off-hand comment at face value. 'Well, like you said, Dad, I might find an attractive French bird at the other end.'

Robert glared at him. This was almost blasphemous. As far as his parents were concerned, Julie could do no wrong. 'What do you mean?' he barked.

'I'm only repeating what you said the other night. So come on, tell me, why don't you want me to go to France?'

'Like I said before, I think you should leave the past where it is.'

Tom expected more, but nothing was forthcoming. 'Is that it? I mean this is your uncle we're talking about. What is it you're so worried about; are you afraid I might unearth some big family secret?'

'No, not at all.' Robert sipped his tea. 'Grim stuff, isn't it?'

'Oh, come on, Dad.'

Robert sighed, but Tom noticed the muscles in his face soften. 'You do as you see fit, son, but don't expect me to get overexcited about it, that's all. It's just that it's part of my life I'd rather forget.'

'But we're talking about your childhood here.'

'Exactly.'

Tom stared at his father. 'Did you get on with your parents?' he asked carefully.

Robert stared into the distance, his memory bounding back through the decades to his childhood years. 'My mother – yes,' he said quietly.

'And…?'

'I suppose as I got older I began to resent how she'd never stick up for me in front of my father. I mean she was always very supportive of me, but whenever Father criticised me, which was often, she'd never intervene on my behalf, always held her tongue. I suppose, like me, she was frightened of him.'

Tom tried to pick his words carefully; knowing he was entering new territory with his father. 'So, was your dad a bit strict then?'

'Dad? I never called him Dad; it was always Father. Oh, I don't know, he was fairly strict, but you know, this was a different generation; most boys were scared stiff of their fathers; it was nothing unusual in those days.'

'If it wasn't unusual, why do you say you prefer to forget about it?'

'If you must know, he was rarely nice to me.' Robert fiddled with the television's remote control as if reassured that if the conversation went too far he could end it with the push of a button. 'In fact, looking back, he was downright mean. It was obvious I was a disappointment to him, but I never understood why. I was never good enough. Never as good as Clarence.'

'You never talk about your brother. He was older than you, wasn't he?'

'Yes, only by about two years.'

'Did you get on?'

'You mean Clarence and me? Yes, we got on. Clarence was always the golden boy; he could do no wrong. My father never kept it secret that Clarence was his favourite. And that was the problem, the thing that blighted my whole childhood and my relationship with my father. It wasn't Clarence's fault, it wasn't as if he tried to curry my father's affection; in fact, he used to try and stick up for me. But you see, Father adored Clarence. People would ask him how Clarence and Robert were getting on, and it was always Clarence is doing this and Clarence did that. And how about Robert, they'd ask. Oh, Robert, well, he's just Robert. He never beat me or anything, I was just ignored. Sometimes the only times he'd talk to me was when I'd done something wrong.

'And Clarence was undoubtedly good at things – he was naturally clever, good at school and good at sports which counted for a lot with my father. The only sport I was any good at was the high jump, and that was only because I was unusually tall for my age, but Father didn't really consider that a proper sport. I remember one sports day at school – Clarence got second place in the hundred-yard dash, but *I* got first place in the high jump. My mother was thrilled for me, but Father? No, it was "just" the high jump after all, hardly counted. Perhaps he gave me a half-hearted "well done", I can't remember, but the real praise was for Clarence, beaten only by a boy a good half-foot taller than him. I suppose the hundred yards has more clout, doesn't it?

'And then the war came. 1939. Clarence and I joined up – the merchant navy. He signed up to be an officer. I had a job in a bank; I didn't want to make a career out of being a sailor so I was happy to remain a lowly seaman. Then Clarence got himself killed – I was there. Our ship was torpedoed by a German U-boat. I'd been granted some extended leave and I returned home to a little cottage in a Devonian village which Clarence and I shared. I went to visit my parents. I'd lost a lot of weight so I'd starting wearing some of my brother's clothes. Clarence had been killed a few weeks beforehand. I just walked straight into the drawing room and Father, although he was expecting me, had dozed off. I made him jump. He saw the jacket, and he thought it was Clarence's jacket, and for a moment his eyes lit up, and in that moment I saw something in Father's eyes I'd never seen before. Of course, he thought I was Clarence, didn't he? And then he realised it was just me, just old Robert, and the disappointment was too much.'

Robert paused and looked down; his eyes damp and carefully focused on the remote control. 'I suppose after the war I thought things would be different. We made up but I was still never able to compete – not with Clarence the martyr. I left the Navy and moved to London, married your lovely mother and got a new job in another bank. For years, I rarely saw my parents. I felt very bitter, you know, knowing as I did that in my father's eyes the wrong son had been killed.'

'Heck, Dad, that's one hell of a thing to say.'

'I know, I know. Funny thing is though, that during his last few years, and after my mother died, his attitude slowly changed. Alec was a baby. Perhaps having given him a grandchild, he sort of finally accepted me. Of course, he never got over Clarence's death but perhaps in those last few years, he felt the need to make peace with me. I was, after all, his only remaining child. It was still painful though, seeing him as a grandfather reminded me of how he was with Clarence. He died just before you were born – the same year.'

'Yes,' said Tom, 'I know.'

Robert took another sip of his tea and placed the mug carefully back on the occasional table. 'Didn't like that at all,' he grumbled. 'I've never told anyone about all this, you know. Your mother knows my father and I didn't get on, but she doesn't know the full extent of it.'

'You never thought of telling her?'

'No, there'd be no point now. You see, I always saw it as a failing in me. Not the sort of thing one wants to brag about.'

'Your father – he was called Lawrence, wasn't he?'

'That's right.'

'So presumably, Guy was his brother.'

'Actually, no. Like I said, Guy had a brother, but Lawrence was his cousin. But we called him Uncle Guy, or sometimes Uncle Hobbly, because of his leg.'

Tom laughed. 'Did he mind you calling him Uncle Hobbly?'

'No. He was always very decent to me and Clarence. You know, after my experience I was always very careful not to show any favouritism between you and Alec.'

'Yeah, I know.'

'I should've got a couple of medals.'

'Really, what for?'

'My time in the navy. Just a war medal and something called the 39 – 45 star. Fairly routine stuff. Never claimed them though.'

'Why on earth not?'

'Well, just the two medals by themselves, lowly ones at that, I just thought it'd look a bit silly, especially next to all the men with their rows of war medals. Uncle Hobbly got a few, including the DCM.'

'Is that good?' asked Tom.

'I'd say. It's a gallantry medal, Distinguished Conduct Medal, he did something to deserve it, but what, I don't know. I certainly couldn't bring myself to ask.'

Tom suddenly thought of an idea. 'Dad, is it too late to claim your medals now?'

'Of course it is. We're talking almost sixty years here.'

Tom was wondering how one went about claiming an overdue medal when his mother reappeared.

'Blimey,' she said, 'turned the TV off then.'

106

Robert looked at Tom. It'd been the first time they'd made eye contact since Robert began his sorry tale. A flicker of acknowledgement passed between them and Tom understood it perfectly. He'd just been allowed access to part of his father's life that no one had ever ventured into before and he felt touched at the thought.

His mother grinned. 'Fancy another pot of tea either of you?'

Chapter 11: *The Unforgiving Sea*

Robert lay in bed. Alice was already fast asleep, her gentle breathing the only sound bar the branches of the trees rustling outside in the wind. The hands of the luminous clock showed half-eleven. Tom's visit and his talk about the past troubled him. The past was a place he never voluntarily ventured to, but increasingly, as the years passed, he found his mind drifting back. Often, as he lay in bed, he'd hear their voices, usually just for a minute or two before sleep claimed him. But tonight, following Tom's visit, he knew they'd be waiting for him – all of them. He knew resistance was pointless; he might as well resign himself to hours without sleep. A streak of moonlight filtered through the gap in the bedroom curtains. He heard a flurry of feline activity as a couple of cats got into a tangle, a yelp and a screech and it was done. He smiled. Silly things. And then it came – the sound that had accompanied his nocturnal wanderings for so many years – the lapping of water against the boat. June 1944. A German submarine. A torpedo. The ship sinking, plunging into the abyss, taking so many lives with it. He remembered the ten of them, including his brother, on that lifeboat drifting for days on end aimlessly on the Indian Ocean. And that sun, that cruel, unrelenting sun, the cold, cold nights, the unforgiving sea. They knew, all ten of them, that without sufficient food and water, they were vulnerable but they had hope – hope that rescue would soon come. And hope, as every man knows, is a huge provider of strength. But like an early morning mist on a summer's day, hope soon evaporated. The first day passed, the second, the third. He saw them in his mind, the ten of them, his younger self included, standing together, wearing only their baggy navy-supply shorts, arms round each other, friends together like a team of footballers. They are smiling, some are flexing their muscles, playing up for the camera in Robert's memory, others sharing a cigarette, but all smiling. The youngest was John Clair, only a boy, jet-black hair, tall, lanky and awkward, as only teenagers can be. Robert remembered the boy asking, 'Are we almost there yet?', his voice as soft as a nervous child. He never got over the trauma of the sinking. He called for his mother, and dreamt of home-cooked dinners, mutton and spuds. He was the first to go, the day of his nineteenth birthday. Second Mate Miles Hodgkin was the most senior man on the boat, so naturally, he took command. His wife, back in the Lake District, was pregnant. Robert could remember him waking up on one of the last days, declaring that his wife had given birth – he could feel it in his bones. And on that same day, he was murdered by Harris Beckett.

After the war, Robert planned to seek out the relatives of those who perished on that boat. Armed with addresses given to him by a navy clerk in Woolwich, he started by finding Hodgkin's widow. He paused outside a flat in a Tottenham housing estate in London and had to fight the urge to turn tail and run. It was June 1948. She came to the door, a little girl clinging onto her skirt, sucking her thumb. She was a slight woman, her features drawn, her hair wrapped up beneath a headscarf. She eyed him suspiciously while using her foot to prevent a ginger cat from escaping. 'Yes, what do you want?' she asked him brusquely.

'Who is it?' he heard a man shout from within the flat.

'Mrs Hodgkin? Hello, I'm sorry to disturb you. My name is—'

'Just a salesman, Ted,' she shouted over her shoulder. 'It's not Hodgkin any more.'

'Oh yes, right.'

'If you're looking for my first husband, he's dead. Now, if you don't mind…'

'I know, it's just that—' He glanced at the girl and felt a sudden pang in his throat – she had her father's eyes, the same colour, the same intensity.

The woman gripped the girl's hand more firmly. 'Look,' she whispered, 'I don't know what you want but I'm not interested.' She stepped back, about to close the door.

'I knew your husband.' She paused a moment and considered him, her eyes penetrating his. 'I was with him when…. when—'

'I told you – I'm not interested.'

The silhouetted figure of the man appeared behind her a second before she slammed the door shut.

'Who was that?' he heard him ask.

He stared at the door, its green paint flaking off, the copper letterbox smudged by years of fingerprints. And he stepped away.

He lay in his bed, clinging onto his duvet, trying to shake the memory from his mind. He never worked out what he hoped to achieve by visiting the relatives. He fancied they'd appreciate knowing that someone, him, was with their loved ones at their ends. But he felt so sullied by Hodgkin's widow and her distrusting expression and her anxious tone, he never tried it again. That girl would be sixty now. He wondered if she ever knew that the man called Ted was not her father, that she had a real dad who'd died on a lifeboat. Too bad Hodgkin hadn't been able to slip away like John Clair and many of the others; too bad that Harris Beckett took a knife to his throat. He'd hated Beckett for years, hoped he'd found himself in Hell where he undeniably belonged. But with time he came to see that Beckett had been as much as a victim as the rest of them. The man had been a carpenter back home in Cardiff when the war had snatched him away. He dreamt of starting all over again. But he never got back. Instead, the waters of the Indian Ocean claimed him, as it did with all of them – all except Robert Searight.

The time was almost one o'clock.

Being back at home in Devon was difficult. He'd been welcomed home as a hero – everyone knew he'd survived the sinking. Why, he'd even been greeted back with bunting and fanfares and a party and a speech. But once the bunting had come down, once all the partygoers had returned home, he'd never felt so alone. No one wanted to know, no one understood. Least of all, his parents. The death of their older son had hit them hard, naturally. He remembered too well returning to his parental home, that morning in July 1944. The first thing his mother, Mary, asked was what day Clarence had died – she didn't know. Did it matter, he wondered, it was just a date. But of course, it did matter; we all need to know where to put the final full stop. 12th June 1944, he told her. Almost a fortnight after the date the German torpedoes had smashed into the *Academic*, destroying her in the time it takes to eat one's dinner. He found his father napping in the drawing room, the curtains drawn. Robert had lost weight over the course of his ordeal, hence his wearing a jacket that had belonged to his brother. His presence was enough to stir his father, who, squinting, opened his eyes on sensing a figure before him. 'Clarence? Clarence, is that you?'

Feeling sickened, Robert said, 'No, Father, it's me, Robert.'

'No, it can't be,' said his father with a nervous laugh. 'Don't be daft. Oh, God, I thought... Oh my, it's you. Oh, my Lord. Clarence, Clarence, Clarence...'

His mother came in, saw the distress in her husband's slumped figure, saw the anguish in her son's eyes. 'Lawrence,' she said, 'it's not Clarence; it's Robert.'

Sixty years on, Robert would still tremble as his father looked at him with a fury in his eyes. 'I can see who it is. It's Robert. Welcome back.'

Over the years, he'd slowly come to terms with the ordeal on the boat, of losing his brother and so much more. But it was that one moment, the moment he realized that in his father's view, the wrong son had survived, that had tormented him day after day, day after day. And still.

The only person who could relate to his experience was his uncle, Guy Searight. He saw him occasionally over the years. Guy had fought in the Great War, had lost a leg and, like him, had survived a sinking ship and, again like him, had lost a brother. He had fired his rifle in anger; he too had seen men mangled for life by war, had seen young men slaughtered in their prime. Lawrence, his father, had never seen action. Guy and his wife, Josephine, had settled near his parents in the Devonian countryside. Guy, bless him, had lived to a ripe old age. Robert went to see him in his final days. It was October 1966, Guy had just turned 78. But he was delicate, having already suffered two heart attacks.

'The next one will finish me off,' he told Robert at that final meeting.

'Don't be silly, Uncle.'

He was sitting in his living room, propped up on several cushions, with his black Labrador, Wilkins, at his feet. He looked pale, had lost some weight, but otherwise looked his usual jolly self, loose strands of hair scraped over his head, his tortoise-shell glasses perched on the end of his nose. It was a cosy space – low beamed ceilings, decorative brass rubbings on wooden pillars, a thick carpet. It reminded Robert of a country pub. The autumnal sun shone through the net curtains, giving the place an almost ethereal feel. Josephine came in bearing tea and cake, refusing Robert's offer of help.

'I'm not complaining,' said Guy. 'We all have to go some time. And I've had more time on this earth than many I've known.' His eyes drifted away.

Josephine and Robert exchanged glances. They knew whom he was thinking of, his younger brother, Jack, killed in action exactly a year before the war ended – 11th November 1917.

'Don't get all maudlin, Guy,' said Josephine in her lilting Irish accent. 'You don't want to be depressing Robert.'

'Hmm? Sorry. You're quite right. Oh, not so much milk, Jo.'

'Now, I'll leave you boys to it.'

'Thanks for the tea, auntie.'

'Robert, you're quite the old man yourself. You don't have to call me auntie.'

'Leave him be. He likes to.'

It was true – he did.

Guy reached down and patted Wilkins as he watched Josephine leave, straightening a framed painting on the wall as she left.

And so it was that Robert and Guy drank their tea, nibbled

on a biscuit or two and talked. They talked children, grandchildren and holidays, they talked medal collecting, cars and lawnmowers, they talked dogs, inflation and football; after all, it was 1966, England had just won the World Cup. But they didn't talk about war, either war, they didn't talk about brothers or fathers. Robert wanted to. He wanted to ask about Jack, about the uncle who'd been killed before he'd been born. But he couldn't; couldn't bring himself to ask the question.

The arrival of the post shook Wilkins from his slumber.

'Silly boy,' said Guy, shaking his head. Wilkins wagged his tail and, trotting up to his master, peered up to see whether there were any biscuits left. Guy obliged. 'Don't tell your aunt,' he said with a wink.

It was time to go, thought Robert; he'd kept his old uncle talking too long. He'd tired him out.

'Well, Uncle Guy, it's been lovely seeing you again.'

'And you, Robert. Give my love to Alice.'

'Of course.'

'Robert, listen, I'm… what I mean to say, I'm sorry if I haven't always been straight with you down the years.'

'What do you mean?'

'I… I guess… You've been a good nephew to me over the years. Perhaps… perhaps you ought to leave before I get all sentimental.'

Robert smiled and patted the dog.

He never saw his uncle again. Guy Searight did suffer a third heart attack, and, as he predicted, this one proved fatal. Aged 80, Guy Searight, veteran of the First World War, recipient of the Distinguished Conduct Medal, died on 1 December 1966.

Chapter 12: *The Presentation*

Friday, the day of the presentation to the council delegation and Tom felt nervous. He had only a ten-minute slot, but he was all too aware that the new library was to be the centrepiece of the council's multi-layered and multi-faceted leisure complex. The firm had one hour with which to present its case. Claudette would open and conclude the presentation, and in between the Project or Assistant Project Managers each had a slot starting with Clive Doherty's proposal for the theatre – a piece of cake compared to the library, thought Tom.

He got to work early. The presentation wasn't until late afternoon, but there were still loose ends to tie up and Claudette wanted the team to do a couple of dummy runs. The office was in a state of heightened anxiety all day. Claudette buzzed around maniacally, shouting at her staff, barking orders, sending and receiving numerous emails and making countless telephone calls. As much as anything else, Claudette's own reputation amongst the firm's senior partners depended on getting this contract, not to mention the hefty bonus. Her department had invested a lot of time and effort in preparing for this brief and the firm would gain kudos and future business if they managed to land the deal.

Before getting down to work, Tom quickly emailed Maria, confirming his time of arrival at St Omer, and telling her how much he was looking forward to meeting her and her husband.

After logging off his email, Tom went through his Computer Aided Design presentation and quietly practised his patter. During his ten-minute delivery, he had twenty slides to show – giving him thirty seconds per slide. Between them, the slides would illustrate every conceivable angle of his proposed library, but he couldn't help but think that something was wrong with it. Claudette checked on him at frequent intervals asking the same questions, checking the same information. Her nervousness permeated throughout the office and by the time they were ready to set out, Tom was a bag of nerves.

Claudette had chosen what they called the Small Committee Room – not too large to be impersonal, but not too small to be claustrophobic. The firm's IT team had set up a PC and overhead screen for the slides. Refreshments were at the ready with someone from the catering team at hand. Tom and the others got themselves set up and prepared. With an hour to spare before the council panel was due, everything was ready. They had nothing to do but wait, and so they trooped back to the main office.

Claudette paced up and down, smoking furiously despite the 'No Smoking' signs placed at regular intervals on the walls. Her team sat together in silence; each lost in their own thoughts. Even Claudette remained silent, unable to think of any more orders to bark out. The atmosphere was what Tom imagined would be like in the dressing room on Cup Final day. He glanced at his watch every couple of minutes, standing up, sitting down, crossing and uncrossing his legs. They'd be here soon. The phone rang in Claudette's office. She threw her cigarette into the polystyrene cup where it sizzled, leaving a small burnt hole in the side. She darted into her office and answered the phone, replacing the receiver with a quick 'thank you'.

'They're here,' she said coming out of the office. 'I'll go and fetch them. Go to your places and good luck to each and every one of you. I want you all to know I've been proud of the way you've all worked so hard towards this. Now, go in there and show them why *we* are the best!' With her brief, football manager's speech over, she turned and walked towards the lift, her corkscrew hair bouncing in time with her footsteps. She could be intolerable at times, thought Tom, but when she got going, she was something to behold. Tom, Clive and the other members of the presentation team made their way back to the Small Committee Room, where they found the IT guys and the catering woman ready at their places.

Clive sidled up to Tom. 'Claudette will be murder if we don't get this and unbearable if we do,' he whispered.

'A rock and a hard place,' agreed Tom.

Five long minutes later, they heard the familiar sound of Claudette's heels on the wooden-floored corridor approaching the room, followed by a series of quieter footsteps. 'And this,' she said opening the door, 'is our Committee Room. Please, come in.'

Tom and the others stood up as three men and two women entered the room, followed by Claudette. She motioned them to their seats behind a table decked with glasses and jugs of water and plates of biscuits. Tom's heartbeat quickened at the prospect of talking in front of these rather dour-looking individuals. Claudette opened by welcoming them to Tooley & Hill and introducing them to the five speakers. Then, the chairwoman from the council introduced her team and the departments they represented. Tom forgot their names instantly, except the chair herself, one Barbara Evans, a frighteningly thin, humourless-looking sort with short grey hair and silver half-moon glasses.

Introductions over and refreshments served, Claudette began. She spoke confidently and with an unusual calmness. She talked of how Tooley & Hill would take the council's brief, run with it and transform their ideas and ideals into an innovative, attractive, community-focussed leisure complex, its foundation based on the traditional, its facilities ahead of its time. It would be the borough's centrepiece, an awe-inspiring model, the benchmark for all other London councils, something the people of the borough could be proud of. What an opener, thought Tom. He felt like clapping; it deserved more than the half-hearted nods of approval it got from the panel.

Clive did his bit first. After Claudette's grand introduction, it was a bit of an anti-climax, plodding and workmanlike by comparison. But nevertheless, he got the job done without a hitch, hesitating only once when one of his slides seemed to take an age to load. Tom was on next. As Clive wound down, Tom took a deep breath and a sip of water. 'Don't talk too quickly,' he told himself. 'Look them in the eye, pause occasionally for effect and don't get flustered. It's only ten minutes…'

'And so,' Clive was concluding, 'I'd like to hand you over to my colleague, Tom Searight, who's going to talk to you about our proposals for the library. Thank you.' He sat down, clearly relieved it was over, and ran his short chunky fingers through his stubbly hair. Tom took his cue and immediately stood up and was about to open his mouth to speak when one of the panel spoke.

'I'm sorry,' it was the chairwoman, Barbara Evans. 'But could I ask Mr Doherty a question?'

A question, thought Tom. He quite forgot they might want to ask questions, he sort of assumed they wouldn't. He sat down again, feeling somewhat foolish. Clive answered his question with unnecessary detail, prolonging Tom's agony.

With no further questions for Clive, Tom returned to his feet. This was it. He introduced himself and his position within the firm and then clicked the mouse for the first slide which, to his relief, came up instantaneously. He talked the panel through the slide and then clicked the second, the third, the fourth. It was going well. He spoke fluidly and with the confidence of someone having done their research. The nineteenth slide, the twentieth, finished. Quick conclusion. Done!

'Any questions?' he asked nervously, glancing over to Claudette. She caught his eye and winked at him. There seemed to be no questions. Thank God for that, he thought. 'Well, in that case, I'd like to pass…'

'Mr Seagrave,' it was that Evans woman again, 'but I do have a question, if I may.'

'Certainly.' Damn you, he thought.

She looked at him over her silver glasses. 'What you've said has been very interesting…' Her fellow panellists nodded and made faint noises of approval, but, thought Tom, go on what's the 'but'?

'But we're concerned with the lack of provision for disabled access. You have made no mention, Mr Seagrave, of the requirements relating to the Disability Discrimination Act.'

'Searight,' muttered Tom. He turned his back momentarily to look at the blank overhead projector screen, just to be able to avert his eyes from the piercing stares of the panel.

The Evans woman continued. 'How do you propose to fit in the facilities in order for us to meet our commitment to complying with the DDA?'

'As the requirements of the DDA affect the whole complex…' said a familiar voice. Tom stepped back and in doing so walked into the table, which toppled over the half-full glass of water. 'Damn, sorry,' he muttered, unable to hide the panic in his voice.

Ignoring Tom's mishap, Claudette continued, '…I'll be covering the subject myself at the end of our presentation. We are, of course, very concerned that full disabled access is an integral and implicit part of the complex, and meeting the requirements of the Act is naturally a top priority in the work we do here at Tooley & Hill. And Mr Searight himself is well-versed with the Disability Discrimination Act, which is a subject close to his heart, having a young, disabled son himself. Are there any further questions for Mr Searight?'

Flustered and red-faced, Tom couldn't help but glare at the panel, as if daring them to try it again. But they didn't. Tom thanked them and sat down, leaving behind a sodden table and a wet patch on the plain blue carpet where the water had dripped down.

His colleague, Sara, another Claudette in the making, took the floor next to talk about the swimming pool facilities. Tom looked over at Claudette, but she kept her eyes fixed on Sara, her face etched with contained fury. A 'young disabled son' indeed. She knew how to manipulate a situation, slamming in the rebound from the missed penalty. But why had she misled him, had she done it on purpose? Why had Clive dismissed Tom's concerns? Without being able to concentrate, Tom listened to Sara's sparkling voice and willed her to go wrong, to stumble, for the computer to crash. Anything to deflect the blame away from him. But nothing happened and Sara finished her presentation with a flourish. The fourth and the fifth presentations came and went without a hitch, the speakers coping competently with the questions asked of them. But none of them referred to disabled access.

Claudette finished the afternoon off. The confidence and naturalness of her opening speech were gone. She was having to do it off the cuff, and it showed, overcompensating for Tom's mistake by referring to the DDA so often, that by the end, it sounded as if the only people ever likely to use the leisure complex would be the disabled. Finally, it was finished. There were no more questions, no further refreshments needed, nothing to add. The council panel gathered their papers and thanked Claudette and her team for their presentation.

As she was putting on her coat amongst the post-presentation small talk, Barbara Evans approached Tom. 'If you don't mind me asking, Mr Seagrave, what sort of disability does your son suffer from?' she asked quietly.

'Spina bifida,' he replied hastily, remembering a friend he went to school with who suffered from it.

'Oh, how sad, how old is he?'

'Fourteen, but he copes; you wouldn't know it by looking at him. He can't do PE of course, but otherwise, he's fine really.'

'He's not in a wheelchair then?'

Tom had only once seen his friend in a wheelchair. 'No, only when he's tired.'

'What's his name?'

'Er, Guy,' he said.

'Guy Seagrave,' she said as if tossing the name around in her head to see how it sounded.

'Yes,' said Tom. 'He won a medal once,' he added gushingly, and immediately regretted his childlike enthusiasm.

'Did he?'

'Yes.' Why did he have to say that? 'For… for swimming,' he said, contradicting his earlier comment about his fictional son's inability to do PE.

Barbara Evans smiled weakly and shook his hand limply before taking her leave to join her colleagues who were waiting with Claudette. Tom rolled his eyes; if she thought he was a bit of a fool, then making puerile comments like that would merely have confirmed it for her. Claudette showed their guests out and escorted them to the ground floor. The team packed up, chatting excitably in their post-ordeal relief.

Tom looked at Clive. 'I did try to talk to you about access.'

'Did you?' he replied blandly, without looking up from his papers which he bundled into his briefcase.

Tom felt a surge of annoyance. Lowering his voice, he said, 'You know I did, but you brushed me off, saying Claudette would deal with it. You never even talked to her about it, did you?'

Clive closed his briefcase with a purposeful click and then looked at Tom directly. 'Not my problem, chum. Wasn't me who cocked up. I'm sure I remember telling you to include it.'

Claudette burst through the door. 'Shit, that was hard work. OK, thank you, team. We'll debrief on Tuesday once Tom gets back from his jaunt to France, but for now, go home, have a drink and forget about it.'

The IT guys dismantled the PC and the catering woman cleared up. One by one, Tom's colleagues bid each other goodbye and left. With briefcase in hand, Tom was also ready to leave, back to Enfield, back to the delights of another evening with his parents.

'Tom,' said Claudette, 'before you go, a word in my office.'

Damn, thought Tom, he thought he was getting away lightly.

Tom entered Claudette's office and Claudette followed, closing the door behind her. She pulled down the blinds, making sure they were properly closed. Tom sat down in the soft upright, brown chair in front of Claudette's desk. Claudette perched herself on the edge of her desk at right angles from Tom, her legs crossed, her black skirt riding up to her knees. She reached down into the drawer behind her and grappled around. Tom noticed, on the top of her in-tray, a letter with Dunstone, Cutler & Maine's logo clearly visible. Claudette pulled out a packet of cigarettes from the drawer, offered one to Tom who refused with a shake of the head, and lit herself one. She remained silent for a minute or two, drawing on her cigarette and idly staring at the year planner stretching on the wall within her gaze.

Eventually, she spoke without turning her head, her voice purposely calm and even. 'How do you think it went, then Tommy?'

Tom never considered himself a "Tommy", but occasionally Claudette called him it whenever she felt the need to assert her authority. 'Bloody awful,' he said.

'She was a bit of an old bat that Barbara Evans, wasn't she?' One of her shoes dangled from her toes; Tom noticed the sharpness of the heel. 'Probably in need of a good rogering, don't you think?'

'I don't know if I'd go as far as that,' he said cautiously.

'She was enough to put anybody off.'

He eyed her carefully; did she really think he was that much of a fool? 'I did try to talk to you about the disability access.

When I tried to speak to Clive about it, he palmed me off, saying you were dealing with it.'

Claudette returned her gaze to the year planner. 'Typical of him. Always passing the buck. He told me you had it all under control.' She drew on her cigarette. 'Hmm, anyone would think he was playing us off each other. I think a quiet word in Mr Doherty's ear is called for.'

'He may be a sullen git but he's not that devious. No, I think it was you who were playing people off each other.'

She spun around and glowered at him. 'What are you implying?'

'I'm not implying anything… yet.'

'Oh, come on, do you know what sort of bonus I'm up for if we get this contract? And what about yourself–'

'What about me?'

'Don't you take any responsibility for this? OK, so the DDA stuff might've been a bit suspect, but the library brief was yours to run with, and rather than just worry about it, you could've shown some initiative.'

'Well…' He hated the way she sat on her desk, towering over him, dominating the situation.

'I think you should search your own conscience first before you go around casting aspersions on others. Why is it always someone else's fault? I mean, it's fairly fundamental stuff, the DD bloody A. I reckon I covered for you fairly well. Neat trick, wasn't it, saying you had a disabled son? Got the sympathy vote.'

Tom guffawed. 'Fairly unethical, if you ask me.'

'But if it did the trick.' Claudette swung around on her desk to face Tom, placing her stiletto shoes on the sides of Tom's chair, either side of his legs. She stubbed her half-finished cigarette in a glass ashtray on her desk, blowing the last mouthful of smoke into Tom's face. 'So instead of trying to make me your scapegoat, I think you owe me one.'

Tom recoiled and tried not to cough. In his peripheral vision, he could see the bright lilac colour of Claudette's underwear within a frighteningly close proximity. He concentrated on keeping his gaze fixed on her eyes as she loomed above him. 'Yes, Claudette,' he said. 'Whatever you say.' He realised he didn't have enough evidence to threaten her with, he needed something else, something more concrete.

'I mean, this is a big tender we have here,' she said leaning forward, her arms folded tightly around her midriff, accentuating the shape of her breasts. 'There's a lot riding on it. Not to mention all the work we've put into it already, there's the big pay-off, the magnificent advertisement for the firm, the kudos, and, lest we should forget, my bonus, a big fat bonus at that. Now why should I want to risk all that?' She leant further forward, leaning her hands on the arms of Tom's chair. Her face was now only inches away from Tom's, her curly corkscrew hair falling forward, almost touching Tom's cheeks. He could smell the cigarette smoke on her breath, intermingling with the delicate scent of her perfume. The smell evoked the memory of his early days with Julie, in the days when she smoked, the mixture of tobacco and cheap perfume filling his nostrils as they made love. But this stuff wasn't cheap, and he found the concoction of smells and the sharp memory intoxicating and, despite himself, arousing. Whether accidentally or purposefully, he didn't know and didn't dare think about it, but Claudette widened her legs a fraction, exposing further the lilac triangle of her silken knickers. 'Claudette, I – I don't think…'

She pulled away slightly. 'What, Tom?' she said softly, brushing a long wisp of hair away. 'What don't you think? Don't you think those disabled folk need their access?'

'It's just not…'

'Ethical?' she said. Then she grabbed Tom's tie and yanked it firmly towards her, pulling Tom nearer to her face, their noses almost touching. He gripped the armrest, astounded by the physicality of her gesture, which in a second, had moved their relationship from the professional to the personal. Determined not to look away, Tom held her gaze, concentrating on the black line of mascara and the convergence of the neatly plucked eyebrows. The space between them was as intimate as the space between lovers, but he knew she was searching for a hesitation, a hint of weakness. Erotic intimidation, sexually charged coercion. So close, her eyes began to lose shape, just a large pool of murky green liquid, the black soulless epicentre. He listened to her breathing, consciously steadied, and noticed the slight flaring of her nostrils. She blinked. Her eyes softened slightly, the hard focus retreated, the eyelids widened but still she remained rooted, her fingers gripped around his tie. Her intimidation had taken her this far, thought Tom, but now she had no idea where to take it next. 'You owe me one,' she mouthed. Tom narrowed his eyes and shook his head a fraction. 'You know sod all,' she added. She was so close, he could almost swallow her words and breathe them back at her.

From behind him, Tom heard the knock on the door. For a moment, he thought Claudette had not heard it but then gently releasing Tom's tie, she lifted her head and barked at the figure on the other side of the door: 'Go away, in a meeting.' Her voice was steady, the tone deep and purposeful. But then like a person coming out of hypnotism with a click

126

of the fingers, she seemed to realise the absurdity of the situation she'd engineered. 'One minute,' she added, her voice now containing a quiver of panic. Quickly, she spun around on the table, hopped off and sat on her chair behind the safety of the desk. Tom swallowed and tried to straighten his tie.

The person outside the office spoke, 'Only me.' It was Clive. What the hell was he still doing here, thought Tom. 'Just going home, but…' Tom glanced around to see the door open as he tried to straighten his tie. 'I thought you'd better see…' Clive had stepped in, faltered for a moment and immediately tried to act as if he hadn't. '…This report before er, going home…' he said, his voice slowing down with each word.

'I thought I'd told you to wait,' said Claudette quickly, unable to look at him. 'Didn't you notice the blinds were down?'

'Sorry,' said Clive looking suspiciously from one to the other, sensing the atmosphere and the awkwardness that drifted like a fog within the four walls of the office. Carefully, he stepped forward, clearing his throat, and placed the file on Claudette's desk.

'I should be going,' said Tom, smiling weakly at Clive as he picked up his briefcase. 'I'll be back on Tuesday.' Clive stepped back to allow Tom to pass, his eyes searching Tom's face for a clue. As he reached the door, Tom paused and looked back at Claudette sitting behind her desk, trying desperately to appear composed while casting her eye over Clive's report. For a moment, just a moment, Tom almost felt sorry for her.

Chapter 13: *France*

Saturday afternoon, halfway to France. Tom looked at his watch and realised he was still on British time. He adjusted it to French time, which made it just gone 3 pm. The papers were still full of Ronald Reagan and now Ray Charles had also died.

Having caught the Eurostar to Calais, Tom then had to catch a train to St Omer, about 50 kilometres south. Arriving in St Omer, Tom waited at the end of the platform, as instructed. Maria warned him she'd be a few minutes late. Despite the time, it was still very warm. He went to get himself a cool drink and with his awkward French managed to buy a can of fizzy orange. Back on the platform, he waited and hoped he'd recognise her from her emailed photograph. People came and went, bustling and rushing to catch departing trains, meeting friends, returning from work. He doubted if any of them could recount such a week as his. He wondered what sort of conversation took place between Claudette and Clive after his hasty retreat. It was typical of Clive: never there when you wanted him, but turns up when you least expect it.

'Monsieur Searight, I presume?'

Tom turned to see a tall, slim man, about 40, maybe 45, in a rust-coloured jacket standing directly in front of him, a

128

tanned man with a bushy moustache and shoulder-length hair, and an earring in one ear.

'Yes?'

He smiled, offering his hand. 'I'm Bernard, Maria's husband.'

'Oh, how do you do?'

Taking Tom's holdall, despite Tom's protestations, Bernard sent a quick text then drove Tom the five-minute drive to the Dubois house, pointing out various landmarks along the way.

Maria was waiting at the front door. 'Tom! *Bienvenue.*'

'*Bonjour*, Maria,' he said, offering his hand.

Ignoring his proffered hand, she reached forward, kissing him on both cheeks. 'We meet at last,' she said. She had friendly eyes and a wide, beaming face, offset by the flow of long, almost black hair. 'Come through. You look younger than you do in your picture.'

'Ah, so that cream does work!'

Both she and Bernard laughed heartily, Maria tilting her head back, exposing her glaringly white teeth. His little joke wasn't that funny, but nonetheless, he felt pleased by their warm reaction, if a little embarrassed.

Tom noticed how casually but stylishly dressed she was. She wore a knee-length purple suede skirt and light moleskin shoes. Barely ten minutes in their presence and he felt very much at ease with them both. She wore no make-up. Compare and contrast with Claudette, thought Tom.

Maria had found Tom a guesthouse he could stay in; just ten minutes' walk from the house. But after half an hour, she and her husband had decided he was either harmless enough or trustworthy enough to invite him to spend the weekend with them and their daughter, Odette. They lived on the outskirts of St Omer in a three-bedroom townhouse with a small garden. Bernard explained that they had two daughters; the eldest, Brigitte, was at college in Bordeaux and their youngest, Odette, had just turned 18. Tom remarked that they didn't look old enough to have two adult children, and then blushed at the crassness of his observation.

Maria laughed. 'I started young. I was only 19 when Brigitte was born. The girls' father – we are no longer together. Many years now. Bernard is their father now.' She reached over and squeezed Bernard's hand.

'And you, Tom,' said Bernard. 'Are you married?'

Tom hesitated. 'I'm separated.' How odd that sounded, he thought, the words didn't seem to ring true. He didn't dare tell them it'd only been three days, but three days or three years, he and Julie were living apart and hence technically 'separated'.

Odette appeared from her bedroom, all made-up, about to go out for the evening. Tom said hello and noticed how similar she was to her mother. Odette was forever going out, Bernard told him. They kissed their daughter goodbye and then gave Tom a guided tour of the house. It was a bright, spacious home, mostly wooden floored and lightly decorated. Tom was to have Brigitte's old room. She was, or had been, a fan of Hollywood film stars. Posters of various pin-ups covered the walls: Johnny Depp, Leonardo DiCaprio, Clive Owen and others he didn't recognise. With the tour completed, Maria sat Tom in the large kitchen and she poured them each a sweet wine, whilst Bernard started on the dinner. Dinner consisted of spaghetti bolognese with plenty of mushrooms and Parmesan cheese together with a couple of full-bodied bottles of red wine which Bernard described in detail. During the rest of the evening, they sat on the sitting room sofa, drinking the remainder of the wine, nibbling cashew nuts and black olives, and talked of their pasts and futures. Tom told Maria about Charlotte and Angus, and his brother and family out in Toronto. Maria talked about her daughters and her work as a travel agent.

After an hour of comfortable conversation, Maria said, 'Let me fetch the things that brought you here.' She disappeared for a few minutes. Tom and Bernard discussed the following day's football match between England and France at the European Championships. Tom sipped his wine and looked around the room. Everything was neatly and tastefully organised, books tidily arranged, tasteful little figurines. The occasional floral print decorated the walls and a large lamp with a deep red lampshade cast a relaxing light over the room. Maria returned carrying a shoebox wrapped with a length of string. She laid it on the coffee table in front of them. 'In this box,' she declared, 'is the life of your ancestor, Guy Searight.' Tom looked at it. 'Aren't you going to open it?' she asked.

Tom slipped off the string and opened the lid. Inside was a padded envelope and beneath it some books, small enough to fit inside the shoebox. Tom lifted out the first book, a notebook. On the cover, written in a small, spidery handwriting, were the words *"Guy Searight, 1914-1921"*. Beneath the notebook were two other books – one an English-French dictionary, the other an old edition of Charles Dickens's *A Tale of Two Cities*. Next, he opened the padded envelope and carefully withdrew its contents. There, in his hands, were Guy's medals – four of them, attached to one another by a thin strip of metal at the back with a thick pin. They were in pristine condition.

'My grandmother used to polish them,' said Maria, reading his thoughts. Three of the medals were round, one cross-shaped. On the back of one of the round medals were the words *"The Great War for Civilisation 1914-1919"*, and on the rim the inscription *"8562 Pte. G.Searight, Essex Reg"*. But it was the first medal that really intrigued Tom. On the front, the bust of George V, and on the back, the words *"For Distinguished Conduct in the Field"*. The ribbon was a dark red colour with a wide blue stripe down the middle.

'"For Distinguished Conduct in the Field". My father mentioned this. I wonder why he got it.'

'I don't know. Perhaps, if you read Guy's diary you might find out.'

'Have you read it?'

'No, the writing is too difficult for me.'

'But why did your archive want to throw away this stuff?'

'It needed space for more of its medieval collections. My grandmother asked if she could keep the diary first. Our family has had them all these years; it's time they went back to where they belong. I don't think they are of much value, but it's the diary and the history of it that makes them so fascinating, *n'est-pas?*'

Tom smiled at the little burst of French. He picked up the diary and ran his finger gently across the cover, feeling the coarseness of the material. He opened it and flicked through the first few pages. He saw it was not so much a diary, but a memoir written after the event. The pages were dusty and dry to the touch and the writing littered with crossings-out and tiny illegible scribbles in the margins. "Uncle Hobbly", his father had called him. Tom wondered whether he would meet his father or Lawrence, his fearsome grandfather, within these pages. Tom had never been one to concern himself with the past and, unlike Charlotte, he hated history at school, and had never taken any interest in his family history. The only time he had ever indulged in nostalgia was a disastrous school reunion party. But now, this French woman had appeared out of nowhere and delivered a huge slice of the past straight into his lap.

'Tom, tomorrow I take you on a mystery tour.'

'Sounds intriguing.'

'I hope so.' She smiled.

*

That night, Tom settled in bed and retrieved Guy's journal from the box. He wouldn't read for long, he decided; after his long day, he'd soon be asleep. He thought of Julie. She'd know by now that he'd gone to a small town in France for the weekend, but she'd have no idea as to why and with whom. The thought gave Tom a tingle of satisfaction, which was quickly tempered by the thought of Charlotte. He'd have to take her out on his return. Perhaps they could go see that new Harry Potter film. He'd ring her tomorrow on the mobile.

Tom turned to the first page. Although faded and small, the writing on the first pages was neat enough for Tom to decipher.

> *My name is Guy Searight. I have decided to commit my story to paper, for I have reached a stage in my life where I am no longer sure how I arrived. I have loved and lost too many times either through the catastrophe of war, injustice or circumstance. I sometimes feel as if I am afloat in a shapeless, unending ocean. A curse touched me many years ago and I live daily within its shadow. Like a plague, everything I touch, anyone I dare to love is equally cursed. I sometimes wonder whether my lack of faith is because of the curse, or whether the curse exists because of my lack of faith. The time has come for me to reconcile my past before I can even attempt to contemplate my future, and with this in mind,*

I need to write my story. It is a story about a young man who goes off to fight for his country in its hour of need. But when I think back to that young ambitious man, he appears in my mind now as little more than a stranger; a man I once knew and still envy. That young man was born into a generation that suffered as no generation had suffered before and, I hope for the sake of humanity, that no generation need suffer like it again. I may have survived the Great War, but the War lives within me still and probably always will.

May God grant me the strength to write my story, and then perhaps, on its completion, to allow me to live again as a man should live......

An hour later, Tom drifted off to sleep, his dreams a mass of images from Guy's description of the trenches. His subconscious had been pricked by a distant voice echoing through the decades, a voice which now, finally, had found its audience.

*

The following morning, Sunday, Tom woke up with a renewed sense of optimism. Banishing all thoughts of work and domestic disharmony, he felt determined to enjoy the unknown pleasures of the day ahead. It was a hot June morning and Maria served up a breakfast of croissants fresh from the local *boulangerie*. Bernard was already out – he was a keen cyclist, Maria told him. She asked how far he'd got with the diary, and Tom felt almost ungrateful having to admit that he'd only managed the first few pages before sleep overcame him.

After breakfast, Maria took Tom on a walking tour of St Omer. It was very much as Tom remembered quiet French towns to be from the occasional French holidays he took with his parents. It had a large central square, La Place Foch, dominated at one end by an imposing Gothic church, big enough to be a cathedral, thought Tom, and seemingly too big for the size of the town. Indeed, according to Maria, it was a cathedral, the Notre Dame Cathedral. The other sides of the square were lined with various cafés, boutiques and antique cum bric-a-brac stalls. Tom was impressed how the town had managed to avoid the influx of high street brand names, which stripped British towns of their individuality, removing any sense of their historic uniqueness. Tom and Maria browsed around the shops. Maria bought a large bouquet of flowers and Tom bought a pair of s–shaped earrings for Charlotte. They stopped off in a café and sat outside overlooking the square, enjoying the sun and calmness.

After their coffees and a large sweet pastry each, Maria took Tom to the cathedral. It took them a few moments to adjust to the darkness inside the church and Tom remarked how cool it was within. It'd been years since Tom had stepped into a church. The far end was dominated by a huge organ, which, according to Maria, dated from the 18th century. The highlight, however, was the impressive astrological clock, which showed the signs of the zodiac and the movement of the stars and sun over St Omer. They strolled quietly up the aisles and Tom admired the murals depicting the descent of the cross painted, allegedly, by Rubens. Before leaving, Tom lit a candle and stared at the flickering flame. He offered a quiet prayer asking that he be guided through his current predicament while apologising for his lack of religious direction.

'Come,' said Maria, 'we need to go for a little drive.' Carrying her flowers, Maria led Tom out of the cathedral and back to her car. They drove about three kilometres southwards on the Abbeville Road until they came to a large cemetery – the Longuenesse Souvenir Cemetery, explained Maria as she parked the car. As they entered the neatly manicured grounds, Tom was hit by the vast numbers of perfectly lined military headstones, rows upon rows upon rows. Maria led the way, seemingly knowing where to go amongst the hundreds of identical rows.

'Over three thousand men are commemorated here,' she said. Eventually, she came to a stop and looked down at a headstone. Following her gaze, Tom gawked at the inscription:

In the memory of Jack Searight, Essex Regiment.
Killed 11th November 1917.

Chapter 14: *The Visitor*

Late Sunday afternoon, Julie was trying to mark her students' GCSE homework, but, sitting at the table with a whole pile of them awaiting her attention, she was having difficulty concentrating. Charlotte was upstairs listening to some music, it sounded like Busted, her new favourite band, the bassline thumping through the ceiling. She was meant to be doing her homework and she had her poetry recital coming up at the end of the week, but how she could concentrate with that noise, Julie didn't know. Another day, she would have remonstrated but since Tom's departure, relations with Charlotte had become strained to say the least, and Julie had no stomach for another argument. Charlotte had become sullen and short-tempered, and recently Julie had noticed the smell of tobacco smoke on her daughter's breath. What was really upsetting Charlotte, Julie knew, was that Tom had made no effort to speak to her and the poor girl was missing him; they both were. Charlotte could do without this upset, especially as she was coming up to the end of her last year before starting on her GCSEs. But when she tried to offer her daughter the comfort she needed, Charlotte merely shunned her efforts.

She gazed at the exam paper in front of her trying to summon the concentration to actually mark it. Where was

Tom now? All Julie knew was that he'd taken himself off to someplace in France she'd never heard of. She couldn't pretend she wasn't worried. They'd never been apart for this long before, at least not in the fifteen years they'd been married, and now she wanted him back – desperately. She wandered around the living room, not wanting to cook or even think about it. She picked up a framed photograph from the mantelpiece of the three of them taken on their Spanish holiday the previous year. She sighed and slumped onto the sofa. If Tom was, in some way, trying to punish her, it was working. She felt miserable. She wanted to ring Alice and Robert to see whether Tom had come back yet, but she daren't; it had only been a couple of hours since she last called. She began to fear the worst. What if he never came back, what if Tom made this 'trial separation' permanent? Seized by an abrupt surge of anger, she threw the photo frame across the room. She couldn't face living without him; she'd rather lose a limb. What would they do? Tom couldn't go on staying with his parents; he'd have to find a place of his own. Or she might be forced to find somewhere else herself. Neither of them could afford the mortgage on one salary; they'd be forced to sell up, uproot and destroy the family home. It was all too big, too depressing to even contemplate.

She wished to God she had someone to talk to – but there was no one. The realisation hit her. She had no friends, no real ones, just superficial people she occasionally had a drink with. Not the sort of women she could talk to. No sisters, no brothers, no one. So wrapped up in her world of work and family, she'd neglected everything else. And now she needed someone, there was nobody.

She heard Charlotte's footsteps coming down the stairs. She picked up an exam paper as Charlotte breezed into the living room. 'Mum, I'm bored. I'm gonna take Angus out for a walk.'

'What about your homework?'

'Finished it already.'

Julie didn't really believe her, but she wasn't going to confront her over it. 'OK, sweetheart,' she said meekly. 'I'll have some dinner ready for when you get back. Anything you fancy?'

Charlotte shrugged her shoulders. 'Dunno. Nothing really, whatever you're having.'

'Will you be long?'

'No, just to the tree and back.'

'OK, then. Be careful.'

Shaking his dog lead, Charlotte called for Angus and then went out. Julie put the exam paper down and sighed – again. She decided to have a whisky. She never drank at this time of day and she rarely drank spirits, but she was shaking and she needed something to fortify herself. The whisky poured, she thought about putting on a CD. She looked through the collection, but every CD was either Tom's, had been bought for her by Tom, or in some way, reminded her of him. In the end, she plumped for classical – Schubert's *Unfinished Symphony*. She sat down, sipped the whisky, enjoying the sensation if not the taste, and listened to the swirling sounds of the strings, the mournful drone of the winds. But instead of allowing the music to free her, it merely focussed her mind even more on the things she wanted to avoid. Unable to bear it any more, she turned the CD off and welcomed back the silence. The music had failed her; the whisky was making her feel worse, and the last thing she wanted to do was to cook. It was going to have to be a ready meal.

There was a knock on the front door. She wondered why they hadn't used the doorbell. Maybe it was Charlotte back already, but no, she had her own set of keys. Surely, it couldn't be Tom. Had he taken his keys with him; she couldn't remember. Maybe he hadn't, perhaps it *was* Tom. It must be; she'd give anything for it to be Tom. Her heart beating with nervous anticipation, she leapt across the sitting room and into the hallway. She took a deep breath, mustn't appear overkeen. The glass in the front door was too frosted to give any clues. Her hand on the door handle, she opened the door. It was Mark Moyes. She couldn't hide her disappointment.

'Hello, Julie,' he said sheepishly, looking more dishevelled than usual, holding his briefcase and a pale green jacket over his arm. 'Your doorbell isn't working.'

'What are you doing here?'

'Can I come in?'

Julie was unsure. She didn't want Charlotte to find him here, and also, although unlikely, what if Tom suddenly reappeared; that really would be it.

Mark could see Julie's obvious reluctance. 'I won't stay for long.'

'Five minutes,' she said firmly.

Julie showed Mark through to the sitting room. He saw the pile of exam papers on the table and on the sofa. 'Practice papers?'

'Mark, I thought we'd agreed…'

'I know. I'm sorry, but… May I sit down?'

'No. OK, five minutes, Mark. Charlotte's gone out for a short walk with Angus; she'll be back soon.'

Mark sat down in the armchair. 'I know, I saw her go.'

Julie remained on her feet. 'What do you mean; were you waiting?'

'Well, not exactly.'

'Mark, are you stalking me now?'

'Of course not, don't be silly. I only waited a couple of minutes.' It had, in fact, been closer to fifteen. He'd sat in his car, waiting, plucking up the courage to knock on her door.

'So why have you got your briefcase? It's Sunday.'

'I always have it. It's got my newspaper and stuff in it.'

'Man bag, eh?'

'If you like.'

'Mark, I thought we'd agreed that it had to end. I *can't* be seen with you any more, it's too risky; I've got too much to lose.'

'So when's Tom back?' asked Mark, watching Julie closely for her answer.

'You know he's gone?'

'Charlotte told me at school last week.'

She sat down heavily on the sofa. She couldn't help but feel betrayed by her daughter's readiness to tell the family secrets to the teacher, but then maybe Mark had coerced the information from her. 'So she's giving you daily updates now, is she?'

'She's upset.'

'Precisely, Mark, she's upset, she's sullen and she's smoking. All because her father's walked out on us, and why do you think that is?'

Mark got up from the armchair. 'Julie, listen…' he said as he sat down on the sofa beside her. Instinctively, Julie's heart skipped a beat. Mark began talking of renewing their affair in the same way as he'd done in the café; they'd just need to be more careful, etc, etc. But while Julie wasn't listening, she couldn't deny the little frisson of excitement she felt at being so close to the man who had, so recently, given her such pleasure. But equally, she felt uncomfortable with Mark being here, she couldn't bear the thought of Charlotte walking in and seeing him in the house. She edged away from Mark; just a fraction, but Mark noticed.

'Oh, I'm sorry,' he said. 'Do I repulse you now?'

'No, of course not.'

'I never used to.' Mark moved closer and placed his arm over the back of the sofa behind Julie's head. 'In fact,' he continued, 'I remember a time, not so long ago, when you couldn't get enough of me.' His hand reached down and touched Julie's hair. He twiddled it around his fingers. Julie moved her head away.

'Mark, that was fun, but this is reality now.' She inched a fraction more away from Mark's encroaching presence. Yes, she still found him attractive, she loved the way his dark, almost black hair curled into the nape of his neck, and under other circumstances, she might have succumbed. But not here, not now.

Suddenly Mark pulled back. 'This is what I find so annoying. One minute, we're going along quite happily, and the next minute, it's bang – you've had enough and that's it; end of story. But what about *me*? I had no choice in this. I feel like a discarded plaything. I bet you've never stopped to think how *I* might feel?' Mark edged closer again. 'Come on; how about we meet up? Just one more time, for old time's sake.' He stroked her hair.

Julie had had enough. She sprang out of the sofa. 'For old time's sake? For God's sake, one moment you're playing the used and abused card, next thing you want one more shag just for old time's sake. Who's using whom here?'

'All right; no need to be so dramatic,' said Mark sullenly.

'Dramatic? Yes, I'm being dramatic, and if you want I'll get hysterical too; it's what women do best, isn't it?' She didn't want Mark in her house a moment longer. 'Get out, Mark. Just… just get out.'

But Mark didn't move. He glared at her. 'What – before Tom gets back?'

'Yes, if you like, before Tom gets back.'

Mark scoffed. 'Come on, Julie, who do you think you're kidding? He's not coming back and you know it.'

Julie grimaced, for the truth in what Mark said had pierced her. It was OK to admit to herself, but not for anyone else to dare even suggest it. 'You bastard,' she seethed. She leaned down and grabbed Mark by the lapels of his jacket, hoping her anger would provide the necessary strength to pull him up. But Mark gripped her wrists tightly and held them still, mocking her lack of strength with his own. Unable to move and almost falling forward, Julie felt enraged by her impotency. Through gritted teeth, she snarled at him, 'Let me go!' But Mark held onto her, enjoying her state of total helplessness.

'Let go!' she screamed. 'You're wrong, you're bloody wrong; he'll be back soon. We've known each other for too long for… for…'

'For what?' Mark shouted back. 'For the likes of me to come between you?' He finally let go of Julie's wrists and pushed her to one side. Julie staggered back.

'Yes, for the likes of you. Now get out. And this time it's final. I do not want to see you again…*ever.*'

Neither of them heard the front door open.

Julie continued, 'You and me – it was a mistake.' She took a deep breath. 'Look…' she said, regaining her composure and lowering her voice. 'You have to understand; I do like you still, but it's finished. I have to put Tom and Charlotte first, I've…'

'Mr Moyes,' said a quiet, confused voice from the other side of the sitting room. 'What are you doing here?'

They turned, aghast, and looked at her. 'Sweetheart,' said Julie unable to disguise the quiver in her voice. 'I didn't hear you come in.'

Charlotte ignored her and continued looking at her teacher. 'I don't understand; why are you here, sir?'

Mark shot a nervous glance at Julie. 'I was, er…'

Julie interrupted. 'Mark – Mr Moyes just popped in because, because I'd left some papers in his classroom. Y'know, after the parents' evening.'

Charlotte was unconvinced. 'Why didn't you just give them to me?'

'Well, I was passing this way, so I thought I'd drop them in as they happened to be in the car.'

Angus trotted into the sitting room, his lead trailing behind him. He saw Mark and made a half-hearted attempt to bark at the stranger. Mark seized the opportunity to change the subject. 'Hello there,' he said bending down and offering his hand to the dog. Angus wagged his tail and sniffed Mark's hand. Mark stroked him. 'And what's your name then?'

'He's called Angus, aren't you, boy? Here!' Angus padded over to Charlotte. She picked him up and ruffled his fur. 'Who's a good boy, then?'

'How old is he?'

'Seven. And you're a little rascal, aren't you, always running off.'

Mark glanced at Julie; he knew his time was up. 'I, erm, I best be going.'

'Yes,' said Julie, 'thank you for dropping the books off.'

Charlotte looked accusingly at her. 'You said papers just now.'

'Well, whatever,' she said feebly, cursing her slip-up. Turning to Mark, she added, 'I don't suppose our paths will cross again, except for the odd school meeting.'

'No, I expect not.' Mark gathered up his briefcase, but Charlotte hadn't finished yet.

Mr Moyes had always been her favourite teacher, and so good-looking too, but here in her sitting room, it was all out of context; something was wrong. Turning to her mother, she asked, 'What did you mean when you said it was all a mistake?'

'What mistake; did I say that?'

'Yes, you did, as I was coming in. You said something like "you and me, it was all a mistake".'

'Did I?' Julie began panicking; she felt cornered and Charlotte was closing in for the kill.

'Yes, come on, Mum, you said something about Dad and me coming first.'

'Well yes…' Julie looked at Mark, but he made no move to help her out. Was it her imagination or did he seem to be enjoying her discomfort? Julie opted for the firm approach. 'I'm sorry, Charlotte, but it's just talk, grown-up talk.' Immediately, she regretted patronising Charlotte in front of her teacher.

Predictably, Charlotte took offence. 'Don't treat me like a child. You're up to something, aren't you? Both of you.' She looked from one to the other, her expression changing from confusion to the horror of realisation. She turned on her mother. 'Is that why Dad left?'

'It's not as simple as that, sweetheart…'

'Don't call me sweetheart,' she said, her voice rising with every word. 'It *is*, isn't it? That's why Dad left, and I thought it was cos he'd done something wrong, but it wasn't, it was *you*, you and… and…' She didn't know what to call him any more.

Somehow, "Sir" or "Mr Moyes" seemed too respectful for him now. 'You and him,' she said, almost unable to form the words through her anger.

Mark had no desire to stay any more. 'I really ought…'

'You've ruined it all,' blubbered Charlotte, 'Dad's gone and it's because of you two.'

Julie sat down; she began to well up. The sight of her daughter clutching her dog whilst her heart was breaking was too much to bear. 'I'm sorry, Charlotte, I'm so sorry…' Rising, she stepped towards her daughter, desperate to hold her.

Charlotte recoiled away from her mother. 'Leave me alone, don't touch me! I want my dad.'

'He'll be back soon, sweetheart.'

'How do you know? He's gone because of you two.' She put Angus down on the carpet, still holding onto his lead. 'Well, I'm going too.'

'Charlotte, love, you can't just go. Really, your dad could be back anytime. I'll ring Granddad now and ask him if he's back yet.'

'Do you really expect Dad to come back while *he's* got his feet under the table? I don't think so.' She turned to Mark who was still poised with his briefcase waiting for the first opportunity to beat a hasty retreat. He was taken aback by the venom in Charlotte's voice: 'I'll see you in school… *Sir*.' She turned and fled out of the sitting room, with Angus close at heel, dragged by his lead, slamming the front door as she left the house.

Julie flopped down onto the sofa, exhausted and tearful. First her husband and now her daughter. If only she hadn't let Mark in.

Mark spoke, his words surprisingly sympathetic. 'I'm sorry. You were right, I was being selfish. Of course, your family comes first, I see that now, I never meant this to happen.' He meant it too. He'd been Charlotte's teacher for almost a year and she was a good kid. It upset him too, to see her like that. He wanted to put his arm around Julie, purely to comfort her, but he knew how inappropriate it would be. 'She'll be back later, I'm sure. I see too many kids from broken homes at school, none of them deserve it, and especially someone special like Charlotte.'

'I know.' Julie looked up at him and half-smiled. 'Thank you.'

'And it was foolish of us, I know that. Imagine if this ever got out. Wouldn't do our careers much good, would it? I will go now unless you particularly want me to stay.'

'No, you go. I think it's for the best.'

'Yes.' As he reached the sitting room door, he turned to look at her. 'I wish you well. I'm sorry to leave you in this mess. It's been nice knowing you.'

'Yeah. And you.'

Mark left. Julie closed her eyes. She wanted to scream, drink whisky, screw up exam papers, anything. But she lacked the strength.

*

Charlotte stormed down the road. She thought about going to her grandparents' house but realised she didn't have enough money for a taxi and it was too far for a bus. She decided to go back to the park, it was another sunny day, sit beneath the shade of the huge oak tree and think it through. Angus pulled on his lead, glad to be out for another walk.

She couldn't believe it; how could they? She didn't know who she resented more – Mr Moyes for splitting up her parents, or her mum for driving Dad out and for showing her up in front of Mr Moyes. Her mum *knew* how much she liked Mr Moyes. All those times she talked of Mr Moyes and all along, she was laughing at her. Christ, she felt stupid. How humiliating. Surely, they hadn't, well, done 'it'? But they must have, and her father must have found out, otherwise, why would he have walked out? The thought of her mum and Mr Moyes together repulsed her. She shuddered with embarrassment at the thought of her own fantasy – how she used to dream she was eighteen and walking hand-in-hand with him and even kissing him. What an idiot she'd been. Perhaps all the other teachers knew and they were all laughing at her in the staffroom. And all those times she'd put her hand up in class and done well in her history homework, and all the while he was seeing her mother. He must've thought she was a right little fool. Not any more, he could stuff his precious First World War and all his bloody history.

And what about her dad? She'd judged him harshly for whatever he was meant to have done. And all along, he must've been really upset to know her mum had been having it off with Mr Moyes. He was still probably too upset to come home. But why had he gone to France, why wasn't he still with her grandparents? Surely he had to come back at some point, what about his work? Was this why parents split up all the time because one of them runs off with someone else? Why bother getting married in the first place? And what would happen to her, she wondered. She had quite fancied the idea of having a weekend dad, but not now, not any more. She wanted her old life back again, with her mum and dad together at home, like it should be. She hated him disappearing for a whole week without even a phone call. Had he forgotten about her already? It seemed so wrong. Her bloody mum had gone and spoilt everything.

Charlotte was approaching the park; she could see the top of the old oak ahead of her. She'd just come from the park and she didn't really want to go back, but equally, she didn't want to go home. What about Gavin? No, she definitely didn't want to see Gavin; she couldn't talk to him about such things, or even Abigail, or anyone she could think of; except perhaps her granddad. She stopped in her tracks. 'Life's shit,' she said aloud, smacking her arms against her sides. At that moment, she momentarily loosened her grip on the lead. The little terrier, pulling as always, yanked himself free. With the park looming ahead of him, he made a beeline for the entrance. Quickly, he darted off, running across the road. A car. Charlotte saw a car. She yelled; her whole body paralysed. 'Angus!'

It seemed to happen in slow motion. The green hatchback skidded. Charlotte held her head in her hands. Angus disappeared beneath the car. She screamed, rooted to the spot. The car screeched to a halt a few yards on. The crumpled heap of Angus lay in the middle of the road. Passers-by stopped and gasped.

The car door flung open; the driver jumped out. 'I didn't see him; he just ran out!' But Charlotte didn't hear him; she couldn't stop herself from screaming.

Chapter 15: *The Photograph*

That Sunday evening, after their successful trip to St Omer, Maria cooked Tom coq-au-vin, accompanied by a fine bottle of Bordeaux, one that Bernard had been saving for an occasion such as this. Their daughter, Odette, had gone out again, promising to be back before eleven. The meal was cooked to perfection and Tom heaped lavish praise on Maria, who responded with modest protestations on how easy it'd been to prepare and cook. Bernard turned on the television with the volume down, and kept an eye on the football game. Tom had never been particularly interested in football but was still pleased to see England were winning.

Meanwhile, conversation flowed easily, from childhood memories to the trials of parenthood and the genius of French painting, Italian opera and English pop. Bernard asked them about their day and, having listened, gave Tom a potted history of the cemetery. In the few hours since the visit to the gravestones, Tom realised that while his present life was falling apart, his past, paradoxically, was fast gaining substance. Something that, hitherto, although he hadn't realised it, had been lacking. Through seeing Jack's gravestone and having Guy's diary and medals, he had acquired a firm foothold in his own history, and with it came the realisation that the name

Searight was not just an accident of birth, but something which had some meaning. Until now, his father had been the full length and breadth of the Searight past, simply because his father had had a childhood best forgotten, thereby denying Tom knowledge of his own past and his place in the Searight story. And knowing something about where he came from gave him a great sense of fulfilment. All that was needed now was a better understanding of where he was going, which for a man not known for taking risks, had, until recently, been fairly assured, at least as much as one can be sure of the future. But now he was adrift in a sea of unwanted possibilities and he doubted whether he would again feel the luxury of complacency. And here he was, with the person who had stepped unexpectedly into his life and had given him a sense of his past, and for that he was grateful.

The game was entering its last couple of minutes. Bernard had turned the volume up. He looked despondent with France losing 1-0. But then, in the final seconds, France's star player, Zinedine Zidane, scored. Two minutes later, deep in injury time, France were awarded a penalty. Bernard sat on the edge of his seat. Zidane stepped up and scored again. Bernard leapt out of his seat, cheering.

Bernard, who was obviously more into the football than he let on, looked relieved and, regaining his composure, heaped praise on Zidane, while Maria sat silently with an affectionate, fixed half-smile, sipping her wine.

Before retiring for the night, Maria had one more surprise for Tom. It was a photograph – a photograph of Mary, his grandmother. Written in ink on the back was the date May 1916, taken on her eighteenth birthday. There she was, eighteen years old, proudly wearing a nurse's uniform, her image filling the picture. She was sitting down, her hands neatly on her lap, her dark hair tied back, disappearing into the cap that sat awkwardly in position. There was something in her hands, a slim shaft of silver. Tom held the photograph closer and peered at the object protruding from her fingers. It seemed to be a crucifix, its silver chain wrapped around her delicate hands. Her nose was long and thin, her lips clasped tightly shut but hinting at a smile as if trying to suppress a fit of earlier giggles. Even through the black and white lens of the camera, Tom could see the glint in her eye tinged with a hint of impatience; the confidence of a young woman on the threshold of life and in a hurry to set forth, tolerating the formality of the occasion.

That night, Tom read about Mary in the pages of Guy's diary…

> …I see her standing before me on board the ship, a girl too young to be burdened with the responsibilities of a uniform, one side of her face bathed in semi-darkness. She turns her head for a fraction as if thinking of leaving, of walking away from me. 'Wait,' I say, my hand outstretched. She stands still but doesn't look at me, her eyes scanning the faraway horizon. I step towards her, careful not to move too quickly for fear of frightening her, as if approaching a stray horse. Unable to move any further yet unwilling to break the spell, I know too well I will replay these few seconds a thousand times in my mind. I whisper her name and finally, she looks me in the eye. I step forward, my shadow encroaching on her. Slowly, I lift my hand and place my palm against her face. She tilts her head into my palm. Her skin feels cold to the touch and she shivers slightly as if adjusting to the warmth of my hand. Trusting that my presence won't offend, I move forward and she seems to lean towards me. I run my hand gently down her hair and she closes her eyes. I kiss her gently on

the cheek, on her nose, on her forehead. Lavender and iodine, how I shall always remember the incongruous mixture of smells, each fighting for dominance. Peace and war. Her lips part slightly, an inkling of a smile. She looks up at me, her eyes searching my face. 'Kiss me,' she whispers, barely audible. Her words echo in my mind again and again. Kiss me, kiss me, kiss me. I kiss her, my arm wrapped around her waist. I feel her fingers run down the side of my face, the smoothness of her fingertips against the coarse textures of my clean-shaven jaw. I feel whole again, I am complete. I am a man. My past is no longer part of me, no longer affects my present, the war is already history, my future irrelevant. Eighty years from now, when I am no more, this moment will still exist between us. I will die with this moment lodged in my mind where it will remain forever more.

Tom put the diary down. But Mary… she was married to Lawrence, his grandfather, not Guy, his father's uncle. Did they have a thing together? Did his father know? Should he tell him? No, he wouldn't want to know. Not now.

*

Chapter 16: *Adam and His Father*

Mark had just left. Julie closed the front door and turned to face the empty house. She leaned against the door and slowly slid down until she was crouching on her haunches. Clenching her fist and thumping herself on the knee, the cancer of seething anger crept through her until it clouded her mind and stripped away the ability of reasoned thought. The anger was all the more unbearable for being directed against herself. She'd been unbelievably stupid; she'd known it before, but not with such alarming clarity as it now presented itself to her. Did she really think she'd get away with it? No, because she hadn't thought at all. She'd subconsciously blocked out the possible consequences as if they weren't things that she needed to bother about. She'd driven Tom away and now Charlotte had walked out. Even the bloody dog had gone. And for what, what had she to show for it? She felt disgusted with herself; disgusted by her own selfish pursuit of satisfaction and annoyed by her needless carelessness, but, most of all, disgusted by her own sense of shame. Ashamed that she'd taken the trust of those she loved most and had tossed it aside, assuming that somehow it would come bouncing back. And soon, the shame would become public. Tom's parents probably knew already. She daren't telephone any of her old friends for fear they'd hear the tone of guilt in her voice. Her colleagues at school often asked, idly, after Tom. They weren't particularly interested in the answer, but how long could she keep up the pretence? Soon, she'd be forced out into the open: she, who had abused her husband and daughter's trust, for the sake of a casual affair. She'd have to wear it like a label – 'shameless woman', tattooed on her forehead – and made to wear her guilt like a hair shirt, never to take it off, even at night-time. Especially at night time, as she lay on her side of her bed, with the acres of cold, empty space next to her, a constant reminder of her wrongful ways.

Julie pulled herself up and staggered back into the sitting room. No doubt, Charlotte would be back soon, but the prospect of living with a resentful daughter filled Julie with dread. Charlotte was already adept at turning the screws whenever she felt the need, but now Julie had given her more thread than even Charlotte would know what to do with. It could go on for weeks, like a trump card to be used at will. The power relationship between mother and daughter was totally turned on its head. Julie would be made to pay – both emotionally and financially. But no amount of pocket money, new CDs and mock designer labels could alleviate this amount of guilt. The only thing Julie could think of that would help turn Charlotte's attention would be a boyfriend, her first boyfriend. She felt tired, tired of everything.

The telephone rang. Julie hoped she'd left the answerphone on, but after six rings, it was obvious she hadn't. Reluctantly, she picked it up. Her tiredness vanished in an instant as Charlotte's panicky voice screeched down the line to her. 'Mummy, Mummy, Angus has been run over. I think he's dead, I don't know.' Her voice could barely cope with her breathlessness and urgency. 'I don't know what to do; you've gotta come.'

'Hang on, sweetheart, I'm coming.' Julie felt seized by the waves of panic clouding her mind. 'Where are you?'

'Richmond Road, at the entrance to the park. Hurry, Mummy, please.'

'I'll be there as quick as I can. Put something over him to keep him warm. Be brave, darling, your Mummy's coming.' She slammed the phone down and tried to think – if he was still alive, where would she take him? She'd never been to the vets; on the few occasions it had been necessary, it was something Tom always did. Her hands were shaking; she doubted if she'd be able to drive, not after the whisky. Mark – she'd call Mark; he wouldn't have got far. She rang his mobile and prayed he'd answer because Mark was one of those types who believed in not answering mobiles when driving. He answered within two rings; thank God for that, she thought.

'Mark, it's Julie, I need you to come back.'

'Why, what's the matter? You sound awful.'

'Angus has been run over. Are you far; can you take us to the vets?'

'Give me two minutes.'

Julie grabbed Tom's phonebook. Yes, it was there – under 'V' for vets, and she knew the road. She reckoned from Richmond Road, they could probably get to it within ten minutes – if they were lucky. She found her handbag, made sure her purse was inside, snatched the house keys and waited outside. Oh God, she thought, don't let the blasted dog die; Charlotte would be distraught. Suddenly, the real reason for her panic hit her like a shameful thunderbolt. Her main concern for the dog's welfare was purely self-motivated, and the thought of it shamed her – again. If it lived, she'd forever have her daughter's gratitude, but if it died, Charlotte would hold her to blame. She couldn't take that as well, not on top of everything else.

Mark pulled up in his battered old Ford Fiesta. Julie jumped inside and, slamming the passenger door shut, directed Mark towards Richmond Road. It was only a couple of streets away and Mark knew the way anyway. She urged him to hurry and not slow down for the numerous speed humps that appeared with annoying regularity. At the end of her road, they needed to turn right, but a mother and pushchair had already started crossing the road. 'Oh hurry, please hurry,' said Julie. Finally, able to move on, Mark pulled out quickly, forcing an oncoming car to brake suddenly and eliciting an angry response of car hooting and mouthed profanities.

'Turn left here,' said Julie quickly. 'This is Richmond Road. She's at the other end, next to the park.'

'I do know,' said Mark, speeding around the corner and hoping nothing was coming the other way. As they came out of the bend, they could see a green hatchback ahead, parked awkwardly at an angle. Mark slowed down as they approached. Julie could see the figure of Charlotte sitting in its passenger seat, rocking back and forth. An England flag fluttered on the bonnet. A short, balding man paced beside the car, glancing nervously at Charlotte. Next to him, stood a red-headed boy, about Charlotte's age but equal in height to what was presumably his father. Julie knew immediately that this was the man who'd run the dog over. Why hadn't he taken the initiative and taken Charlotte and Angus to the vet himself? The man and his son looked up at the sight of Mark's Ford coming to a halt. Julie swung open the car door and charged out. From inside the man's car, Julie could hear the pitiful sound of her daughter crying, almost wailing.

'I'm sorry,' said the man, 'I'm afraid he's, erm…'

Julie clenched her eyes shut. 'Shit,' she muttered. Taking a deep breath, she approached the hatchback. Charlotte hadn't seen her yet. Julie opened the car door and there, on Charlotte's lap, half-wrapped in her daughter's jacket, lay the limp body of Angus, his white fur congealed with blood. Charlotte looked at her, her eyes red with tears and anger, her cheeks sodden, traces of blood on her hands.

'He's dead, Mummy; Angus is dead.'

Julie had to hide a sigh of relief; she'd expected an immediate accusation of responsibility, but equally, felt pained at seeing her daughter so visibly distressed. 'Oh, Charlotte, I'm sorry.' She wanted to put an arm around her but she realised how wary she'd become of her own daughter. She hovered nervously next to the car trying to think of the appropriate words. 'My poor darling; I can't tell you how sorry I am.'

Julie turned towards the solemn-looking, bald-headed man who was explaining to Mark how it'd all happened. 'Why didn't you look where you were going?' she said to him vehemently.

The man looked genuinely taken aback by Julie's assumption. 'I – I couldn't help it, I had no chance… really.'

'You were going too fast, weren't you?'

'No, honestly, he just ran out…'

The red-headed boy interrupted, 'It's true. Dad wasn't going fast at all. Angus just appeared from nowhere.'

Julie was surprised by the boy's familiar use of the dog's name.

'Mum, Adam's right,' said Charlotte quietly from inside the car. 'It was no one's fault.'

Julie looked at the boy. 'Adam?'

The boy nodded. 'Me and Charlotte are in the same year at school.'

Charlotte's crying took a turn for the worse, reminding Julie where her attention should be. She placed her hand on Charlotte's head and stroked her hair, all dishevelled and damp from sweat. 'Come on, let's go home.' Julie reached down to take the dog off her daughter's lap, but Charlotte swivelled her shoulder to prevent her mother's interference.

'No, leave him,' she said. 'I'll take him, he's mine, I'll carry him home.'

Julie put her arm around Charlotte's fragile shoulders as she steadied her daughter out of the hatchback. Charlotte was shaking with shock and cold, clutching the little dog's body close to her chest. Mark raised his eyebrows at Adam's father in resigned acknowledgement of the man's misfortune and went to open the back door of his car. Julie helped Charlotte in and then gently closed the door on her. She leaned back against the car and closed her eyes. She wanted to scream and she wanted and *needed* Tom to come back, to be by her side – for Charlotte's sake, as well as her own. She opened her eyes and realised there were three pairs of sympathetic eyes watching her. But she didn't want their sympathy; she just wanted Tom. If ever she needed Tom, it was now. Where in the bloody hell was he?

'Take us home please, Mark,' she said quietly.

Chapter 17: *Returning Home*

The Eurostar was fast approaching Waterloo. On the seat next to him was a copy of *The Times* with a picture of Tony Blair and George W Bush shaking hands on its cover.

Tom felt immersed in a warm glow of contentment but tainted with a sense of dread. With each mile the train took him further from France, the glow evaporated slightly, and with each mile closer to London, his anxiety increased. He tried to focus his mind on the weekend he had just left behind: the day trip to St Omer, the diary, the medals, the name Searight on the headstone. He had never seen his family's name inscribed on a headstone before and the vision of it made him shudder. It was now early Monday afternoon. Tom and Maria had spent the Sunday sightseeing. She took him to the St Omer museum, and later, Bernard joined them for a walk in the local forest. In return for their hospitality, Tom took Maria and Bernard out for an expensive meal in a pleasant restaurant in the town. They staggered in late, giggling. It felt as though he'd known them all his life. It was like rediscovering long-lost friends, an echo of a past life. But delightful as it was, he knew it was no more than a distraction, a means to escape. They got up late on the Monday and Maria accompanied Tom to the train station at St Omer. They kissed goodbye and promised each other to keep in touch by email.

But now with Waterloo only twenty minutes away, Tom's reality hit him square between the eyes. First, there was the little matter with Claudette. He tried to tell himself, it'd been to his advantage, but Claudette was Claudette, and he couldn't shake off a sense of foreboding about the whole affair. And then there was Rachel. For a while, he experienced that old desire for her but her ham-fisted attempts to interfere in his life reminded him how unpredictable she could be. But the more he thought about the women at the periphery of his life, the more his mind went back to the woman at the centre of it. If Maria was a distraction, Claudette a threat, and Rachel an intrusion, then what was Julie? Julie was his wife and the woman he loved. It was still less than a week since he'd left with a vague promise to be back by the weekend, but during that week, he'd realised that perhaps more than ever, he still wanted Julie. Yet, the thought of her with Moyes made him screw his eyes shut with pain. His old life, which seemed so ordinary, so pedestrian, now faded into the distant past like a bygone idyll. And his heart drowned at the thought that at the centre of it, laid one enormous lie, one huge deceit. She'd said it'd been going on for a year or so. He cast his mind back over the previous year and a half, and tried to compare it to the time before. He expected to find a time, a dividing line between black and white but found nothing but continuity, a constant grey. Just the life of an ordinary couple. He remembered their Spanish holiday; the photograph of Julie and Charlotte he kept on his desk at work. The smiling sunburnt faces, the splatter of dried sand on Charlotte's cheeks, the hint of white lines around Julie's eyes where the sun hadn't permeated. Their heads touching, a fusion of blonde hair, bleached further by the Spanish sun. It was a year ago, just one year. It was already going on, already happening. He imagined her writing secret postcards to him, sneaking away to post them, thinking about him as she lay in the sun.

He missed her and he missed his daughter. He really needed to see Charlotte again, if only briefly, to make sure she was all right. She had her poetry recital coming up and he wondered how she was getting on with her preparation. He felt a stab of guilt. The presentation had been such a big part of her life and he'd tried to make it part of his. Somehow, it never seemed to work; perhaps he'd tried too hard. He could almost hear her tutting, a mixture of exasperation and embarrassment.

It was only then that he remembered he'd forgotten to phone her. He dialled her number. No answer. Instead, he phoned home but again no answer, just the answerphone; his own voice asking the caller to leave a message. He cringed at the sound of his diction and told Julie he was going to pop in. Tom knew that his visit home could involve a painful confrontation and that Julie would want to pin him down to discuss 'things'. Could he face it? Yes, he decided, he had no choice; it was part of the process. The future had to start somewhere if only to sweep away the past. He'd been away long enough; he'd made his point, and sufficiently intruded on his parents' routine. His plan, as well as his future, was simple enough. It was time to go home.

Facing his Waterloo, Tom read a bit more of Guy's diary. His great-uncle had got himself injured and his brother, Jack, had rescued him. But trench warfare proved too much for Jack – he deserted.

I went to see him on his last night on this earth. I cannot describe the feelings of despair that raked my soul as I said goodbye to my little brother. He was executed the following day, 11th November 1917. He was just 19 years old. May he rest in peace.

Tom noticed how the small elegant writing diminished to a minuscule scrawl as Guy described the aftermath of Jack's death at the hands of a firing squad. He tried to imagine his great-uncle writing the words, his eyes welling up, his hand shaking. How strange it was to think that one's forebear had been shot for desertion; the family name sullied in the annals of war. He wished he knew the names of the men who sat on the court-martial, the men so convinced of Jack's guilt, so sure that their brutal justice would stand the scrutiny of history. He imagined meeting one of their ancestors – shaking their hand, accepting their apologies. Tom remembered himself when he was nineteen, in his second year at Leicester University, his immature head full of grandiose ideas and fantastic schemes. He closed the diary, the date was 14 November 1917. Guy was leaving France, knowing he might never return. Tom knew the feeling. He stared out of the window as the train pulled into Waterloo.

By now it was half past five. He was about to unlock the front door and walk straight in, but something held him back. He rang the doorbell but it didn't ring. He tried again, but no – definitely not working. Instead, he knocked – quite gently the first time and then progressively louder – but still no response. Blow this, he thought, and unlocked the door and walked into his hallway.

'Anyone home?' he cried out. No answer, not even Angus. They'd probably all gone out for a walk, which was unusual for Julie. He went through to the sitting room. He felt uneasy;

how odd it was to be back. It'd only been a few days, no time at all, but already he felt like an intruder, a stranger amongst familiar things. He looked wistfully at the room as if taking it in for the first time: the 'honeybee' yellow painted walls with its dado rail, the beige carpet; the old fireplace with its wooden surround adorned with various family photographs, and a silver framed mirror above the mantelpiece; the heavily loaded bookshelves, his neatly organised CD rack. Only the Schubert *Unfinished Symphony* lay out of place. He glanced at the family photographs from one to another – photos of the three of them together or individually. And of course, Tom and Julie's wedding photo. Wiping an invisible film of dust off the frame, Tom couldn't help but smile at their cheesy grins, the romantic but painfully self-conscious pose. He looked up at his passive reflection in the mirror above the mantelpiece. The occasional grey streak seemed less occasional now, the lines on his face more pronounced. A man doesn't age this quickly, he thought, but the realisation of ageing can be alarmingly sudden.

It was then he noticed it in the reflection – lying on the sofa behind him. He spun around, hoping that reality would contradict the evidence of what he saw in the mirror. But no, it was still there. He went over to the sofa, picked it up, and looked at it. Faded brown in colour, made of leather and battered; yes, it was the same briefcase all right. He looked up at the ceiling. Surely, they weren't upstairs again. A surge of angered panic coursed through his veins. He flung the briefcase back onto the sofa, and ran quickly out of the sitting room and upstairs, bounding up the stairs in twos, across the landing and towards the spare bedroom at the back of the house. He threw the door open and almost fell inside; convinced he would find them there. But the room was empty. He felt both foolish and relieved, but at the same time, somewhat disappointed to have been denied the opportunity to vent his simmering anger. He looked around the bedroom – the bed neatly made, all clothes put away, nothing out of place. Tom stepped back and gently closed the bedroom door, noticing again the crack in the doorknob. It wasn't his concern any more. But if the briefcase was here, then surely Moyes couldn't be far away. Perhaps, he thought, they'd all gone out for the walk together – the image revolted him. It wasn't so much the thought of Julie and him still together; it was the idea of Moyes ingratiating himself into Charlotte's life which he found particularly irksome. Or perhaps, he thought, they were in the garden; it was, after all, a lovely hot day. He missed his garden – it was unusually big for the area, which was one of the house's main appeals when he and Julie bought the place all those years ago. He returned to the spare bedroom and looked out into the garden.

'What the…' he said aloud, astonished by what he saw. 'What *are* they doing?' At the back of the garden were Julie and Charlotte, just standing silently. Charlotte seemed to be holding something in her arms, wrapped in a blanket. But what really puzzled Tom was the sight of Mark Moyes digging a hole in the lawn, just in front of the laurel hedge.

Tom charged back down the stairs, ran through to the kitchen and into the garden. 'What are you doing?' he shouted at them as he stepped outside. Julie and Charlotte jumped; Moyes stopped digging. The three of them turned to see Tom marching across the lawn towards them.

'Tom,' said Julie, unable to hide her surprise. 'What are doing here?'

'I left a message, but what're you doing for goodness sake and what's *he* doing here?'

'I'm afraid something dreadful's happened.'

Tom's stomach flipped. 'What? What's happened?'

'Oh, Daddy,' said Charlotte, her voice cracked with despair. 'It's Angus...'

Tom looked from Charlotte to the shallow hole in the ground and back to the wrapped bundle in her arms. 'Oh no, not Angus. How... how did it happen?'

'Run over,' said Charlotte quietly.

'Oh, God.' Most of the time, Tom had simply tolerated the dog, but the sight of his forlorn daughter made his heart lurch with pity. He looked at the silent Moyes who looked suitably awkward for being there and then at Julie. 'Where?' he asked Charlotte.

'Richmond Road.'

'Were you at the park?'

She nodded. 'He must've seen something on the other side of the road and he just ran off and he got hit by Adam's dad.'

'Adam?'

'Boy in her class,' said Julie.

'Was he not on the lead?' Tom immediately regretted the implied reprimand in the question.

'Of course, he was; he just lunged forward and I wasn't able to grip the lead on time. Sorry.'

'Sorry?' Tom put his arm around her. 'It wasn't your fault; there's no need to say sorry, sweetheart.'

Charlotte began to sniffle. 'Yes, but he'd done it before, a couple of weeks ago. I should've been more careful.'

Finally, Mark spoke. 'Erm, I'll carry on then.'

Julie said: 'Charlotte wanted us to bury Angus here, in the garden.'

'He liked it up here,' said Charlotte. 'Always sniffing around.' She smiled at the memory.

Tom glared at Mark. 'So Mr Moyes just happened to be passing, I s'pose.'

Julie's face flushed. 'I phoned him.'

'So you phone him before you phone me now, do you?'

'Oh, come off it, Tom. I didn't know where you were. I mean, you disappeared, not a call, nothing. All I got from your parents was that you'd gone off to France or something and you hadn't come back. *That's* why I called Mark, OK?'

Tom turned to Moyes. 'And you came running like the proverbial lapdog, I suppose.'

'At least I was around,' said Mark.

'How convenient.' Tom was beginning to regret the irrevocable descent into pettiness, but he couldn't stem the flow of sniping. He looked disdainfully at the hole. Moyes had obviously only just begun digging. 'I can take over from here,' he said holding out his hand for the spade.

'No, no, it's OK,' said Mark, shielding it.

Tom stepped up to him and spoke quietly so as to not be overheard by Charlotte. 'Listen, matey,' he said through gritted teeth. 'It's *my* daughter's dog here, and *I* will bury him.'

'Bit late for all that now. Where were you when she needed you most? When they both needed you?'

Tom hadn't punched anyone since school, but he'd gladly have punched Moyes now. 'Not as readily available as you, obviously. Now, if you don't mind…'

'Oh, stop it,' cried Charlotte, 'just stop.'

Mark and Tom looked sheepishly at her. Julie took Tom's arm and led him swiftly to one side. 'Tom, simmer down. Do you really think your behaviour is appropriate given the circumstances? You can see how upset she is, and you sizing up to Mark is not helping matters.'

Tom heard the sound of Moyes's spade hitting the earth. 'OK, OK, I'm sorry.'

'We were having a quiet, respectful little ceremony here. It's important we do it properly for Charlotte's sake; it's not as if we can simply throw the dog out with the rubbish; he meant a lot to her. Now, you can stay if you behave, but I'm not sending Mark away. When Charlotte phoned me from the park, I was in such a state, I couldn't think. So I rang Mark, and yes, he did happen to be nearby, hardly surprising when he doesn't live far. And I asked him back today – I needed someone to dig a hole, and you weren't exactly available. Frankly, I couldn't have done all this without him.'

Tom wasn't convinced but he knew he had little choice but to accept it. The sound of Moyes's digging began to irritate him. Each mound of earth dug out seemed to undermine his parental role and emphasised his sense of having been cast out. He hated the thought of standing around watching Moyes diligently digging under the grateful eyes of his wife and daughter. It was like having to call in an expert to fix the simplest DIY task, the humbling effect it had on one's standing as the 'man of the house'. It was humiliating and, despite Julie's warning, Tom wasn't prepared to have his role undermined. He ambled nonchalantly over to Moyes, who continued digging away. 'Really, I'll take over. Please.'

Mark stopped and straightened up, his face glistening with sweat. 'No, it's all right, I'm halfway there now.'

He watched as the spade pierced the earth and wondered what he had to do to make Moyes stop. He clenched his fist and tried to contain himself, but the ownership of that spade had taken on a meaning of gigantic proportion. 'Look, give me that spade.' Mark shook his head and was about to resume digging when Tom reached out and seized it. Both men stood facing each other, each gripping onto the spade, wanting to yank it out of the other's hand but restraining themselves for the sake of decency and the fear of looking pathetic in front of Julie. This was primeval men's stuff; they both knew it but couldn't acknowledge it. It was Tom who broke first. Gripping firmly, he jerked it. It was enough to unbalance Moyes who, on being pushed back, stepped into the shallow hole he'd just dug, his leg disappearing halfway up to his knee. He slipped and, with arms flailing, landed on his backside on the edge of the hole, his back scraping against the laurel hedge. Witnessing this undignified spectacle, Charlotte turned her back abruptly and, still cradling the blanket, stood facing the opposite direction.

Julie yelled at Tom, 'Have you not listened to a word I said? For goodness sake, you're still at it.' She paused and then, in a quieter voice, added, 'I think you should leave.'

'What, me? Or him?'

'You, Tom. You,' she said firmly.

Tom looked from Julie to Charlotte, willing her to turn around. He knew he'd behaved like a fool and had overstepped the mark, but he couldn't help himself. He rubbed his eyes and groaned. 'OK, OK, I'll go.'

'Yes, I think it would be for the best.'

He placed his hand on Charlotte's shoulder and wondered whether to present her with the earrings he'd bought in St Omer. She made no attempt to shrug his hand off but equally remained firmly rooted to the spot. He decided it wasn't the time for gifts. 'I'm sorry, Charlotte. And I'm sorry about Angus.' He suddenly realised how much Angus had been part of the family life and how much he was going to miss the old thing. Everything seemed to be slipping away from him. He trudged back across the lawn.

As he reached the outside door to the kitchen, the sound of digging had started again.

*

It had taken a few days to sink in. But now Rachel realised Tom was little better than some of the other losers she had wasted her time on over the years. She never had much luck with men. She could attract them all right; problem was she usually attracted the wrong sort. Adrian was typical. Decent enough but too self-obsessed and not in the slightest bit interested in Abigail. If she wanted to settle down, and she did one day, she needed someone who could make a difference in her and Abigail's life; she could barely survive on the wages of a part-time job in an antique stall and the occasional odd job. It all started to go wrong the day Abigail's father upped and left one autumn morning twelve years ago. Abigail had only just been born. He went off to be a roadie for a second-rate rock band and never came back. What a spineless git he turned out to be. Never heard from him again and except for the odd cheque or present, neither did Abigail.

It was late, past one in the morning. She wondered whether to open another bottle of wine; she somehow managed to polish off the first one fairly quickly. She rubbed her eyes; she really ought to go to bed. The music playing gently on the stereo soothed her aching mind. Adrian had lent it to her. Something called *I Giorni*, according to the CD sleeve, by a composer called Ludovico Einaudi, a solo piano playing lots of gentle arpeggios with sweet, lilting melodies on top. Modern-day Satie, she thought to herself. She opened the second bottle of wine and filled her glass. She sat on the floor, rested against the settee, and reached out for her packet of cigarettes. She had stopped smoking two years back but had recently taken up the habit again. She picked up the small silver gun beside her and looked at the reflection of her eyes in the shiny barrel, her finger resting gently on the trigger. She smiled and squeezed. A little flame shot out. She lit her cigarette.

The lighter had been a jokey Christmas present from Tom seventeen years ago. Or was it eighteen years? It was naff of course, it was meant to be. She pulled the trigger again and stared at the flickering flame. It was a day or two after Boxing Day, and she and Tom had gone out for a meal in an Italian restaurant in Islington. Tom had heard good reports about it and indeed, the food was delicious, the atmosphere perfect. He presented her with his tongue-in-cheek present, which was only meant to be a witty extra. What the main present was, delivered before Christmas, Rachel couldn't remember. But she remembered how the smile on Tom's face soon disappeared when a guitarist suddenly appeared and circled the tables singing romantic Italian ballads in a flat croaky voice. The man hit upon the couple and sang for their benefit. Tom was mortified and sat there with a fixed grin while Rachel fell into a fit of giggles at seeing him so embarrassed. The guitarist in his tight black trousers and frilly white shirt, took their reaction as an endorsement of his playing and subjected them to (what felt like) his whole repertoire. By the end, Tom could barely contain his embarrassment and Rachel's cheeks were wet with laughter. The man finished with a flurry and then presented Rachel with a single red rose.

Rachel grinned at the memory. She drew on her cigarette and flicked the lighter on and off, on and off. A gun-shaped lighter, a fake red rose and a flat serenader; she had never known such a convergence of naffness in one evening, but equally she had rarely known such an unforgettable one. Arm in arm, they stepped out into the cold night air but the warmth of romantic contentment surged through her every vein. She always remembered that moment, that feeling when everything felt gloriously right and natural. Right there, at that moment, she would have done anything for that man. Anything.

They caught a taxi back to hers and made love. It wasn't passionate or urgent, it was more exquisite than that, it was soft and gentle, a love of unsurpassed desire and warmth.

A few months later, she left him.

She lit another cigarette. She stared down the barrel of the lighter and she knew. It wasn't over with Tom yet. He reacted badly when he found out about her visit to Julie's, but he was still in shock about Julie's affair. And he hadn't had time to realise that she still wanted him, was still waiting for him. He would have had time to think, time to remember the party in Lewisham, the Italian restaurant, their lovemaking, the laughs they had, the affinity that drew them together. He'd know now where his destiny lay and it wasn't with Julie. She didn't understand him; what with her neatly ordered house and her compartmentalised life. Tom was just another accessory. Rachel ran her finger up and down the length of the shiny barrel. Julie had her teacher; she could keep him. But it was time that she knew the truth, the whole truth, that it wasn't just a drunken kiss at a party, it wasn't just a shirt that smelt of 'cheap' perfume. It was time to try again. She pointed the lighter at the window and pulled the trigger. On and off, on and off.

Chapter 18: *Suspension*

The plan had seemed so simple; he'd half expected an emotional reunion, tearful apologies, a romantic night out. But he hadn't reckoned on Moyes lurking around, and he hadn't expected to be upstaged by the dog in the emotional stakes. After his ignominious exit, Tom found himself phoning Maria, asking if he could visit again – the following Friday. Her initial lack of enthusiasm immediately made him regret his haste and his face flushed with the embarrassment of his impetuousness. But perhaps there was something in his tone that made her relent. Tom thanked her, promised only to stay the one night and felt it necessary to explain that the traumas of separation had prompted him to seek refuge. Have you no other friends? He could almost hear it in the tone of her voice. Well no, he thought, not friends who didn't know him as part of a couple. He switched off the phone but still found himself shuddering with embarrassment. He'd made a fool of himself; he wanted to phone back, say he'd made a mistake, but of course, that seemed worse. So having committed himself to it, he bought another Eurostar ticket to Calais.

*

Tuesday morning. Tom was dreading the prospect of going to work and having to face the inevitable discussion and analysis of Friday's presentation. As he walked through the open-plan office, he kept his eyes firmly on the floor. The surreal, tense atmosphere of Friday had given way to the usual chaotic ambience of an ordinary working day. He plonked himself down and smiled weakly at Gabrielle sitting at her desk next to his. Gabrielle asked politely after his weekend and passed on a couple of telephone messages. Tom logged onto his computer and read his emails, which included one from Claudette requesting a meeting with all her project managers at two o'clock to discuss Friday's presentation. Tom groaned inwardly, but it was only to be expected. There were numerous other messages which he settled down to deal with. He worked steadily and had managed to kill half an hour before he was noticed by Clive, who suddenly appeared behind his chair.

'Ah, Tom, pleased you could make it.'

Suppressing the urge to tell him to piss off, Tom merely grinned lopsidedly.

Clive continued, 'Did you see the England game?'

'No,' he lied.

'Good game. We were unlucky – losing like that.'

'Not that interested, to be honest.'

'Your loss. The council rang Claudette. Reckon they could let us know within the week. Pity about the DDA stuff; would've thought you'd know all about that.'

Tom swivelled around in his chair to face his boss looming above him. 'You may recall, Clive, that you said not to worry about it, Claudette would be dealing with it.'

'Did I say that? I don't think so.'

'You know damn well you did.'

Clive puffed his chest out. 'What are you trying to say, Tom?'

Tom ignored him and pointedly returned his attention to the screen in front of him.

'So is that what you went running to Claudette about?' Clive grinned.

'No.' He wasn't prepared to talk about it.

'It must've been some meeting. You could've cut the atmosphere with a knife; what were you two talking about?'

'Incompetent managers,' snapped Tom.

'Heated conversation, was it? You both looked somewhat dishevelled when I walked in.'

Tom remained focused on the screen, hoping Clive would take the hint and give up. It seemed to work. 'I'll leave you to it then,' said Clive as he strode off. Tom sighed and wondered how much Clive was bluffing.

Within seconds, Clive reappeared. 'Oh, I forgot to say, Lewis wants to see you at ten.'

Heck, thought Tom, it was a rare "honour" to be hauled in by Mr Lewis. Mr Lewis, Claudette's boss, was a company director and had a large office on the top floor. 'What for?'

'Don't know,' replied Clive, barely able to suppress his glee, 'but I wouldn't want to be in your shoes.'

'Ah, it's probably about my bonus,' said Tom.

'Yeah, right.'

It was still only twenty to ten, so Tom worked through a few more emails. A few minutes later, Gabrielle went off to get them both a cup of coffee. It was time to make a quick phone call. He didn't know Adrian's surname but by describing his blue beard the receptionist at Dunstone, Cutler and Maine soon tracked him down. As he waited to be put through, he started doodling.

Adrian was apologetic. 'Look, I'm sorry, mate, that stuff about you and Rach, it happened years back, didn't it? She made it sound as if the two of you still had a thing going.'

Typical Rachel, thought Tom. 'No, she finished with me years ago.'

'Yeah well, she's dumped me too now.'

'Oh…'

'Nah, don't worry about it; she was too neurotic for me anyway. So, mate, how can I help?'

Tom glanced around the office and spoke closely into the mouthpiece. 'Listen, is it true that my boss, Claudette, Claudette Tyler, has had talks with your people?'

Adrian lowered his voice. 'Ah, can't really comment on that right now.'

'Your lot are filching her, aren't you?' There was a silence at the other end. Tom drew a doodle of a wheelchair. 'In fact, she's probably already working for you, that's why she was flippant about our tender.' Tom heard the sharp intake of breath at the other end. 'Come on, Adrian, just one word – yes or no.'

'Put in a good word for me with Rach?'

'Course, mate.'

'You promise?'

'Absolutely.'

'Yes, she is. You didn't hear it from me, right?'

'Absolutely.'

'Your coffee, Tom.' Tom jumped. It was Gabrielle.

The phone went dead. 'See you later, sweetheart,' he said replacing the handset. He smiled weakly at Gabrielle. 'My daughter.' He looked at his watch, gulped a few mouthfuls of coffee, and decided it was time to go, time to face his maker in the rarefied air of the top floor.

A minute to ten, Tom knocked gently on Mr Lewis's door. On being told to enter, Tom stepped into the large, spacious office, its walls a pale green colour, a large solid wooden desk dominating the room. Behind it sat Mr Lewis, besuited in a dark double-breasted suit and bespectacled with thin, silver-framed glasses slipping down his long thin nose. Various silver-framed photos adorned his desk, a packet of cigars lay unopened on one side.

'Tom, come in, take a seat,' said Mr Lewis, gesturing to the red leather chair in front of his desk. 'Give me a moment, just let me send this email off.' Tom sat down. Mr Lewis clicked his mouse and smiled at Tom. 'Life seemed so much easier before the advent of emails. People email me with the most mundane of matters, things that before, they would've just got on with. Ah well, that's progress for you, I suppose.' His whole demeanour reminded Tom of a kindly but authoritative doctor, who, as a well-respected pillar of the community, was nearing his retirement. Mr Lewis took a file from his in-tray and opened it. His eyes quickly scanned the page while Tom straightened his tie. Finally, Mr Lewis looked up at him.

'Tom,' he sighed. 'I won't pretend this is going to be easy, so I'll get straight to the point.'

Tom's stomach lurched. The "point"; what "point"?

Mr Lewis's face had suddenly lost the look of the friendly doctor and took on the look of someone with an unpleasant duty to deal with. 'Ms Tyler came to see me yesterday morning and told me about this unfortunate business on Friday.'

Tom sat bolt upright, his face flushed. 'Unfortunate business, sir?'

Mr Lewis sighed again and fixed Tom a solemn stare. 'There's no point in denying it; I've also spoken to Clive Doherty.'

Tom stuttered. 'I'm s-sorry, sir, I don't understand.'

'Mr Doherty has backed up Ms Tyler's claim.'

This was beginning to sound like a stitch-up. 'Claim?'

'Oh, come now, has your memory faded already? Do I need to spell it out for you? Mr Doherty says that when he entered Claudette's office on Friday evening, he knew immediately that something was not quite right. He said you both seemed awkward and flustered. After your hurried departure, he asked Ms Tyler if everything was OK. Ms Tyler told him, as indeed she has subsequently told me, that you made an inappropriate pass at her. I think Clive's exact words that you tried to "jump her". Is that the correct terminology?'

They really had got their story straight, thought Tom. 'No, sir, that's not right at all.'

'No? In that case, I'd be interested in your version of events.' He leant back in his chair and peered at Tom over his spectacles.

Tom blushed. 'It's not as you say, sir, she was trying to… to intimidate me.' He paused wondering how to describe the scene.

Mr Lewis rested his elbows on the chair rest and placed his fingertips together in an arch. 'Intimidate you? Ms Tyler?'

Perhaps, thought Tom, he'd said too much already. He tried to think. Yes, he had the ammunition but he hadn't had a chance to work out how best to use it. Would Lewis believe him if he told him about Claudette's treachery? He had no real proof yet, only Adrian's say-so and that wouldn't cut much ice while Claudette had Mr Lewis neatly wrapped around her finger. 'Claudette tried to blame me for Friday's fiasco.'

Mr Lewis snorted. 'Oh, the infamous cock-up over the DDA. Yes, I must say I was disappointed to hear about that. Could be costly. So, how do you account for it?'

'Account for it? I think you should ask Claudette.'

'Oh but I have, and frankly I have no reason to doubt the validity of her version of events. After all, Ms Tyler is a well-respected and loyal employee of this company—'

'Is she? And I'm not?'

'Be that as it may, but all this takes us away from the point, which is this very serious allegation. Now Ms Tyler is an undeniably attractive young woman. I mean, hell man, it was unprofessional and bloody stupid, but I can't in all honesty say I blame you.'

Tom slumped back in the leather chair. Mr Lewis's mind was already made up and there was nothing he could do, at least not for now.

'You'll be pleased to know, at least,' continued Mr Lewis, 'that Ms Tyler has, after careful consideration, decided not to take this matter out of the department…' That's big of her, thought Tom. 'But naturally, there will have to be an internal investigation.'

'Naturally.'

'Therefore, until we have time to convene such an investigation, I have no option but to suspend you on full pay—'

'You've got this so wrong, Mr Lewis—'

Mr Lewis ignored him. '…to take effect immediately.'

'What, now?'

'I'm afraid so. I'm sorry, really I am. You're a good man but you've blotted your copybook, whatever way this goes. When an allegation like this has been made, I have no option but to follow it through. You will be escorted out of the building. If you need to collect anything from your desk, you may do so, but strictly personal items only. Your coat, briefcase, photographs, that sort of thing, but you are not permitted to touch anything belonging to or concerning the company and your work. You will not be allowed to touch your computer, not even to turn it off, nor the telephone, your paperwork or files. Do you understand?'

'Yes, I understand.'

'Very well.' Mr Lewis pushed a button on his intercom and requested a security guard to escort Tom out of the building. He looked at Tom and with a wry smile said, 'Next time, at least wait until you're out of work.' There was a knock on the door. 'Enter.' The security guard stepped in and stood, expressionless, next to the door.

'Well, Tom, wait until you hear from us.' He nodded at the guard. 'Now, if you'll excuse me…'

Tom rose wearily from the leather chair. He looked at the security guard and thought how painfully white the man's shirt was. Tom decided to walk down the three flights of stairs rather than face the prospect of standing silently in the lift with his escort. The guard followed three paces behind. Tom paused before entering his floor and took a deep breath. 'Here goes,' he said to himself.

As Tom approached his desk, Gabrielle looked up from her computer. 'Oh, Tom, you got a couple of messages while you were out…' She saw the security man standing directly behind Tom, his arms folded, his head disappearing into his neck. 'Oh, nothing that can't wait…' she said, her voice trailing off. She glanced nervously at Tom, who shot her an apologetic smile. He looked briefly at the two photographs on his desk and decided to leave them. The whole office had come to a standstill. Voices fell silent, telephone conversations were cut short, the perpetual sound of fingers tapping on keyboards evaporated. Tom was fully aware that his every move was being carefully watched by the dozens of incredulous staff. He picked up his briefcase and was ready to go. He nodded at the guard and began the slow, humiliating walk down the long, silent passageway through the centre of the office. He kept his eyes fixed on the exit door ahead of him but, in the corner of his eye, he could see someone standing with her arms folded in her glass-fronted office. It was, of course, Claudette. The blinds were up.

*

Tom caught a tube and a train back to Enfield and surprised his mother with his unexpectedly early appearance. He told her he'd taken the rest of the day off to enjoy the sun and, indeed, the rest of the week, and did she mind if he stayed on for a few days more. No, of course she didn't. Much to his relief, his father was out – playing his weekly game of bowls. He offered to make his mother a cup of tea and listened while she complained about next door's cat. As he passed her her tea, he asked, 'Any messages while I was away?'

'Oh yes, I almost forgot, Julie rang.'

'Really?'

'She's concerned about Charlotte and thinks the two of you should meet up and discuss it. But you'll have to phone later; she's going out to meet a friend for a pub lunch.'

Tom groaned inwardly. 'She wasn't meeting up with a man called Mark by any chance, was she?'

'No, don't you worry; it was a girlfriend.'

Tom sipped his tea. 'Good.'

'I think she said her name was Rachel.'

'Shit!' said Tom, spluttering on his tea.

'Thomas!'

'Mum, I've got to go. Can I borrow your car?'

'My car?'

'Thanks, Mum. She didn't say which pub, did she?'
'No. Why? You're not going to find her, are you?'
But Tom had gone.

Chapter 19: *The Pub*

Julie wasn't overly pleased to be meeting up with Rachel again – especially in the middle of the school day, but Rachel caught her in an absentminded moment, and she seemed insistent. First, she was coming round for coffee and now she was inviting her to the pub for a lunchtime drink. It all seemed slightly odd and yet, intrigued, she'd accepted. Julie was sitting alone at a window table in the Rose and Crown nursing a bitter lemon, waiting for Rachel. The pub, only five minutes away from school, was big, depressing and largely empty but already a fug of smoke hung in the air. A jukebox played quietly in the background and Julie found herself humming along to a song by The Walker Brothers. The red flock wallpaper was bedecked with numerous black and white local history photographs. Julie stared at one entitled Holloway High Street, circa 1917. She looked at her watch, Rachel was late. She had less than 40 minutes before she had to head back to school.

Julie was casually casting her eye down the lunchtime menu of bar snacks when Rachel appeared, looking flustered and muttering several apologies. The two women offered to get each other drinks and deliberated on what to eat, deciding in the end not to have anything. Neither was hungry.

*

While Julie and Rachel argued over who was buying what, Tom was haring down the A10 in his mother's ancient Vauxhall estate. The car had trapped the heat of the day and with no air conditioning, Tom soon broke out in a sweat. The thought of the two women having a cosy chat over lunch appalled him. He had to get there. The speed limit was forty. Tom was doing fifty-five. What exactly he would do once he found them, he had no idea, but somehow he had to stop Rachel from opening her mouth. He cursed the day he met Rachel under the red oak in the park. Why had he told her; why hadn't he realised it would only lead to trouble? She'd always been a liability, threatening to spill the beans, to ruin it all for him. But after so many years, he would have thought it was well and truly forgotten, but no, obviously not. He didn't know what he wanted any more but he enjoyed the illusion of occupying the moral high ground over his wife. But it was more than that; he didn't want Julie to know because he still loved her. Was that enough now? Probably not.

A speed camera flashed at him. He tried to think of the repercussions of his suspension. The first one, he concluded, was obvious – he'd be sacked. With his word against that of Clive's and Claudette's, two against one – what chance did he have? They were both his senior and, in the spirit of positive discrimination, Claudette would benefit as a woman. But worse, the directors all thought the sun shone out of her backside, they'd want to hang onto her, whatever the cost. The job market beckoned. He'd been tempted to look elsewhere anyway, but now it was going to be difficult, bloody difficult. 'So, Mr Searight, why did you leave your last post?' 'Change of direction, greater challenge, blah, blah, blah.' 'But it says here on your reference that you were dismissed for "jumping" – is that the right terminology? – your power-crazed, attractive female boss. Is that not correct?' 'No, she was clinging onto my tie.' 'Hmm, likely story. Thank you, that'll be all.' No one was ever going to believe him – 'no smoke without fire' and all that. Did former employers disclose that sort of information? Probably not. Perhaps he could strike out on his own and start up a new company. But with what? Half of a £6,000 savings account he shared with Julie? £3,000 would hardly have Tooley & Hill quaking in their boots. No, whatever way he looked at it, he was up the creek without a paddle. So, what was he to do with no job and potentially no home? Abject poverty stared him in the face. The middle and fast lanes were congested and Tom was overtaking in the slow lane. He turned left into Green Lanes and headed south swearing at the slightest impediment to his progress. Any moment now, Rachel would open her mouth and the quicksand beckoned. Maybe it was for the best. Maybe it was fate, or destiny as Rachel called it.

The lights at Turnpike Lane changed from green to amber. Tom pressed on the accelerator. The light turned red, the car in front broke it. Tom almost braked and then went for it. Cars were already turning in from the right. The first one had to brake while Tom swerved violently to the left. The second car hit the first. But Tom ignored them and prayed he'd have enough of an empty road to make good his escape. He did. There was of course Charlotte, he thought, as he approached Hornsey. That was tougher. But kids these days were resilient. Half the kids in the school were probably from broken homes. She'd be OK.

*

The two women talked. Pleasant as it was, Julie was aware that it didn't feel natural. She couldn't put her finger on why – but a couple of times she found herself struggling for something to say.

Rachel, however, seemed more than happy. 'It's so nice we've become reacquainted, don't you think? So, tell me, how is Charlotte? Such a polite girl.'

'Oh, she's fine, thanks. She's… Well, actually, Angus was run over on Sunday. Got killed. Charlotte's ever so upset.'

'Oh, how awful for her, the poor love.'

'Yes. Yes, it is awful.' Julie thought of her, of Charlotte placing the dog, still wrapped in her jacket, into the hole dug by Mark. Staring down, she offered a little prayer as Mark and Julie stood silently behind her. Their next-door neighbour but one began cutting his lawn, the sound of the electric mower slicing through their thoughts. He'd been a good dog, a faithful, happy little chap. Only six years old. Charlotte had had him for almost half her life. She fell into her mother's embrace as Mark slowly piled the earth back into the hole.

Julie sighed. 'Truly awful. The timing couldn't have been worse.'

'Why? What's…'

'Everything seems to be going wrong at the moment.'

'Oh, Julie, I'm sorry to hear this. What's the matter? What's happened?'

From the Walker Brothers to the Righteous Brothers, the barman had turned up the jukebox and was singing along to 'Unchained Melody'. The song got to her; its desperate lyric and its mournful, slow melody permeating her heart, wrenching her emotions. She could feel her resistance crumbling as the singer sang of his hunger 'for your touch'.

She ran her finger around the rim of her glass, staring at the melting ice cubes within her drink. 'Tom's left me.'

'Oh my God.'

'Yes, he's left me.' She'd said it, and to Rachel of all people; fey, hippy Rachel. But hell, there was no one else; no one else she could talk to. Just saying those words lifted her somehow, eased the burden on her heart.

Rachel placed her hand on Julie's sleeve. 'Tell me. Talking is good. It will help.'

The feel of Rachel's hand on her arm melted something inside her. And so she talked. She told Rachel, her new best friend, about a serious misunderstanding that resulted in Tom leaving and staying with his parents; how he'd disappeared to France and she had no idea why or who with; about Charlotte and the death of Angus; of how damn difficult life was. 'Has Charlotte said anything to Abigail?'

Rachel shook her head. 'If she did, Abigail wouldn't tell me.'

'She seemed all right for the first few days but then I began to see signs. She came back the other day with her breath stinking of smoke and then disappears for a couple of hours at a time, usually with Angus, poor thing. When I ask her where she's been, she refuses to tell me. I try to insist and she storms off to her bedroom. She wasn't like this when her dad was around.'

'So how long has Tom been gone for?'

'Not that long really, but Charlotte's decline has been rapid. I'm sure she wasn't smoking before that. And then what with Angus getting run over, well... you can imagine.'

'That must have been a shock.'

'God, yes. She's devastated. I said we'd get a new dog but that didn't help, of course, she just wants Angus back.'

'It's understandable.' Rachel sipped her tomato juice. She really fancied a cigarette but felt as if she couldn't, not in front of Julie.

'Yes, I know. I don't know what to do. I tried phoning Tom, I need to discuss things with him, but he's not with his parents and his mobile's switched off. I haven't heard a peep out of him since he left.' She decided against mentioning his brief appearance at Angus's 'burial'.

'I'm sure it'll sort itself out – one way or the other.'

Julie felt odd – surprised at how much she'd opened up to Rachel. 'I'm sure he'll be back soon. I just hope so for Charlotte's sake.'

'And yours.'

Julie looked at her and hinted at a smile. 'Yes. And mine,' she said, finishing off her bitter lemon.

Rachel felt inside her handbag for her purse. She felt the smoothness of the lighter. 'Another drink?'

Julie looked at her watch. 'No, I ought to be going soon; I've got Year Eight at two o'clock.'

*

'Get out of the bloody way.' Tom's fuse was short. Panic and the heat were taking their toll. He was almost there but the traffic on Holloway Road was predictably dense. He was so regretting that kiss at the Lewisham party. He remembered it all too well – the beach-themed tiles, the roll-top bath with its ornate legs, sitting on the toilet with the lid down, she straddled on his lap, her musky perfume, the smoothness of her blouse. It was all so clumsy and sordid but wonderfully desperate. Ten minutes later, they emerged from the bathroom to be greeted by a small queue of people waiting for the toilet. Rachel giggled, Tom blushed. He remembered the meal out at the Italian restaurant – what a painful experience that was; the beginning of the end. That was the time he gave her that silly lighter in the shape of a gun. Once they recovered from the crooning serenade, Rachel was unnaturally happy, ecstatic almost, dancing in the street with her red rose. At first, he put it down to the drink and the occasion, but he soon realised her joy had a far deeper meaning. He'd liked her – but not that much. He began to distance himself, made up excuses, whatever it took. And then he met Julie. Rachel broke it off but not without the hysterics and the threats. He was so annoyed with himself for allowing Rachel back into his life. 'Get a move on!' he shouted, slamming his fist against the steering wheel in frustration.

To his left was the bus lane – empty. He checked his rearview mirror, indicated left and eased out onto the red tarmac lane. He knew it was risky, especially in Holloway and could earn him a hefty fine to add to the earlier speeding one, but what the heck, he had to get there. He sped down the bus lane and managed to squeeze back into the main flow of traffic beyond the next set of traffic lights. It was 1:45; five more minutes and he reckoned he'd be there. He was banking that they were at the Rose and Crown. It was the nearest pub to Julie's school; it had to be that one. He just hoped he wasn't too late. Surely Rachel wouldn't launch straight into a blow-by-blow confession, she would feel the need to build up to it first, get Julie relaxed, on her side. He swung left into Sydney Street. Just a few back roads and he was there.

*

'Tom is a very special man. I don't understand why he'd walk out on you.'

'I know.' Yes, thought Julie, Tom was a very special man. 'I know,' she repeated.

'I don't see so much of you both now…'

'I'm not sure we saw that much of each other in the first place. Apart from toddler groups and children's parties.'

'Well, perhaps I meant Tom.'

'Yes. I never knew you two were such good friends; I don't remember it at all.'

'I suppose if I'm honest with you, Julie, you wouldn't have.'

Julie frowned. 'What do you mean?'

'Look, let me just nip to the loo. I'll be back in a minute.' She paused. Then, with a wink, she added, 'And then I'll tell you everything you need to know.'

*

Tom parked his mother's Vauxhall. Dreadful old thing, he thought, he wished they'd get something newer, something with air conditioning. The Rose and Crown was just around the corner. He stuffed a few coins into the parking meter and started walking quickly towards the pub. His heart was thumping, he had no idea what he was walking into or how he would explain his unexpected appearance. It was too late to think up a story now. He began jogging and broke into another sweat as the adrenaline flowed. He reached the pub, pushed open the door and staggered into the dark, smoky atmosphere. He glanced around, adjusting his eyes to the darkness, catching his breath. A few men propped up the bar watching the horse racing on an overhead television, trying to hear the commentary over the music. An elderly couple sat in silence in the corner. At another table sat an unkempt youth reading a tabloid, smoking a roll-up. Tom peered around the bar. There she was – sitting alone next to the window. For a

190

moment he felt relieved, perhaps Rachel had stood her up. But then he saw the glasses on the table in front of her. How forlorn she looked, somehow out of place in this dreary pub with its dreary clientele. He approached the table cautiously and noticed how the sun streamed through her hair, accentuating her natural blondness. 'Hello, Julie,' he said quietly.

She jumped at the sound of his voice. She turned and looked bewildered by his sudden presence. 'Tom?' She almost smiled but seemed to check herself. 'What are you doing here?'

'My mother said you phoned...'

'Yes, but you didn't have to–'

'Hi, Tom.' Tom spun round to see Rachel. 'How nice to see you.' If she was surprised by his appearance, she certainly didn't show it.

Despite knowing she was there, he, in turn, still felt surprised at seeing her. 'Hello, Rachel, I was just passing, as they say.'

'What a coincidence.' She sat down. 'Might as well join us. Want a drink?'

'What? Yeah, sure. Water. That'd be fine. Thanks.'

'OK,' said Rachel cheerfully. 'I'll get it.'

He sat down, his back to the bar, and glanced furtively at his wife.

'So what does bring you here?' she asked coldly.

'My mother said you needed to speak to me about Charlotte. She said it was urgent.'

'Yes, but not so urgent you had to come all this way without phoning first. Anyway, I was just having a nice drink with Rachel.'

'So I see. How's Charlotte?'

'Missing you, wondering what she's done wrong.'

Tom grimaced. 'And, erm, are you missing me?'

She stared out of the window for a few moments, as if tossing his question around her mind. 'Tom, listen, I want you to know–'

'One water with lots of ice,' said Rachel sitting down. 'My treat – two words I never quite managed to teach Adrian.'

Tom seized on the opportunity to steer the conversation. 'I was talking to Adrian today – good bloke; you could do worse, Rachel, a lot worse.'

'I know; thank you for the advice. But I also know I could do better; a lot better.'

Tom's cheeks flushed. He gulped down his water, the coldness jarring against his teeth.

Julie spoke, 'Rachel was just saying how you two used to hang out together. I didn't know you two were such good friends. I thought it was just through the girls.' She laughed.

Tom glanced at Rachel, his eyes pleading for her to keep her silence. But Rachel was enjoying herself; this was, he knew, some sort of watershed for her. She giggled. 'It was more than that. It was fun, wasn't it, Tom?'

Tom held his tongue and twirled the ice around in his glass.

Julie was watching both of them when it hit her. Like a thunderbolt striking her, she suddenly realised what was happening. Her stomach flipped. Gripping the table, she turned to Tom, fixing him a piercing stare. 'Well, Tom? Was it fun?'

He noticed there was the slightest hint of lipstick on the rim of his glass. His mind was spinning, trying to work out how to deflect the conversation but knowing it was already too late. Julie continued.

Julie could see it in his face – something had gone on between them. She glanced at Rachel, clocking her smug expression. So, that was what it was all about – this sudden need to be friends. They were having an affair and Rachel wanted to expose it. How could she have been so naïve? How had she let this woman worm her way in? She felt betrayed; hurt that she'd exposed her inner self to this woman. Her heart hammered as the surge of anger rose within her. 'OK, as Tom's memory seems to have conveniently lapsed,' she said loudly, trying to contain herself and speaking quickly, 'let me put it another way.' She looked at Rachel. 'Rachel, I hope you don't mind my asking,' she said, adopting a softer tone. 'Are you having an affair with my husband?'

Tom felt the sweat running down his collar. He remembered those words – she'd used exactly the same words he had used with Moyes at the parents' evening. He shot a look at Rachel who produced a cigarette and the gun-shaped lighter. She could barely constrain the smile, thought Tom. Julie waited patiently while Rachel lit her cigarette. She blew out a mouthful of smoke, which lingered within the beams of sunlight streaming through the window. Tilting her head to one side, she grinned. 'No,' she said calmly. 'But before you, we were together; an item, as they call it.'

Tom noticed Julie clench her jaw. 'It was before we were married…' he said.

'Don't forget what happened at Lewisham, Tom dear,' interrupted Rachel.

'That was years ago.'

'Only three years, Tom.'

'It meant *nothing*.' He looked at Rachel to see whether his harsh words had wiped the grin from her face.

It had, but only momentarily. 'That's not what you said at the time. If I remember rightly, you were more than happy to–'

'Stop being so self-deluded. Did you really think for a moment I would–'

'Shut up, both of you.' Julie snarled her lip. 'You sodding hypocrite.'

'Takes one to know one,' said Rachel.

'What? You…' She turned to Tom. 'You told her?'

'Julie–'

'I don't believe it. You bastard.' Julie picked up her handbag and turned to face Rachel. 'That was it, wasn't it? That was the reason for your pathetic attempts at being friends? So you could gloat, you sad bitch.'

Rachel smirked. 'You don't know anything, least of all Tom, you simply don't understand him.'

Julie rose from her seat. 'How dare you preach to me, you scheming little cow.' She picked up Tom's half-full glass of icy water and threw it at Rachel, slammed the glass down on the table, and stormed out.

Rachel screeched, then laughed. Tom jumped out of his seat. 'Julie, wait…' By now the whole pub was watching intently as Tom ran after her. He caught up with her outside. 'Julie, please wait a minute…'

She stopped, spun round, and for a moment Tom thought she was going to spit at him. 'Kept that one a bit quiet, didn't you? I was full of regret, up to here with self-loathing for what I'd done, and all the while you'd been at it with… with *her*. Puts a bit of a new perspective on it, doesn't it, you bastard.'

'Julie–'

'All this prima donna stuff running off to mummy and daddy. And to think I was desperate to have you back. Well not any more, matey, you can sodding stay there and stew for all I care.'

'Will you–'

'I can't believe you told her; how dare you? Got another shag in while you were at it, did you? Christ, she's all over you like a rash–'

'Will you shut the hell up? I've not slept with her since… since–'

'I don't want to know. I'll shut the hell up but I'm not hanging around to listen.'

'Julie, you have to hear me out–'

'Do I, Tom? No, I don't think so; I don't have to listen to you because I don't want to hear it. Understood?' She turned and walked quickly away. But then she stopped and flung around to face him. 'And no, I'm not missing you.'

Tom watched her leave, watched her as she strode purposefully down the street, around the corner and out of view. He remained still, vaguely gazing at the space where her presence had been, this stranger who used to be his wife. He looked up at the blue skies, the sun reflecting off the roofs and noticed a hot air balloon drifting gently across the sky.

He stepped back into the dark atmosphere of the pub, his polished shoes echoing on the wooden floor. His return drew a sudden silence from the regulars who turned to watch him in full expectation of further excitement. 'A Whiter Shade of Pale' now played on the jukebox, its doleful organ ringing around the interior. He marched back to the table to find Rachel dabbing her blouse with a handkerchief, a lighted cigarette in the other hand. She smiled at his approach. 'I'm sorry, Tom, but it's best out in the open,' she said in her high-pitched voice.

'No, Rachel, it isn't.' He glanced around, conscious of being watched by the whole pub with the horse racing and Procol Harum in the background. He lowered his voice and spoke through clenched teeth. 'Julie's right, you're a scheming little cow. What exactly was this meant to achieve?'

'Come on, we both know…'

Tom hovered above her. 'No, no, you've got it wrong. I admit there was a while back then when perhaps… but not now. I don't fancy you, I don't need you.'

She looked hurt; this wasn't part of the plan. 'Tom…'

'You finished with Adrian because of me, didn't you? That was a mistake because he still wants you but… I don't. You do understand, I don't, and I don't want to see you again.'

Her face crumpled. She threw her cigarette on the wooden floor. 'You don't mean that.'

Tom tried to keep his voice steady. 'Believe it.' He turned to leave; his eyes fixed on the exit.

Rachel stood up abruptly and with the final chords of 'Whiter Shade of Pale' fading away, yelled his name across the pub. 'Tom! Tom! TOM.'

He paused at the door and looked back. Tears were streaming down her face, her make-up running, the smoke still whirling in the sunbeams, the stunned silence gripping the puzzled audience. She looked so pathetic, so crumpled that for a moment he felt pity for her. He was tempted to say he was sorry, but decided against it; that would have been too spineless.

Chapter 20: *The Drunk*

20th October 1917.

This day was the last day of my war. Today I killed a few German soldiers close to, effectively lost my leg and earned my medal. It is not a day I cherish but the date is indelibly carved onto my mind as clearly as the date of my birth. I think of it often, either consciously or subconsciously. I have no control over it.

A party of about 30 men took part in a raid. The objective was to collect German prisoners to aid our intelligence before the coming battle at Cambrai. Not that we knew anything about the imminent assault, of which I certainly would have been a part of, if it had not been for a stray German bullet that caught me in the back of the knee.

The raid was exciting and terrifying by turn. My mind went a complete blank hence my memory of it is vague. Fuelled by some instinctive bloodlust, I had never been so keen and willing to kill – or be killed. All but one of the men I killed are faceless.

The Germans were there for the killing, I forget how many lost their lives at my hands. But there was one I remember all too well – a boy I bayoneted to death. His face comes back to haunt me frequently and at the most unexpected of times or places. As he lay dying, he pulled out a photograph of his family. But I had no time to feel either pity or mercy. I bayoneted him one more time

— to make sure. I was on my way back when the bullet brought me down. Unable to move, I expected to die. But under the cover of night, Jack and our Sergeant Wilkins came to my aid and hauled me in. Jack saved my life under almost impossible circumstances. When later the tables were reversed, I was unable to return the favour.

A few months later, I received my DCM for taking a trench that was probably retaken within hours, for playing my part in providing invaluable intelligence, and for denying a few more German mothers from seeing their sons again.

Such is war.

Tom closed the diary with a sigh and picked up the medals lying at his side on the bed. 'Such is war,' he said to himself. It was Wednesday, mid-morning, the whole day stretched before him and he was at a loss as to what to do. He was feeling bored, on edge and inadequate. Bored – because he couldn't put his mind to anything; on edge – in case Mr Lewis phoned to haul him into work to face the music; and inadequate – for having been such a useless father to Charlotte. St Omer seemed like the only bright spot on his bleak horizon but even the thought of that now made him cringe. He'd bulldozed Maria and was now regretting putting her on the spot. Shaking it from his mind, he decided he had to do *something*. He put Charlotte's earrings in his pocket, trotted downstairs, politely declined his mother's offer of lunch, and went out. He decided to go and have lunch in a pub. He walked to his parents' local, not that they had ever stepped into it, and ordered a ploughman's and half a lager. It was the sort of pub that provided newspapers for their customers, so after finishing his lunch, which frankly wasn't particularly nice, he ordered another half and settled down with a copy of *The Mirror*. He read it from cover to cover while refreshing his glass three maybe four times. He then finished off with the supplement and another half – or two. He looked at his watch – he had been in the pub for two hours and had consumed so many halves, he'd lost count, and he still had enough time to catch a train down to Holloway and meet Charlotte from school. But first, another half. Twenty minutes later, Tom emerged from the pub into the heat of the day, feeling decidedly woozy.

Tom was outside the school gates a good ten minutes before home time. He sat down on the pavement near the main entrance and waited. He hadn't met Charlotte from school since primary school. He imagined that she might be embarrassed in front of her friends, but inside she'd be delighted at his unexpected appearance. He'd take her out to a café where they could have a talk. He needed to talk to her and clear the air. He needed to apologise for his childish behaviour on his visit home, to commiserate over Angus and to remind her that, whatever happened, he was and would always be her father. He remembered that on Friday it was Charlotte's First World War performance. He wondered whether she was still bent on doing a poetry recital. Tom felt a twinge of nervousness on her behalf and thought back to his own recent performance in front of an audience. He thought back to their trip to the Imperial War Museum. It had been the last thing he'd done before everything started to go wrong.

In the distance, the school bell sounded. It was three-thirty. Tom stood up clumsily; feeling nauseous, his stomach churning. Taking his place next to the school gates, he hoped no one would notice. The first set of children, mostly the little ones, suddenly appeared in a mad dash to escape school. After the initial rush came the deluge – what seemed like hundreds upon hundreds of schoolchildren of varying sizes and races. A sea of black blazers engulfed him. He would never spot Charlotte among this lot, especially in his current state of dizziness. He kept his eyes peeled for her blonde hair, but his fuzzy mind couldn't keep up with the waves of shrieking, chattering, excitable children. Who'd be a teacher, he thought. Some of the big boys were taller than him and all but a few seemed to possess an arrogance that he found slightly threatening. He saw a spotty, overweight youth who had unbuttoned his white school shirt to reveal underneath a black tee shirt with the words "Swivel on it" emblazoned in red lettering. Charming, thought Tom.

Tom heaved and for a horrendous moment, thought he was going to be sick. The crowd of schoolchildren was beginning to thin out and Tom assumed he had missed her. He waited for a few minutes more until barely a handful of children remained. Tom gave up and realised he had probably hung around at the school too long to try and catch her up on her way home. He was just turning to leave when he saw her. She was walking alongside a gangly red-headed boy and, much to Tom's irritation, Mark Moyes. He stepped into the playground. The three of them were deep in conversation but they were too far away for Tom to hear what they were saying.

Moyes saw him first. 'Charlotte, your father's here.'

Charlotte looked up and shot her father a filthy look. 'Dad? What are you doin' here?'

'Nice to see you too, sweetheart. I wasn't doing anything, so I thought I'd come and meet my lov-er-ly daughter from school.' Tom realised he hadn't said a word to anyone since leaving the pub and his speech sounded slurred. He looked at the red-headed boy. 'Who's this then?'

'Adam.'

'Hello,' said Adam politely.

'He's in my class,' added Charlotte.

'Well, Adam, nice to meet you, to meet you...' Oh stop it, you fool, thought Tom. He was beginning to act like a drunk.

'Dad, are you OK?'

'Couldn't be better, my love.' He took a deep breath. 'Couldn't be better.' He reached inside his pocket. 'Look, I've bought you a little present, not much really.' She took the little box and flipped open the lid. Tom watched her, hoping for a spark of enthusiasm but was disappointed by her blank expression. 'They're in the shape of a snake, you see?'

Moyes looked at him accusingly. 'You're drunk.'

'No, I'm not.'

'Yes, you are; you're drunk.'

'Oh-no-I'm-not,' said Tom, adopting a pantomime voice.

Adam looked embarrassed. Tom decided it was best if he took Charlotte away before he made more of a fool of himself. 'C'mon, sweetheart, I'll take you out for a Coke and a big sticky bun. Hmm? You'd like that.'

'No, not much.' Charlotte glanced up at Moyes as if seeking his help. He was only too glad to intervene.

'You're not taking her anywhere,' he said firmly, stepping forward to place himself between father and daughter.

Tom couldn't believe his ears. 'You what?' he said threateningly.

'You're drunk and I'm not prepared to entrust Charlotte's safety into your hands. I think you should leave.'

A mixture of rage and humiliation sobered Tom in an instant – how dare he speak to him like that. 'OK, I may be a bit drunk; can you blame me? But she's still *my* daughter and I'm *not* leaving without her.'

'Dad, please, you're showing me up.'

Adam mumbled to her, 'I won't say anything.'

Tom cast his eyes around the playground. Beyond a few teachers and an odd group of schoolchildren, the place was almost empty. 'C'mon, Charlotte,' he said, sidestepping Moyes and offering her his hand. But Charlotte stepped back a pace and shook her head.

Moyes stepped forward again. 'I think Charlotte has made her feelings quite clear. Now, I *really* think you ought to leave.'

'No,' said Tom impetuously. He was aware that their argument was beginning to attract attention.

'In that case,' said Moyes, 'I shall escort Charlotte home myself.' He turned to her, 'You ready, Charlotte?' She nodded. The teacher started to walk forward, but Tom moved to block him, his face only inches away from Moyes's, eyeball to eyeball. In the corner of his eye, he saw another teacher, at least he assumed he was a teacher, coming over.

'Oh no you don't,' seethed Tom. 'You took my wife; you're not taking my daughter too, you bastard.'

'I'm only escorting her home, you fool.'

From the near distance, Tom heard the approaching teacher call out. 'Are you OK, Mr Moyes; do you need any assistance?'

Keeping his eyes fixed on Moyes, Tom took a half step back, clenching his fist.

Moyes shouted back to his colleague, 'Yes, I'm fine thanks, Mr Searight here is just going—'

Tom hit him. Weeks of resentment surged out of him; he hit him with as much force as he could muster, catching Moyes on the cheek. Charlotte screamed, Adam put his hand to his mouth; Moyes staggered back clutching his cheek. Tom grasped his own hand, surprised by the surge of pain inflicted by Moyes's cheekbone.

The second teacher ran towards Tom, his arm outstretched. 'Oi, what do you think you're doing!' he shouted. Moyes fell onto one knee, still holding his cheek. Tom sidestepped the teacher and hovered above Moyes with his fist clenched again, waiting for Moyes to get up so he could hit him a second time. Some instinctive code of honour, gleaned from a childhood diet of Hollywood films, told him not to hit Moyes while the man was still down. The teacher pushed him to one side. Tom caught his balance and glared at the teacher who stepped back for fear of also being hit by this demented parent.

'Stop it!' screamed Charlotte. 'Stop it, just leave me alone, Dad.'

The sound of Charlotte's desperate voice immediately diffused Tom's aggression. He turned and looked at his daughter. The second teacher went over to Moyes and helped him back to his feet. Adam simply looked awkward, wanting to walk away but unwilling to desert Charlotte. Charlotte began crying. 'Dad, I know what happened between Mum and Mr Moyes. I wish I didn't know and I wish it hadn't happened. But it did happen and you're just making everything worse. I don't need a dad who disappears and then comes back drunk and hits people. I just want…' Her voice trailed off.

'Go on, Charlotte, what do you want?'

'I just want you and Mum to get back together. I want Angus back. I want to go back to how we were.'

Moyes was listening. Tom looked at him. He wanted to say "see what you've done", but circumstances told him this wasn't the time to score petty points at Moyes's expense.

Charlotte turned to Adam and wiped her sleeve against her nose. 'Come on, let's go.'

Adam looked nervously from Tom to Moyes, as if needing both their consent before he could escort Charlotte out of the school. Both men nodded. With her schoolbag trailing behind her, Charlotte turned to her father, 'See you sometime, Dad.'

'Are you still doing your thing on Friday?'

'My thing?' She nodded and with Adam beside her, she walked out the school gates. Tom and the two teachers watched her go. As she exited the school, Tom glanced at Moyes who had a small trickle of blood running down from the small cut in his cheek. He deserved more, thought Tom.

'Do you want me to call the police, Mr Moyes?' Mark shook his head. 'If you're sure. We'll need to report it to the head in the morning.'

Without a word, Tom left. He began to feel nauseous again. He belched. At least, he thought, he hadn't been sick.

Chapter 21: *Loud Music*

Charlotte and Adam walked in silence; both too embarrassed to know what to say. Frankly, Charlotte was relieved. She needed to be with someone, but she had no desire to talk. Adam's silent companionship was ideal. Although she had known Adam since they both started at the school, she'd never had anything to do with him, at least not until his father had run over her dog. She had spoken more to him in the last couple of days than in the previous three years. And she liked him; he was nice. A bit square and a bit quiet, but nice. Presently, they came to Adam's house; he lived nearer to the school than Charlotte. They hovered around Adam's front gate for a while, not sure how to say goodbye. Eventually, Adam asked Charlotte in, but she declined. She wasn't ready yet to meet the man who had run over Angus.

Charlotte walked on alone. She could tell that Adam had been relieved she hadn't accepted his invitation. She was beginning to really resent her father. First, he disappears, although she could understand that now, but not to call her? That was too much; it was as if he was denying her existence. And when he does show up, he's an embarrassment, fighting over a spade or violently drunk. This wasn't the father she loved. She ambled along Valentine Road, past the library, the left side of the street bathed in dazzling sunlight. She didn't know what to do. She didn't want to go home. Mum had said she was staying on late at school because of some staff meeting, but equally, she needed to do something, just to take her mind off things. She fancied going to the park, but she couldn't face it – not without Angus. She thought of all the times she used Angus as an excuse to meet Gavin. She smiled at the thought of Angus sniffing around while she and Gavin had a quiet smoke. Gavin – that was it! If ever she needed a smoke, it was now. Yes, what a good idea, she thought, she'd go and see Gavin.

With a new-found purpose in her stride, Charlotte turned back on herself and made her way to Gavin's house. She'd never been inside before but she knew where it was. Chances were, she thought, he'd be out; he'd probably found himself a new chick to impress with his illegal substances, but it was worth a try. Ten minutes later, Charlotte was standing outside his house. She rang the bell. There was no answer, but she tried again. Presently, she heard footsteps scurrying down the stairs. The door swung open. Standing there, barefoot, was Gavin himself wearing his "Swivel on it" tee shirt. 'Bugger me, she's back!'

'Hello, Gavin,' she said meekly.

'Watchya.'

'I was jus' passing and, erm, jus' thought I'd see if you were around.'

'Sure. Come up, if ya like.'

Charlotte stepped into the hallway and followed Gavin to the foot of the stairs. She looked around. She was struck by how squalid everything was. The wallpaper in the hall and up the stairs hung off in huge strips, the carpet was filthy and threadbare. A full but untied bin liner was propped up against the wall; its sordid contents spilling out.

Gavin charged upstairs. 'What's up?' he shouted from the top.

'Your mum not at home?'

'Nah, she's at work. Won't be back for ages; I'm on me tod. You coming up or what?'

Charlotte climbed the stairs and followed Gavin to his room. As he opened the door, huge whiffs of sweet-smelling smoke came billowing out. 'Bloody hell, Gav, you've been at it.'

He laughed. 'Yeah, got loads at the moment. Want some?'

'You sure?'

'Course.'

She stepped gingerly over the clutter of discarded clothes, glossy football magazines, scattered CDs, crushed cans, crisp packets and bits of rubbish. Posters of semi-naked women and football stars adorned the walls. Gavin plonked himself down in a large, red beanbag in the corner of his room and finished off a joint he'd been smoking. Charlotte looked around – there was nowhere to sit, so she perched herself at the end of his bed, trying to disguise her look of distaste. Next to her was a table covered with more magazines, an old computer and bits of paper and on which sat a small CD player. While she took in her surroundings, Gavin rolled a joint, quickly followed by a second. He passed one to Charlotte.

'What, all of it?' she asked.

'Yeah, get it down ya.'

Charlotte gazed at the daunting size of it; she hadn't smoked weed for a while and knew it would go straight to her head. Gavin lit his joint and then handed her his pornographic lighter and an unopened can of cider. She opened the can, placed it carefully between her knees and lit hers. She took a few gentle puffs, sipping from the drink between each draw.

'Hey, I got a good mark for my homework,' said Gavin.

'Blimey, that must be a first. What homework?'

'Y'know, Great Fire of London.'

Charlotte laughed. 'Oh yes, that one.' She wondered whether she ought to offer to do more in return for the joint. She'd smoked almost a third of it before it started having any effect. She let out a deep breath and grinned. 'That's better,' she said quietly to herself.

'How's the mutt?'

Charlotte really did not want to discuss it with him. 'Oh, he's all right.' But then it seemed terrible lying about it, not because of Gavin, but for her own sake. 'Actually, he got run over,' she said dispassionately as possible to discourage further conversation. She took another draw and gulped down a mouthful of cider.

'That'll teach 'im.'

Did he not understand? 'No, no, he's dead, Gavin.'

'Oh, sorry,' he sniggered.

The effects of the grass were taking over and she actually found Gavin's lubricious reaction quite funny. Despite herself, she started giggling. Gavin, in turn, guffawed which made Charlotte giggle more. And once she'd started giggling, she found she couldn't stop until she crescendoed into an outright belly laugh.

'Stop', said Gavin. 'What's so bloody funny?'

Charlotte neither knew nor cared. She tried to catch her breath. 'I don't know,' she said breathlessly.

'I thought you were meant to be sad when your dog kicks the bucket.'

'I am, it's just the way you said "that'll teach him". It just made me laugh.' She was coming to the end of her joint and felt pleasantly light-headed but had to concentrate on coordinating her hand with her mouth. She began to feel dizzy and slowly the pleasantness gave way to queasiness. She belched.

'Oh shit,' said Gavin. 'You're not gonna be sick again, are you?'

'No, no,' she slurred. 'It's just the cider.'

'I know, let's 'ave some music.' Gavin pulled himself up from the beanbag and almost fell back with the effort. He crawled across the floor, reached up to the portable CD player on the table near Charlotte, and pressed 'play'. The music was loud and aggressive and the thumping bassline reverberated through Charlotte's stomach.

'Turn it down a bit,' she shouted.

'Nah, it's good.' He stood up and started dancing, the drugs having stripped him of his inhibitions. But he had no sense of rhythm – his feet moved about clumsily while he jutted his shoulders violently and, with clenched fists, punched his arms out in unison vaguely in time to the music. How ridiculous he looked, thought Charlotte, hoping he wouldn't try to persuade her to follow suit. The first track finished but led directly into the second, denying Charlotte the relief of even a few seconds' peace.

For a moment, she thought she was about to be sick. Not again, she thought, how uncool. She tried to stand up but fell back on the bed. Fortunately, Gavin was too busy punching the air to notice. 'I'm just going for a piss,' she yelled above the music. She staggered across the landing, opened a door, only to find it was another bedroom. A woman's bedroom, far nicer than Gavin's shithole but, for reasons she couldn't articulate to herself, still incredibly depressing. She found the bathroom and locked the door behind her. The bassline thudded through from Gavin's bedroom. She wondered how the neighbours put up with it. She knelt down in front of the toilet and retched. But nothing came, just a few dribbles of cider and bile. She pulled herself up and, cupping her hands under the cold water splashed her face and had a drink. Feeling slightly better, she made her way back wearily to Gavin's room. The music was loud as ever, but Gavin had gone. She went back onto the landing and called out his name.

He had gone downstairs. He shouted back up, 'Got the munchies. Want any?'

'No,' she shouted back. She returned to Gavin's bedroom and realised she was feeling dizzy again. She stood in the middle of the room and closed her eyes. The music pounded in her head, making the room seem smaller, more claustrophobic. She put her hand to her throat, opened her eyes momentarily, tried to breathe and then collapsed onto Gavin's bed. She lay there groaning, unable to move, her head swimming. She desperately wanted to leave, to get some air, but her own weightlessness held her down to the bed. She was just falling into a nauseous sleep when she was vaguely aware of Gavin's presence. He said something, but she couldn't make out his words. Then suddenly, he was on top of her.

The smell and heaviness of his body, the sensation of being suffocated, brought her back to consciousness. 'What... what're you doin'?' she spluttered. Her body trembled with revulsion as she became aware of his wet lips against hers. She turned her head away, but he persisted. She shook her head either way, trying to escape his repugnant kiss. She felt his hand cup her breast. She tried to push him off but he was too heavy, too strong. The drink and the spliff had sapped her strength. The rhythm of the music continued to pulsate aggressively in her head; the warm, unpleasant smell of his breath revolted her. With his weight pinning her down, he ripped violently at her blouse, tearing off the top buttons, exposing the plain whiteness of her bra. She tried brushing his hands away and twisted and writhed beneath him, trying to make it as awkward as possible for him. She felt his clammy hand on her thigh, attempting to hitch her skirt up, his breath becoming quicker and more urgent as he fumbled with his fly. With his other hand, he grappled with the front of her bra, trying to lift it over her breasts. The constriction in the back of her throat prevented her from screaming and she thought she was going to be sick. Suffocating still under his pressure, her mind began to go blank. She had to hold on, she had to fight. She thumped him as hard as she could on his back, but it had no effect. To her horror, she felt the warm flesh of his penis against her leg and the revulsion was complete. She retched and could feel the vomit at the back of her gullet. She retched again. She stuffed her fingers down her throat and heaved as hard as she could. Suddenly, with a violence that stretched every tendon and convulsed her in pain, the vomit gushed out in torrents splattering over Gavin's face and her chest. 'What the hell…' screeched Gavin. He arched up and struggled to move away from her, furiously wiping away the vomit with his sleeve and retched himself from the smell and the sensation of someone else's sick on his clothes and skin. Charlotte took advantage of his distraction and pushed him away. He lost his balance and fell back against the wall. 'You bloody cow,' he screeched. Charlotte rolled off the bed, landing heavily on the floor. Instinctively, she jumped straight back up. She started coughing violently but seizing her chance, grabbed her schoolbag and reeled out of the room before

Gavin had a chance to react. She rushed down the stairs, almost losing her balance, the frightening music fading as she threw open the front door and rushed outside.

Clutching her blouse together and dragging her school bag, she staggered halfway down the street before stopping, unable to go on. She bent over, panting and coughing. Eventually, the coughing subsided and she was able to catch her breath but she couldn't stop shaking, her teeth chattering. She glanced back but there were just a few ordinary people going about their business. A woman walking a dog passed and studiously ignored her. Gathering her strength and wiping away the worst of the vomit, Charlotte slowly made her way home, barely able to keep a straight line. The walk back to her house seemed interminable. Twice she had to stop and rest, perching against a low garden wall. Sweating from the heat and effort, she staggered on, zigzagging across the pavement. Eventually, she was home. As she fished around in her schoolbag for her house keys, she remembered her mother would probably still be out at the staff meeting. She stepped into the house, leaned back against the front door and wrapped her arms around herself. For a moment, she half expected to see Angus bounding up the hallway to greet her. Her heart dropped at the thought of not seeing him again. She called out her mother's name. To her relief, there was no answer. Still shaking, she climbed the stairs on all fours, the tears coming, and fell into the bathroom. She turned on the taps. As she waited for the bath to fill, she took off her clothes and threw them in the corner. Wiping away the steam from the mirror and the tears from her eyes, she looked at her reflection. She realised, quite suddenly, how much she hated her life.

Chapter 22: *The Compromise*

She phoned him before nine o'clock on the Friday morning and asked if they could meet up for a coffee. At first, Tom was reluctant, but there was something in her voice that, for once, sounded sincere, desperate even, and so Tom relented. They arranged to meet at eleven in a small café Tom knew on Upper Street. He spent the next ten minutes trying to decide what to wear. Should he look casual – as if relaxed and at ease with life; or should he go smart-casual implying he was getting on with things; or should it be simply smart – as in one ready to get back to normality at the drop of a hat. Having had a shower and a shave, he decided to go for the middle option. Before going out, Tom made a couple of phone calls. He rang the Army Medal Office in Droitwich in Worcestershire about how one went about claiming a medal, and a local stonemason about getting a plaque for Angus.

As he was about to leave, Tom's parents returned from a morning trip to the supermarket. Tom offered to pay for half of it. He told his parents he would soon be looking for somewhere else to live. This only had the effect of upsetting his mother who assumed Tom would be returning to his proper home – with Julie and Charlotte. But it was obvious now that Mark Moyes was still very much on the scene and

Tom had to resign himself, and his parents, that the split was going to be more than the temporary affair he'd initially anticipated. What option did he have? No, he was going to have to face living without her, without his daughter, and without employment. Bedsit land beckoned. He still couldn't bring himself to tell his parents why he and Julie had separated because, despite everything, he didn't want to drag Julie's name through the quagmire. But the consequence of his honourable silence was that his parents still assumed that it had all been *his* fault, that the guilt lay firmly at his door. Somehow, without going into details, he had to think of a way of relieving them of such a presupposition. But whoever was to blame, he knew his parents were finding the novelty of having their youngest son back at home wearing thin. It was, he concluded, time to leave. It was also, he realised looking at his watch, time to make tracks – he had a date to keep. As he left, he thrust a few notes into his mother's hand, brushing aside her semi-sincere protestations, and promised he'd start looking for alternative accommodation that afternoon.

*

Tom arrived at the café soon after eleven. He saw her immediately, sitting at the table next to the goldfish tank. She too had gone for the smart casual look, looking stylish but, for once, not overdressed. Her make-up was reduced to a minimum, her eyes stripped of their usual layers of mascara and her skin free to breathe without the copious amounts of foundation. As a result, she looked more attractive than usual; proving that she didn't need all that gunk. Despite smoking, she looked elegant and composed; sitting with her legs neatly crossed, reading a newspaper. Tom resolved himself not to be taken in by her obvious allure. She was, after all, still a scheming, devious woman who had as good as lost him his job.

'Hello, Claudette.'

She looked up from her newspaper and flashed him a broad if slightly embarrassed grin. 'Tom, thank you for coming,' she said stubbing out her cigarette. 'Let me get you a coffee.'

Tom sat down as she attracted the attention of a waitress.

'Fancy a Danish?' asked Claudette. Tom shook his head. 'Just two coffees then.'

Tom wondered what Claudette had in store for him; this was going to be more than a casual chat over coffee. She would have taken time off from work to come up to Islington. She was after something.

'You don't smoke, do you?' she said, reaching for the packet.

'No.'

'Do you mind if I do?'

'Well…'

'It's just, you know…' She lit her cigarette. She blew out a mouthful of smoke. 'How are you then, or is that a silly question?'

'What d'you think?'

'Still, you've had some nice weather for your week off.'

'Yes, but somehow I wasn't quite in the mood for sunbathing.' She was an intelligent woman, thought Tom, but sometimes she could say the most inappropriate things.

Realising her tactlessness, Claudette smiled weakly. 'Yes, of course. Sorry.'

'So, tell me, why did you do it?'

'I don't really know,' she said as she drew on her cigarette. 'I suppose if I was honest with myself, it was probably just a knee-jerk reaction, y'know.'

'Running scared, were you?'

'Perhaps.' A thin, Italian-looking waitress with a pierced nose returned with their coffees and plonked them on the table. They both reached for the sugar. 'After you,' said Claudette. 'You see, when Clive walked in, I was mortified and of course, he immediately jumped to the wrong conclusion. So I just blurted something out and made it sound as if, erm… it was your fault. You know Clive, he's an old sod and he would never have kept it to himself.'

'Great, thanks a lot; saved your own skin nicely, didn't you?' said Tom, as he stirred his sugar.

'I understand if you're angry, Tommy.'

'Bloody right I am, and don't call me Tommy. So what happened then, what made you go to Mr Lewis?'

'It was Clive's idea and I sort of went along with it.'

'Naturally. I can see it now – you go running to the boss, put on your best little girl act and blame that nasty Tom, eh? And no doubt Mr Lewis lapped it up.'

'Something like that, yes.'

'And now it's my word against yours and Clive's. I don't stand a chance, do I? You've got it fairly well sewn up, haven't you? I mean, I don't understand, why did you want to see me anyway?'

Claudette stubbed out her half-finished cigarette. 'Christ, Tom, draw it out, why don't you? Isn't it fairly bloody obvious?'

'Not to me, it isn't.'

'To say I'm sorry, right? There you are, I've said it, I'm bloody sorry.' She gulped her coffee.

'Oh, so you're sorry, that's all right then. I've come all this way for you to say sorry.'

'I thought you lived nearby.'

'Not at the moment, I'm in Enfield.'

'Why, have you–'

'It doesn't matter,' he snapped. Tom was certainly not going to relate his domestic affairs to Claudette.

Claudette stared idly at the multicoloured goldfish. 'Actually, there's something else too.'

Ah, thought Tom, now this is the rub. 'Go on,' he said.

'I've dropped the allegation.'

Tom sat up. 'What?'

Claudette turned to look at him. 'Yes, I couldn't go through with it. I know you think I'm a heartless bitch, but I felt… I don't know.'

'Guilty? Is that the word you're looking for?'

'Is that the smell of burning flesh?'

'What?'

'The burning flesh of a martyr.'

'Oh very funny, Claudette, very funny indeed.'

'Well, come off it; you're milking this for all it's worth.'

'What if I am? So, tell me, apart from suddenly discovering your conscience, what made you drop your "allegation"?'

'I went to see Mr Lewis and told him that perhaps I'd been a bit hasty and maybe it'd been more a case of six of one, half a dozen of the other.'

'Couldn't you have told him the whole truth; that it was a full dozen.'

'Oh come on, I did fairly well to go that far, I didn't have to do it.'

'Yes, you did – remember, your conscience?'

'If you let me finish, you should receive a letter in the next day or two, inviting you to return to work, with your record clean and your reputation unblemished.'

'And Clive?'

Claudette grinned. 'He'll keep his mouth shut.'

'Bonus?'

'Something like that.'

Thank God for that, thought Tom, what a relief. He opened his mouth to thank her but then thought better of it, she didn't deserve his thanks. Instead, it was time to move to his own agenda. 'Claudette, I've been giving some thought to the brief and the DDA stuff–'

'Not that again.'

'Yes, that again. You ignored it on purpose, didn't you? You wanted us to lose; you want Dunstone, Cutler and Maine to get the contract.'

'Rubbish. You haven't got any proof.' She sipped her coffee.

'No? What about your little visits to DCM, eh?'

She choked. 'You bastard. How do you know about that?'

'I have my sources, as they say.'

She looked him squarely in the eyes. 'So what? I'm being headhunted, nothing wrong in that.'

'There is when you're purposely throwing a contract in favour of your would-be employers.'

'Bollocks.'

'Does Mr Lewis think it's bollocks?'

'He wouldn't believe you.'

Tom fished out his mobile from his pocket. 'Well, let's find out.'

'What are you doing?'

He started tapping a number. Claudette merely grinned at him. 'Hello… Yes, could you put me through to Mr Lewis's PA please…? Yes, I'll hold.' Claudette's grin was quickly fading. 'Hello, I wonder if it's possible to have a word with Mr Lewis… yes, it's urgent…'

'OK, OK, it's true.'

'Oh, sorry, wrong number…' He switched the phone off, smiling at the thought of his mother wondering why her son had not realised she was neither a receptionist nor a PA and had no idea who this Mr Lewis was.

Claudette reached for another cigarette, then decided against it. 'And to think I dropped the allegation against you.'

'You expect me to be thankful for that?'

'So, what do you want me to do?'

'Fairly obvious I would have thought. Tell DCM, thanks very much but I'll stick with good old Tooley and Hill.'

'Oh, stop being so bloody virtuous. How about if I offer you a bribe?'

'Christ, Claudette, don't you know when to stop? What sort of bribe?'

'OK, right, I might as well tell you,' she said. 'Clive has been angling to leave for months now, so I'm in the process of negotiating a generous redundancy for him and frankly, I can't envisage any problems. So, before I leave I'll be interviewing for his replacement. The job's there for the taking. All you have to do is say so.' She paused and looked at him carefully. 'Fancy it?'

Tom thought for a moment. 'No.'

'You sure? More responsibility, good salary, lots of bonuses.'

'OK, I'm not sure. Let me think about it.'

'Yes, Tommy, you do that, you think about it.'

Chapter 23: *The Hero*

Tom's father was trying to find his membership card for the bowling club. He'd looked everywhere downstairs and, feeling exasperated, hadn't found it in his bedroom either. He heard his wife calling from the kitchen. 'What did you say?' he shouted back.

'I said, would you like a cup of tea, Robert?'

'No thanks. You haven't seen my bowling card, have you?'

'No, but you could try that box of odds and sods in Tom's room.'

Robert noticed how recently the spare room had become "Tom's room". He hadn't stepped in there since Tom had come to stay, so he doubted he'd find the card in there. But it was worth a try. He walked in and noticed the various items of Tom's wardrobe laid out neatly on the bed. He found the box Alice had referred to and rooted around inside. Oddly enough, the card was there. 'Eureka!' he said to himself. As he turned to leave, he noticed the train ticket next to the ancient-looking book on Tom's bedside table. Why was Tom jaunting off to France again so soon, he wondered. Intrigued by Tom's reading material, he picked up the book and ran his finger along the lettering: *"Guy Searight, 1914-1921"*.

He'd purposely not shown any interest in the diary, and he was already regretting having told Tom of his unhappy childhood. Why had he exposed himself like that? He didn't feel any better for it. So much for this modern-day claptrap about *talking*, getting it off one's chest. He'd learnt years ago to accept it, to forget about it. But because of Tom's passing fad, all the old wounds had reopened, and forgotten and suppressed memories surfaced with painful clarity. Why *had* his father been so distant with him? It was all water under the bridge now and it didn't do any good thinking about it – when he did, it kept him awake at night. He had no desire to discuss further that distant time in his life, let alone read his uncle's diary. Nevertheless, he felt drawn to the small neat handwriting – a style not too dissimilar to his own. He sat down on the edge of Tom's bed and carefully turned the pages, stopping occasionally to read a sentence or two. One particular page took his attention:

> *20th October 1917.*
> *This day was the last day of my war. Today I killed a few German soldiers close to, effectively lost my leg and earned my medal. It is not a day I cherish but the date is indelibly carved onto my mind as clearly as the date of my birth. I think of it often, either consciously or subconsciously. I have no control over it…*

So, that was how his uncle lost his leg. Uncle Hobbly! He turned a few more pages.

> *20th January, 1919.*

Mary and baby Clarence came to see me again today. (Ah, thought Robert, his mother and his brother.) *Alas, Mary brought me sad news – my father has died. He went to his grave tormented by the war, as effectively as one who'd fought in it, deprived as he was, of both his sons. Will I regret my decision not to take over his business, I wonder? I think not. I could not bring myself to a reconciliation with my father whilst he refused to recognise that Jack too, had been his son. Finally, in his last days, he did reconcile with Jack.*

I pray God reunites them and that when my time comes, He reunites us all.

Robert was intrigued. He knew about Jack being executed; he remembered his mother mentioning it, and always with great sadness, but why the falling out with their father? Robert was hooked. He resolved that after Tom had finished with it, he would read the whole journal from beginning to end. He turned a few more pages, wondering what, if anything, his uncle had written about the day of his birth. He found the entry and read:

6th February, 1921.

Today should have been a day of celebration, for on this day Mary gave birth to a boy – Robert Searight. (Indeed, thought Robert, swelling with pride at seeing the occasion of his birth marked in his uncle's diary but why, he wondered, the downbeat mood?). *I could not be at the birth and neither was Lawrence, who refused to see the baby for a whole week.* (Robert's heart lurched at this sentence. Often, as a child – and many times since – he'd wondered what he'd done to so antagonise his father. Now, he knew. He'd done nothing. His father had been angry with him from the moment he left his mother's womb, possibly even before. How could it have been, thought Robert, how can a man resent a baby, his own flesh and blood?)

But then, who could blame him? Robert's birth would have been a great embarrassment had the truth ever been known. (Truth, what truth? wondered Robert).

About six days later, Mary came to see me with Clarence and the baby. I shall never forget her words as she held Robert up for me to see. She said 'Guy, this is Robert – your son; Robert, this is your father. Say hello'.

Carefully, Robert closed the journal and placed it back on Tom's bedside table. The walls seemed to be closing in on him, his head felt light, butterflies churned in his stomach, his heartbeat hammering away. For a moment, he thought he was going to faint. Memories of the sport's day came flooding back – his first place in the high jump eclipsed by Clarence's runner-up slot in the hundred-yard dash, beaten only by a boy "a good half-foot taller". He put his head in his hands. He remembered the war, his war, not Guy's. The ship, the U-boat, the torpedo. Surviving on a lifeboat adrift for days on the Indian Ocean. Ten men, all dead except for himself, the sole survivor. Robert let out an audible groan as he visualised his father in tears having mistaken him for Clarence. Now, over half a century later, Robert finally knew why. His father was crying, not because the *wrong* son had been killed, but because his *only* son had been killed. It was all so frighteningly clear now. A lifetime of confusion, of wondering, clarified in a few words written at the time of his birth. His father had had to live with an impostor all his life, a constant reminder that his wife had a child, not by just another man, but by his own cousin. Every day, a constant reminder of his failure and her infidelity. Every time he saw his impostor son, he saw Guy. No wonder his father had resented him all his life.

Robert clenched his eyes, desperately trying to stem the tears, a whole lifetime's worth of insecurity seemed to both disappear *and* intensify simultaneously. If *only* he'd been told, he would have understood. He could have forgiven. But no, he had to wait until his grandchildren were almost grown up before a chance letter from a woman in France had revealed the truth. The enigmatic Uncle Guy, Uncle Hobbly, had been his father, his real father. He leaned over and picked up the journal again. All he knew about his real father, or was about to find out, was contained in these pages. And there were also the medals. Where had Tom put them? Robert looked on the bedside table, lifting the Dickens novel, and yes, sure enough, lying under the book, were the four medals – Pip, Squeak and Wilfred – that's what they used to call the three Great War campaign medals. And attached to them, the DCM "for distinguished conduct in the field". He ran his finger over the metal, feeling the lettering inscribed on the reverse. He pictured Guy showing them proudly to *his* parents. What mixed feelings they must have had – one son a hero, the other executed. Robert looked at the inscription on the rim of the medal: 'Pte. G.Searight. Essex Reg'. His father, his real father, had been a hero.

Chapter 24: *The Red Oak*

On his way back from meeting Claudette, Tom stopped off at an estate agent to get a rough idea of how much rented accommodation cost. It was all as expensive as he feared. But what option did he have? He couldn't go on living with his parents and he couldn't go back home. When he first left, he fully expected Julie to come to her senses and come begging for him to return. Not only had it not happened, but she seemed more together with Mark Moyes than ever. So much for it being a casual affair. All that stuff about not fancying him and not seeing him any more was just talk. Maybe it had been true at the time but as soon as his back was turned, she tugged the string and Moyes came bouncing back, pandering to her every whim and playing surrogate father to Charlotte. Well, as far as Tom was concerned, Moyes was welcome to Julie – they deserved each other, but he was damned if Moyes was going to usurp him in Charlotte's affections. Tom knew he hadn't exactly been a model father since his departure. He couldn't help not being around when Angus got run over but he hadn't helped his cause by thumping her teacher like that. That had been a mistake. Immensely satisfying, but a mistake. He missed Charlotte. In fact, he missed them both and he missed his old life. But Julie had betrayed him and then rubbed salt in the wound, and he couldn't forgive her for that. How could he ever go back now? What a waste; twenty years since they met, fifteen married. How rapidly their mutual past had been made extinct by the present that held it in such little esteem.

As he caught the train back to Enfield, Tom's thoughts turned to Maria. It annoyed him that her grandmother had never tried, as Maria had done, to track down the Searights. From what Maria had said, she had never even attempted to. She had held a secret from his father, who, had he known, would have been spared a lifetime of torment and unanswered questions. His father had always, at the best of times, been morose and in possession of a quick temper. As children, Tom and his brother, Alec, had been terrified of him and as adults wary of their father's fluctuating moods. Tom now knew why. His 'grandfather' Lawrence had loved his son Clarence to the total exclusion of Robert, the product of his wife's illicit union with Guy. Nowadays, people would understand the sort of psychological scars that would leave on a person, but his poor father had kept it all pent up, festering inside him. Should he tell his father? No, it was too late now. His father was well into his eighties; the truth wouldn't alter anything and, indeed, could make things worse. But that wasn't Maria's fault. He thought about getting off the train in a few hours' time at St Omer and being met by Maria or Bernard. He couldn't wait to start another blissful weekend away from London.

Tom ate lunch with his parents – an awkward affair, his father being particularly silent and morose. Soon after lunch, it was time to go to Charlotte's school for the much-anticipated First World War performance. His father looked rather unkempt, his hair out of place. Suggesting to his mother that his father should perhaps comb his hair, Alice reminded

Tom that Robert hadn't looked at himself in the mirror for many a year.

Tom quickly packed his holdall for the weekend, threw it in the back of his parent's car, and picked up his passport and Eurostar ticket, which he stuffed into his back pocket. His parents had arranged to drive via Tom's house to pick up Julie, even though she lived within easy walking distance of the school. This, thought Tom, was a taster of their future relationship – the occasional united front for the sake of their daughter. Tom drove the Vauxhall. His mother sat in the front, with the window wide open, chattering away about the latest bargains she'd found in one of the big department stores and complaining about receiving a speeding fine when she never broke the speed limit. His father sat in the back, sporadically offering Tom the benefit of his driving experience and complaining of the draught.

Julie was waiting for them outside the front gate. She'd dressed up for the occasion in an outfit Tom had always liked – a smart pair of pinstriped trousers, a black top and a sixties-style green leather jacket. She looked lovely, and despite himself, Tom's heart lurched on seeing her. She took her place next to her father-in-law. She seemed on edge, but whether she was on edge on Charlotte's behalf or because she had to spend the afternoon with Tom and in close proximity to Moyes, Tom didn't know. Probably a combination of both, he thought. The ex-couple managed a cordial acknowledgement but otherwise, the tension remained palpable and not helped by Robert's sullen silence. The drive from the house to the school was mercifully brief. Tom parked on a side street near the school. The four of them made their way through the school playground and into the main hall.

Tom liked the main hall; it reminded him of his old school. It was imposingly large with a wooden floor and dark oak panels that stopped halfway up the wall. It had a high ceiling and the far end was dominated by the large four-foot-high stage, currently obscured by a thick purple curtain. The hall was decked with row upon row of black plastic, interlocking chairs, leaving a long central aisle. The place was a cacophony of noise and milling schoolchildren. The youngest ones sat at the front and their ages graduated towards the back. Behind the oldest children were the seats reserved for parents and guests. Most of the reserved seats were already occupied but there was a convenient run of four empty chairs directly behind the children and next to the aisle. Robert spotted them first and dashed ahead to claim them, followed quickly by Alice. It left Tom and Julie with no option but to sit next to each other.

Tom turned around. Two rows behind him he saw Rachel, catching her eye. But she pretended not to notice and turned to speak to Adrian, whose blue beard was now pink. Pinkbeard didn't seem to roll off the tongue so neatly, thought Tom. The big white clock on the wall showed ten minutes to three. The performance was due to start on the hour. As various parents, teachers and children milled around, the Searights flicked through the crudely produced programme. Charlotte's solitary moment of glory was due to be the second act, directly after the Passchendaele Sisters. At least, thought Tom, Charlotte would get her bit over and done with. As if reading his thoughts, Julie said, 'Poor girl, she'll be a nervous wreck by now.'

'I feel a nervous wreck for her.'

'Yes, so do I. I've got awful butterflies.'

'How is she?'

'Oh, she was in a dreadful state this morning what with all this, but generally, she's very down at the moment. You could have called her, you know; she's missed you desperately. She thinks you don't love her any more.'

'Hell, does she? I tried to meet her from school–'

'But you were drunk and you hit Mark, you idiot. She doesn't need that, poor girl.'

Tom nodded and resisted the temptation to ask where it all started. His thoughts were interrupted by a voice rising loudly above the din of the hall.

'Quieten down now please.' It was Mr Nolan, the head, standing on the stage in front of the curtain. He was a suitably severe-looking man, with a neat beard and glasses, who spoke in a flat, even tone. 'That's enough, thank you.' He waited patiently until the noise subsided to a muffled silence, but there were still plenty of audible whisperings to one side of the hall. 'I am waiting,' he added until he got the silence he wanted. 'That's better, thank you.' He paused, ensuring he had everyone's undivided attention. 'Welcome everyone to our summer term's special performance by Year Ten and a special welcome to parents and carers; thank you for coming. As you all know, the theme for this year's display is the ninetieth anniversary of the start of the First World War. It's been the focus of a wonderful collaboration between the history, music and art classes, so a big thank you to those teachers involved – Mr Moyes, Miss Grossman and Mrs Moore respectively. Now, a few practical points I need to mention. School today will finish directly following the end of the performance. That does *not* mean to say I want to see a huge scrum for the exit as soon as the curtain comes down, is that understood? You will wait quietly in your seats until you are given permission to leave in an orderly fashion.' He paused for a few moments to allow his instruction to sink in and then informed the parents where the fire exits were. 'Right then,' he said, 'to start the proceedings, I will hand you over to Mr Moyes, Year 10's history teacher. Mr Moyes…'

Mark ran up the side steps to the stage and waited for his head to exit gracefully back to his seat at the side of the hall. 'OK, thank you, Mr Nolan, and welcome everyone to our commemoration of the beginning of the Great War of 1914 to 1918, otherwise known as the First World War, which started ninety years ago this month. We hope today to be able to give you a small taste of what it was like to be in the war through songs, poems and re-enactments. The kids have worked really hard towards this, so please show your appreciation and give them lots of support and encouragement. Now, if you've read the programme, you'll know our compère for this afternoon will be Adam Sixsmith. So, with no further ado, I present to you, ladies and gentlemen… the First World War!' With his arm outstretched, Mark stepped back to the side of the stage as the thick purple curtain slowly rose to reveal a huge, impressive backdrop depicting the dark barren landscape of No Man's Land. The teachers began the applause, followed by the children and parents.

'Isn't it good?' remarked Alice clapping.

'Yes,' replied Tom. 'I especially like the gruesome bodies.'

'Painted with obvious glee,' added Julie.

At the front of the stage stood three microphone stands. A red-haired pupil appeared on the stage and approached the middle microphone. Tom recognised him as the boy who was with Charlotte the day he hit Moyes. 'Ladies and gentlemen,' he mumbled, 'today's show will…'

'Speak up,' shouted an older boy in the row directly in front of Tom and diagonally to his left. The boys on either side of him giggled.

Adam stopped, looked worried, coughed and tried again. 'Ladies and gentlemen,' he said too loudly so that his microphone squealed with feedback. Adam stepped back and glanced nervously to the side of the stage. He tried again. 'Today's show will start with two songs from the First World War with Miss Grossman on the piano. Please give a warm welcome to the Passin– Pass*chen*daele Sisters…'

The hall erupted into a huge noise of clapping, whoops and cheers as Adam made way for Abigail and two friends dressed in khaki, sparkling in excessive make-up and glittery hair, their faces brimming with confidence at the welcoming applause. They took their places at the microphones and waited patiently for the noise to die down. Abigail announced the first song, a number called 'There's a Land'. Miss Grossman began on the piano and after a short introduction, the girls launched in. Tom found himself tapping his feet in time, enjoying the musical spectacle, although one of the voices, he couldn't tell which, was slightly flat. A second song, called 'Come Under My Umbrella', included a short piano solo in the middle, during which the girls performed a synchronised dance, much to the delight of the male portion of the young audience. In no time, the songs were finished and the girls bowed and then slipped away smiling at the rapturous handclapping. Tom clapped heartily but inside his stomach churned. It was Charlotte's turn next.

Adam returned to centre stage. 'The Passchendaele Sisters… thank you. We will be hearing more from the Sisters later.' He waited for the applause to stop. Tom noticed that, having warmed to his task, Adam was smiling now. 'And now to our second act. Ladies and gentlemen, for an introduction and recital of First World War poetry, please put your hands together and give a warm welcome to…' He paused for effect. 'Charlotte Searight…!'

The four adult Searights led the clapping as a terrified-looking Charlotte walked onto the stage and took her place at the middle microphone. She had tied her hair back and wore a long, dark blue skirt and a pale blue blouse. She looked really nice, thought Tom. He noticed she was wearing a pair of earrings, he hoped they were his. How could she think he didn't love her any more? The applause stopped abruptly. Charlotte stepped forward, clasping a piece of paper. Tom rubbed his hands and noticed his palms were wet with sweat. He had to overcome the temptation to reach for Julie's hand. He felt acutely conscious that all eyes were on his daughter and that she was standing there in front of this silent sea of people, very much alone.

Charlotte glanced at her notes and began. 'Wilfred Owen, Siegfried Sassoon, Rupert Brooke. These three names are the most famous of the First World War poets…'

'Never 'eard of them,' muttered the boy in front of Tom.

'But there were many, many more. These were soldiers who felt so moved or frightened by what they saw, they needed to write down their experiences of war, death and fighting. The poems were written by soldiers who were still fighting, so they never knew if the poem they were writing would be the last. Many of the poems were written on a scrap of paper or on the back of an old envelope or in letters home to their family and loved ones.' She's doing really well, thought Tom. 'Sometimes, poems were found in the uniforms of men who had been killed, because not all of them lived. Siegfried

Sassoon did survive the war and died in 1967, aged eighty-one…'

'Old git,' sniggered the boy in front, loud enough to be heard by the nearby rows, who tittered at his remark. Tom hoped to God that Charlotte hadn't noticed the silly ripple of amusement.

'But Rupert Brooke died in 1915 and Wilfred Owen was killed in November 1918, exactly one week before the end of the war…'

'Served 'im right.' With each comment, the boy spoke louder and found a widening circle of barely muffled appreciation, which only served to encourage him more. Tom looked to see whether there were any teachers at hand, but they all seemed to be stationed at the front of the hall. He caught Robert's eye and his father looked as if he'd explode any moment.

'I am now going to read you a poem by each of them…'

'Oh Gawd, must you?'

'Will you be *quiet*!' said Robert quickly but loudly enough to be heard throughout the hall. It felt as if every head turned to see what was going on. The mutterings and giggles provoked a chorus of 'shushes' from the teachers standing at the sides of the hall. Even from the back, Tom could see the look of panic sweep across Charlotte's face. Whatever confidence she'd gained from the opening would now be unhinged.

'First… first, I will read a po-poem by Wilfred Owen called '*Dulce et Decorum Est*', which means death with honour, which Wilfred Owen calls the old lie…'

Tom waited for another sarcastic remark, but a couple of teachers had edged their way down towards the end of the hall and the boy remained silent.

'The poem goes like this…'

Taking a deep breath, Tom psyched himself up. He caught Julie's eye, her face etched with worry. 'This is terrifying,' she whispered. Tom nodded.

'"Bent dou-double, like old beggars under sacks, knock-knee, coughing like hags, we cursed through sludge…"'

And so she continued but Tom couldn't concentrate on the words, he could only listen to the sound of her voice, listening with trepidation for the slightest quiver or hesitation.

'"Gas! Gas! Quick boys! An ecstasy of fumbling…"'

'Ecstasy!' called out the vile youth in full voice. 'Fancy some E next time, Charlotte?' The children collapsed in giggles. Tom could have gladly hit him and for a moment, he thought his father was going to. The nearest teacher merely clicked her fingers at the boy. Charlotte stopped and looked up nervously and then tried to focus on her piece of paper.

'"But someone still was yelling out and stumbling…"' Her voice was trailing off and Tom could no longer hear her above the fidgety audience. The teachers glared at the pockets of distracted pupils until they managed to silence the restless mirth and Charlotte's voice could just about be heard as she reached the end of the poem.

'"To children ardent for some desperate glory, the old lie: *Dulce et Decorum est pro patria mori.*"'

The parents and teachers clapped. The children followed suit but their applause lacked the previous enthusiasm. Tom leant over to Julie. 'One gone, two to go.'

'The next poem was written by Siegfried Sassoon and it's called 'Aftermath'.'

Tom braced himself, at least he knew this one, not that it could in any way help his daughter exposed up there on the stage. But Charlotte seemed to be taking an age to get going.

Tom moved to the edge of his seat, urging her to start, but Charlotte remained silently rooted, staring at the piece of paper in her hand.

The boy in front yelled out, 'Get on wiv it!' The hall collapsed in laughter.

The teacher nearest to Tom finally approached the boy. 'Shut up, Gavin. One more word out of you and it's detention every lunchtime next week. Got it?'

With the hall still simmering with barely stifled giggling and the teachers shushing and glaring, Charlotte began. '"Have you forgotten yet?"' The tone of her voice took Tom by surprise. '"For the world's events have rumbled on…"' Charlotte was shouting above the barely restrained noise. Tom could see it in her expression – her fear had been replaced by anger, she seemed on the verge of tears, but she was fighting on. Tom felt seized by a sudden surge of pride. He wanted to stand up and yell out 'keep going, Charlotte; to hell with the lot of them, the ignorant sods'. He was desperate for her to reach the end, to get to the final stanza, the lines he could still recite.

But the more Charlotte shouted, the more the children laughed and the more the teachers tried to restore calm, the more they seemed to lose it. Tom turned nervously to Julie. 'What can we do?'

'There's nothing we can do, we just have to sit through it.'

'QUIET!' The head's voice cut through the huge hall, which fell immediately into silence. 'I will not tolerate this a moment longer. Now, show some respect please.' Charlotte waited, looking nervously at Mr Nolan. 'OK, Charlotte, please continue.'

Charlotte looked from the Mr Nolan to her piece of paper. Then slowly, she rolled it up into a ball and threw it into the front rows before leaping off the four-foot high stage. At first, the children were shocked into silence, but as she started running down the central aisle, the children burst into a deafening round of laughter and cheering which quickly reached a crescendo as she fled. Julie leapt out from her seat at the end of the row, but Charlotte sidestepped her, flapping away her mother's outstretched arms. Reaching the end, she pushed open the large double doors and charged outside. Julie called out her name as the doors swung back into place.

'Leave her,' said Tom standing up.

Julie looked at him as if trying to decide what to do. 'I can't; she needs me,' she said. 'She needs *us*.'

Tom watched her as Julie chased after her daughter and out of the doors. He heard his father mutter 'bloody savages,' as Mr Nolan restored order and castigated his children for their "unforgivable behaviour". Tom turned around to see Mark Moyes jogging up the central aisle, past him and out into the playground. Adam was already back on stage waiting for Mr Nolan to finish so he could introduce the next act. Tom looked at the scene before him and he hated it, he hated *them*. The final words of the Sassoon poem came back to him. As the last of the noise faded away, he heard himself shout out loud. '"Have you forgotten yet?"', his voice filling every corner of the hall. Everyone turned around to see where the voice had come from. His parents looked up at him with a mixture of surprise and understanding. '"Look up,"' he seethed, '"and swear by the green of the spring that you'll *never* forget" you ignorant little...' His words were greeted by an absolute silence. He turned to leave and caught sight of Rachel, who smiled at him and silently clapped her hands. Pinkbeard gave him the thumbs up. He walked slowly out of the hall, conscious of the noise his shoes were making against the polished wooden floor, but deeply satisfied that on Charlotte's behalf, he'd got the last word.

Tom slammed the double doors behind him. The playground was deserted except for the solitary figure of Mark Moyes hovering at the school gates, staring down the street. Tom caught up with him, noticing close-to the thin red line on his cheek where he'd hit him. 'Where did they go?' he asked brusquely.

'Down that way; towards the park,' answered Moyes.

They'd probably gone to the oak tree. He decided to follow them. As he passed Moyes, he paused. 'Are you still sleeping with her?'

'No.'

'I don't mind, because I don't care,' he said. 'I just need to know, that's all.'

'No, I'm not. I wanted to, but she said no.' Tom turned to leave, but Moyes called after him. 'She said she loves you too much.'

His words stopped Tom in his tracks. He turned to face the teacher. 'She said that?'

'Yes. Yes, she did.'

'Oh.' He absorbed the words. 'Thank you,' he said.

*

It was still warm and by the time Tom reached the park, he felt hot and breathless. The park was busy but free of schoolchildren. Another twenty minutes or so, the place would be teeming with them – playing their noisy games, eating their fast food takeaways and leaving a sprawl of litter in their wake. Perhaps he was being overly cynical he thought, but having seen how they behaved during Charlotte's recital left Tom feeling less than enamoured with tomorrow's generation. He walked quickly along the tarmac path beside the green wicker fence and past the small café. Shrieking toddlers splashed around in the paddling pool while their parents, sitting on the white plastic seats, sipped their coffees. Tom stopped and gazed up at the huge red oak tree with its long, outstretched arms of twisted branches, the resolute, sturdy trunk layered with its brittle bark, the roots disappearing into the grass. He could see them, about a hundred yards away, sitting on the grass, embraced by the tree's mottled shade. He left the tarmac path and cut across the grass, which, again, had just been cut. He breathed in its smell, and inched carefully towards the tree, his eyes fixed on them. Approaching, he slowed down, almost walking on tiptoe, not wanting to make his presence known. Julie was kneeling, her back facing him, and Charlotte was lying, foetal position on the grass, her head in her mother's lap. Somehow, thought Tom, they looked pathetic and so vulnerable under the solid security of the red oak. Tom could hear Charlotte trying to talk between sobs, her whole, delicate body shaking with the effort. Tom crept to their side, about twenty yards away, conscious of his voyeuristic presence. Julie was stroking Charlotte's hair, talking in soothing tones, trying to soothe away her daughter's tears. It took Tom right back to when Charlotte was a little girl, sucking her thumb while huddled up on her mother's lap listening to the stories Julie used to make up on the spot with such ease.

Tom felt as if his heart was being squeezed from inside at the sight of them together now and the memory of those cherished times. He had never lost anyone close to him, but recently he had been prepared to throw away the things more precious to him than life itself. What must it have been like to know one's child was growing up without you? What must it feel like to say goodbye to one's child? He could feel his heart paining at the mere thought of it. How does a man kiss goodbye to part of himself? A brother condemned to die, a child condemned to a childhood without fatherly love and a lifetime of doubt and insecurity. How could a man ever love again when one has already died from the within? What Guy and his father would have given now, thought Tom, to be in his position, to have that second chance, to have one's future so clearly mapped out in front of one. Guy would have married Mary, the mother of his child and the love of his life; Robert could have had a father's love.

It had been just over two weeks since the trip to the Imperial War Museum. It felt like months, years even, but it was just two and a bit weeks that separated his old life from his new. And in that relatively short amount of time, Tom had allowed his resentment to take him so far from what was important. And in the process, he had learnt nothing that he didn't know already, except to realise that he'd never wanted to leave at all. This was *his* aftermath; the haunted gap in his mind was filled. The words of the poem echoed back to him now with such clarity – he, Tom Searight, had been reprieved, he was ready to go, to claim back his past and grab his future.

He edged closer. In the background, he could hear children playing at their games, the rasping music of an ice cream van, a woman calling for her dog, a couple giggling over a game of Frisbee, the distant rumble of traffic, and then, in the far, far distance, reaching back over the decades, the simultaneous sound of eight rifles taking the life of a blindfolded young man. Charlotte's fragmented words came clearly to him now as her mother wiped away the tears of a shattered girl while trying to offer words of reassurance. He heard certain names between the sobs, like stones being thrown into a pond, the ripples from which had brought her to this point of breakdown – Mr Moyes, Angus, Gavin, Daddy. *Daddy*. Tom knew there had been too many tears during his absence. That of Charlotte's and Julie's, he'd seen his father's anguish, Rachel's longing, and, from the faded pages of a journal written almost half a century before he was born, he had heard so many more. But he, himself, hadn't cried, hadn't dared allow himself the luxury of such introspection. He was always too frightened of what he might have found. Perhaps, he should have listened to himself a long, long time ago. But now, as he listened to Julie speculate on how she and Charlotte were going to have to learn to live without him, Tom felt as if he was eavesdropping from Heaven and finally his eyes reddened.

Slowly, Julie became aware of his presence. She looked at him and brushed away a wisp of blonde hair from her face, a face engraved with maternal concern. Tom so knew that look, the look of a mother who so wants to alleviate the suffering of those too young to know why love should hurt so much, they would gladly welcome their child's pain. Tom tried to smile. 'Hello, my sweethearts,' he said.

At the sound of his voice, Charlotte pulled herself up from her mother's lap and twisted around to look at her father. 'Daddy,' she said wiping her eyes with her sleeve.

'Yes, sweetheart?' Tom edged forward. 'Are you OK?' He noticed the curling earrings. His shadow fell over his daughter.

Charlotte ran her fingers through her untied and dishevelled hair. 'Thanks for the earrings.'

'That's all right, my lovely.'

'Are you coming home?' she asked quietly. Tom noticed Julie screw her eyes shut at the directness of Charlotte's matter-of-fact question.

Tom knelt down beside them both. 'Yes,' he said. 'If it's OK with you and Mum, I would like to… very much.'

Julie opened her eyes, swallowed and smiled. Tom stepped over Charlotte, leant down and kissed his wife gently on the lips, cupping her face in his hands. She tried to say sorry, but Tom held his finger to her lips and gently nodded. There was no need for her to say it; he had just as much to be sorry about. He turned to look at his daughter and kissed her on the forehead. Above them, the leaves of the red oak rustled in the gentle summer breeze.

*

As they walked home, the three of them arm in arm with Charlotte in the middle, Julie said, 'I thought Alice said you were going back to France this weekend.'

Tom pulled the ticket out from his back pocket. He looked at it and studied the details of departure time and seat number. He shook his head as he rolled the ticket up into a ball before throwing it accurately into a bin.

'What was that, Daddy?'

'Oh, nothing. Nothing at all.'

Charlotte shrugged a shoulder and linked her arm back into Tom's.

'What made you come back to us?' asked Julie.

Tom considered the question for a few moments. Then, choosing his words carefully, he said, 'I suppose it was all down to someone I met just recently.'

'Really, who was that?'

Tom smiled. 'Oh, just an old soldier who taught me a thing or two. An old soldier who lost his leg back in 1917.'

Epilogue
Sunday, 6 February 2005

Tom stood at the head of the dining room table, a glass of white wine in his raised hand. 'So, everyone, after three. Ready? One, two, three...'

Together they sang Happy Birthday – Tom, Julie, Alice and Charlotte, while Robert sat at the opposite end of the table, his finger scratching at the white tablecloth, an embarrassed grin plastered on his face as he contemplated the flickering candles on Alice's homemade birthday cake in front of him.

They'd all insisted on having a mini-party for Robert at his Enfield home. It was now three in the afternoon on a bitterly cold February Sunday, the lawn outside white with frost. They'd eaten a huge roast dinner, drank wine, and Robert had opened his presents which now lay piled up on the floor next to the armchair – a jumper, chocolates and various books on the war. Alice stood behind him, her hands on his shoulders. Tom led the singing, his face a little red from too much wine. Julie looked lovely in a new dress and Charlotte, bless her, seemed so much more grown-up now. The armchair opposite had been claimed by Charlotte's dogs, Toby and Goliath.

'Happy birthday, Dad.'

'Yes, happy birthday, Robert,' added Julie.

'Thank you. Thank you all of you. This is lovely.'

'Sorry we couldn't find 85 candles, Dad.'

'Hey, only 84, if you don't mind.'

'Go on then, dear,' said Alice. 'Aren't you going to blow them out?'

'And make a wish, granddad.'

'A wish? I wish–'

'You're not meant to tell us.'

'Oh but, Charlotte, I want to; it's fairly obvious anyway – I wish Alec was here.' He sighed. 'Right, here goes…' Rising to his feet, he leant over the dining room table. Apart from wishing his eldest son and family lived nearer by, he had finally, at the age of 84, nothing else to wish for, he had everything he wanted. With a big puff of his cheeks, Robert blew out the candles eliciting a round of applause.

'Shall I cut the cake?' asked Julie.

'Not quite yet,' said Tom in a whisper.

'Why don't you come with us, granddad?' asked Charlotte as they resumed their seats.

'What – all the way to Canada? Don't worry, your father has already asked me. But I can't, Charlotte; I'm too old for such gallivanting. Aren't we, dear?'

'Speak for yourself,' said Alice.

'Oh? Well, if you–'

'No, no, you're probably right. I couldn't face the journey. Anyway, Alec assures us they'll be visiting soon.'

'When you get there, Charlotte, will you give them our love?'

'And take lots of photos,' added Alice. 'Go on, you two, off you get.' Reluctantly the terriers tumbled off the armchair. Alice leant over and began talking to Charlotte while Tom and Julie, holding hands, talked of Canada.

Robert looked at each of them and felt a contentment he hadn't felt for years, if indeed he'd ever felt it. What a relief that Tom and Julie were back together again. It filled his heart with joy to see them there talking so animatedly and holding hands at every opportunity. Whatever it was that drove them apart during the summer was all but forgotten. They seemed more together now, more in love, than ever. Tom seemed to be enjoying his new job and the greater responsibility at Tooley and Hill, and his old nemesis at work had, by all accounts, transformed into a model boss. Funny how things turn out.

And what about Charlotte? Thoroughly enjoying school at last. She's even got a boyfriend now – a red-haired boy called Adam, nice lad. And then there's Toby and Goliath. Having one Highland terrier was bad enough, but two…? But, she says, she'll never forget Angus – he has his plaque at the end of the garden, just beneath the laurel hedge.

'Dad…' Robert noticed his son and Julie exchange a worried glance.

'Yes? Something wrong?'

'Dad, there's one more present.'

His son sounded serious, leaving him to feel faintly anxious all of a sudden as he watched Julie hand Tom the present. 'Dad,' said Tom, passing it on to his father. 'This is for you.'

Wrapped in relatively sombre blue paper, Robert carefully opened the present. Inside, was a wooden presentation box, mahogany perhaps, about five inches by eight. His heart lurched. Surely not, he thought, surely not now…

'Dad. Are you OK?'

'Tom, I don't think I can do this.'

'Yes you can, Dad.'

Alice and Charlotte fell silent. 'Is anything the matter,

245

Robert?' asked Alice.

'Go on, Dad, open it. Open the box.'

With trembling fingers, he did. Inside were three war medals – and he knew immediately that they were his medals, three gleaming medals with their colourful ribbons.

'How… how did you get them?' Robert asked quietly.

'Quite easy once I'd worked out how.'

Alice took Tom's hand and smiled. Charlotte stroked one of the dogs.

'Oh my,' said Robert, unable to take his eyes off them.

'You can wear them on Remembrance Sundays, granddad,' said Charlotte.

'And wear them with pride,' added Julie.

Robert looked up at his granddaughter. 'You're right, Charlotte, I will.' Turning to Tom, he said, 'I don't know what to say, except… except to say thank you, son, this… this…' He couldn't speak, his words lost in a fog of emotion.

'You don't have to say it, Dad. I know.'

Robert looked at each of them. The dogs were chasing each other under the dining room table, the silence punctuated by their little yelps of excitement. Carefully, Robert placed the medal box on the table, next to the cake and the empty glasses of wine. 'Do you mind if you excuse me a minute?'

'That's fine, Dad.'

Inside his bedroom, he sat on the little stool in front of the dresser, its top laden with Alice's perfumes and paraphernalia. He closed his eyes and listened to their muffled voices coming from downstairs to the sound of Charlotte playfully berating the dogs. 84 years old. How did he become so damn old? God had allowed him the chance to grow old, to have his family, his grandchildren, to be surrounded with love. Their faces came back to him, the nine of them. God, for whatever reason, had not been so merciful to them. The sea, the terrible sea, the unforgiving sea, had claimed them all, had denied them all the chance to live life as he had lived it. He had lived and breathed with their memory daily for sixty years. For six decades he had lived with them, remembering their suffering, the agonies they had all endured. Sixty years. He had lived with them for long enough. Perhaps now, he could finally lay them to rest.

Opening his eyes, he forced himself to look at his reflection in the dresser's mirror. He rarely looked at himself, subconsciously it was something he always avoided. Who wants to be reminded of the inevitability of their ageing? Yet now, scrutinising himself for the first time in years, he reminded himself of his father, his real father, "Uncle Hobbly", during Guy's final years. The realisation took away his breath. Had he always looked like Guy? No, people always thought he resembled his mother but now, now in his fading years, like a thread through time, it was Guy Searight looking back at him through the dresser mirror. Both had survived their wars, both had lost their brothers to war, but it was over now.

He heard his granddaughter's shrill laugh coming from downstairs.

He finally understood Lawrence – learning the truth had finally put his mind at rest, had eased some of the torment that had festered inside him for so long. He had spent his whole life resenting the man, trying to fathom out what he had done to so antagonise him. But now that he knew, he already found it within himself to forgive. He never realised he could be such a forgiving man. It hadn't been Lawrence's fault, and he had had a mother who loved him and, nearby, he had a real father who had loved him too. It may not have made up for his forced absence, but now, as Robert lived out his twilight years, it somehow provided a consoling postscript to his life. He had, after all, been conceived out of love, albeit a forbidden one.

A soft knock on the door. 'Dad? Are you OK?' Tom perched himself on the side of the bed.

'Tom, tell me, how long is the flight to Toronto?' asked Robert, speaking to his son via the mirror.

'Eight hours or so.'

'Eight hours. It's not so long. Have you booked the tickets?'

'No, I was going to do it tomorrow evening after work. Why? Are you tempted?'

'More than tempted. Let me speak to your mum about it and I'll let you know for sure by tomorrow.'

'That'd be so great, Dad. There's nothing I would like better.'

'Me too.' Turning back to his reflection, Robert smiled. 'I'll let you know by this time tomorrow.'

THE END

The Searight Saga:

PART ONE: *This Time Tomorrow*
'Two brothers. One woman. A nation at war.'

Vast in scope and intimate in the portrayal of three lives swept along by circumstances, 'This Time Tomorrow' moves from the drawing rooms of Edwardian London to the trenches of the Western Front and to the uncertainty of post-war Britain.

PART TWO: *The Unforgiving Sea*
'Ten men adrift on a lifeboat. Only one will live to tell the tale.'

A sequel to This Time Tomorrow, The Unforgiving Sea, set in World War Two, is, on its surface, a tale of murder, survival and loss, while at its core we find a story of deep love, loyalty and forgiveness.

PART THREE: *The Red Oak*

Rupertcolley.com

Novels by R.P.G. Colley:

The Love and War Series
Song of Sorrow
The Lost Daughter
The Woman on the Train
The White Venus
The Black Maria
My Brother the Enemy
Anastasia
Elena
The Mist Before Our Eyes
The Darkness We Leave Behind

The Searight Saga
This Time Tomorrow
The Unforgiving Sea
The Red Oak

**The DI Benedict Paige Crime Series
by JOSHUA BLACK**
And Then She Came Back
The Poison in His Veins
Requiem for a Whistleblower
The Forget-Me-Not Killer
The Canal Boat Killer
A Senseless Killing

Rupertcolley.com

Printed in Dunstable, United Kingdom

72654564R00150